A Nutcracker Nightmare

Also available by Christina Romeril

Killer Chocolate Mysteries

A Christmas Candy Killing

A Nutcracker Nightmare

A KILLER CHOCOLATE MYSTERY

Christina Romeril

CROOKED
LANE

NEW YORK

This is a work of fiction. All of the names, characters, organizations, places and events portrayed in this novel are either products of the author's imagination or are used fictitiously. Any resemblance to real or actual events, locales, or persons, living or dead, is entirely coincidental.

PUBLISHER'S NOTE: The recipes contained in this book are to be followed exactly as written. The publisher is not responsible for your specific health or allergy needs that may require medical supervision. The publisher is not responsible for any adverse reaction to the recipes contained in this book.

Published in the United States by Crooked Lane Books, an imprint of The Quick Brown Fox & Company LLC.

Crooked Lane Books and its logo are trademarks of The Quick Brown Fox & Company LLC.

Library of Congress Catalog-in-Publication data available upon request.

ISBN (hardcover): 978-1-63910-491-8
ISBN (ebook): 978-1-63910-492-5

Cover design by Mary Ann Lasher

Printed in the United States.

www.crookedlanebooks.com

Crooked Lane Books
34 West 27th St., 10th Floor
New York, NY 10001

First Edition: October 2023

10 9 8 7 6 5 4 3 2 1

For all the mystery fans who grew up
wanting to be Nancy Drew

Chapter One

Murder may not be good for some businesses, but for the Murder and Mayhem: Killer Chocolates and Bookshop it was essential. The shop's customers loved donning their sleuthing caps to unravel the many murders committed in the books lining the shelves of the specialty store, currently decked out for the holidays with an abundance of vintage ornaments and twinkle lights.

Co-owner Alex Wright stirred a saucepan of cream heating on the stove. She reflected that making the tasty confections their store was known for was both an art and a science. She and her identical twin sister were creative alchemists developing flavor combinations that were original, decadent, and daring—yet always perfectly balanced.

Their chocolates needed to capture the senses, beginning with appearance and aroma. The thin chocolate shell needed a glossy shine and crisp snap that allowed the delicious, oozy filling to spill out with the first bite. The right combination of textures ensured the experience would be satisfying. Secondary flavors had to enhance rather than overpower one another, to provide a harmonious finish to the encounter. In the tradition of mystery, each chocolate was named after some kind of poison from the popular genre novels.

Alex poured the simmering liquid over the waiting chocolate in a glass bowl on the kitchen island and placed the pot on the shiny granite countertop. A minute later Alex whisked the remaining ingredients into the ganache. The mixture was silky smooth, the perfect texture for the Gingerbread Gelsemine truffles. She was getting ready to pour the ganache into a dish when Maggie Fletcher, the twins' only employee, banged open the kitchen door, announcing her arrival.

"Have you heard yet?" Maggie was breathless. Alex wondered if the energetic sixty-one-year-old had run all the way from her bungalow, three blocks away. Living close to work was one of the advantages of living in the small village of twelve hundred, nestled in a valley at the foot of the Rocky Mountains in Montana. Harriston didn't have any claim to fame aside from its sunny views of the Swan Mountain Range and the glorious tree-lined lake it sat beside. But that didn't stop a steady throng of tourists from finding it every summer. Cottages dotted the perimeter of Echo Lake, and their owners provided an influx of business for Harriston's merchants.

"Heard what? I've been preparing these truffles for the past half hour." Alex was usually the first one in the shop each morning. She loved the solitude and the crisp scent of paper and ink mingled with hints of evergreens, chocolate, and vanilla as she began her day. While she loved summer, Alex adored Christmas. There were numerous hand-painted glass ornaments and little festive touches of pine and cedar tucked onto shelves and among the homemade candles and jars of jam they sold.

"Miss T just broke the story wide open."

Before Maggie could say more, a slender blonde with cool gray eyes, which looked almost green today, came in from the back hall, carrying a stack of chocolate boxes. She set them on the island beside Alex and set a paper shopping bag on the counter by the sink. "What story? And who the heck is Miss T?" Alex's twin, the store's other owner, Hanna Eastham, started unpacking the contents of the grocery bag.

She held up a glass bottle. "I got the real Canadian maple syrup. The clerk at the Black Currant ordered it for me from a small business in Ontario weeks ago, and it finally came. Did you know it takes forty gallons of sap to make one gallon of maple syrup? I once went to the Elmira Maple Syrup Festival and got to see how it's made. I've been dying to create a chocolate with some of the real stuff."

"I'm looking forward to tasting it. Are those chocolates for tonight?" Alex gestured to the stack on the island as she placed the ganache in the fridge.

"Yes. There are two hundred chocolates there. Most of them are Strychnine Strawberry. So, who is this Miss T?"

Maggie had finally caught her breath and continued with her news. "Miss T—it's short for Tattle—found out that the cute little chocolate shop in Missoula that was the favorite to win the Festive Foods Chocolates Competition has been cheating! They've been buying some of their chocolates from a specialty shop in Spokane and passing them off as their own."

"What!" Alex knew of the chocolate shop two hours south of Harriston. The other shop was far enough away not to be a real competitor for sales, but Alex knew they would be the shop to beat in the chocolate competition next weekend.

"Miss T exposed the cheating scheme in yesterday's blog in the *Harriston Confidante*. She said they used those chocolates in the Monde du Chocolat competition in Portland and won. The Festive Foods organizers put out a statement on social media this morning, saying they'd investigated allegations of cheating against Missoula's Choco Choco and verified it had happened. Choco Choco withdrew their entry in the competition late last night. Can you believe it?"

"This Miss Whatshername must be quite the investigative journalist?" Hanna was opening one of the bottles of maple syrup. "I wonder what the Monde du Chocolat competition will do. Do you think they'll strip them of their title like what's been done with sports figures after they've been found doping?"

"I wouldn't be surprised. They might even have to give back the prize money they won." Maggie tapped her finger on the counter. "Cheaters never prosper. I always taught my kids that."

"Well, I hate to be a Debbie Downer, but I'm pretty sure that proverb has been proven wrong lots of times." Alex stood beside her twin and looked at the new maple syrup. "Our culture rewards whoever is at the top. It seems a lot of people think it's worth cheating because of the possible rewards. And let's face it, not everyone gets caught."

"That's probably true, but I still think the possible consequences aren't worth the risk. Duncan tried to write the answers to a test on his hands once, I caught him and he had to have daily study sessions with me for a month. I don't think he ever tried to cheat again." Maggie's three grown children had all been born and raised in Harriston. Duncan, the oldest, was a deputy sheriff with the Lakehead County Sheriff's Department and had moved back in with his parents several years ago.

"I'm going to win the competition the old-fashioned way. Hard work. And this grade A dark robust maple syrup is going to help." Hanna opened the bottle of syrup and poured a bit on a spoon. Her lips curved upward as she sampled the sweet liquid. "Perfection. I can taste notes of caramel and brown sugar. I've been experimenting with a new chocolate for the competition next week, using the maple syrup I had on hand, but this will make it a winner."

"I'm more worried whether we'll be able to keep up with demand for the chocolates in the store." Alex and Hanna had been churning out their specialty chocolates like Santa's elves the past few weeks for their busiest season. Hanna had committed to providing chocolates for the community's high school reunion dance and alumni dinner. The reunion weekend was to celebrate the completion of renovations on Harriston's K–12 school gymnasium. Many of the school's alumni had donated generously to make the needed improvements that weren't in the budget.

The reunion weekend had been scheduled for Valentine's Day, but because the renovations took much longer than expected, the date had been pushed back four times. That was how the event ended up being on December tenth, just fifteen days before Christmas, not an ideal time for Alex and Hanna.

Months ago, before she'd realized all the events would culminate at the same time, Alex had also convinced Hanna to enter her handmade chocolates in the competition next weekend in Whitefish.

Alex was watching Hanna as she walked back to the island, and didn't see the pot handle sticking out into the aisle. Her arm caught it, and knocked it into the stack of finished chocolate boxes. The boxes teetered for a moment. At the last second Alex dove for the boxes.

At the same time Maggie tried to race around the counter to save the boxes from hitting the floor. Instead of catching the chocolates, she and Alex banged heads and both ended up sprawled on the ground next to the confections.

Alex looked at the scattered chocolates. "Do you think the five-second rule counts in this situation?"

"Absolutely. I won't tell if you won't," Hanna deadpanned.

All three women burst out laughing. Maggie rubbed her head as she stood up. "I think my pride is hurt more than my head."

"I'm so sorry, Maggie. I'm a walking disaster. I think my mother was right when she used to call me a *Trampeltier*." Alex's first words had been German. Their family had insisted on speaking their native language at home, and English everywhere else. Alex and Hanna still spoke German to their parents and Oma on their weekly call.

Hanna put on a pair of gloves and picked up the chocolates that were on the floor. "I wouldn't call you a clumsy oaf. Then again, you did manage to trip Mr. Olafson, our eighty-year-old neighbor, when you were trying to help him shovel his snow."

"I was eleven, and to be fair he wasn't all that sure on his feet at the best of times." Alex took stock of the mini disaster. "Anyway, I think we can salvage the chocolates that didn't come out of the boxes. We can take the others home with us. I'll still eat them."

"Are you going to be short chocolates for tonight?" Maggie bent down and picked up the few boxes with chocolates still safely ensconced.

"No. I can use some of the one's for the alumni dinner tomorrow night. That will give me time to make more chocolates. Let's figure out how many of these we need to scrap." Hanna grabbed a tray from the counter and started creating rows of chocolates while Maggie went to open up the shop.

"I count one hundred and eleven chocolates that have to be replaced," Alex said.

"That's not as bad as I thought it would be. I was going to come back after the dance and work for a couple hours anyway. I'll just add this to my list." Hanna wrote *111* on the large blackboard hanging on the wall of the all-white kitchen. There was already an extensive to-do list.

Hanna had been tasked to oversee the food at the reunion dance that night, and Alex had been asked to help her sister at the last minute, when one of the organizers had to back out. "We'll both come in and work—that way it will get done twice as fast." Alex wiped up the last of the chocolate crumbs on the floor as her phone chimed, signaling an incoming text message. Alex glanced at the phone sitting on the counter. "Eudora is wondering who I got to teach the line dancing class. *Rats!* I completely forgot I was supposed to ask someone to do that. When we decided to scrap the speed dating, I volunteered to find someone, but I forgot to write it down. My memory seems to be on Christmas vacation already. Who can I get on such short notice?"

"I bet Isabelle would do it," Hanna offered.

"That's a great idea. I'll call her right after lunch. I know she teaches a yoga class on Friday mornings." Alex slipped the phone into her pocket. "I should check on Watson and see how she's doing."

"Don't forget we've got the volunteers meeting here this afternoon before they head to the community center to finish decorating for the dance," Hanna reminded her sister.

Alex went into the small conference room next to the kitchen and rubbed their Staffordshire terrier behind her ears. The fawn and white dog was lounging on a bench they'd had built under the window. The dog, adopted three years earlier from a rescue shelter, let out a rumble that sounded almost like purring. Alex was beginning to think Watson identified as a cat. The medium-sized canine had her eyes glued to a television playing a videotape of a German shepherd rescuing a woman from a burning building.

Back in the kitchen, Alex washed her hands and started measuring ingredients for the Strychnine Strawberry chocolates from the recipe card Hanna had set out.

"It's a good thing you've been improving your chocolate-making skills this past year." Hanna lined up polycarbonate molds on the counter.

Alex had learned the rudimentary aspects of chocolate making growing up, but it was Hanna who was the true chocolatier. Hanna was an artist and had been teaching Alex to refine her skills so she could help out more on the confection side of the business.

"I need to work on the chocolate for the competition." Hanna started coating molds with the shop's new wheel tempering machine. The tabletop machine had been a splurge but was proving a good investment. It had allowed them to keep up with the increased demand for their chocolates.

"Are we going to give some of those chocolates from this morning's spill to the volunteers meeting here later?" Alex examined the chocolates closely.

"We can use the ones that didn't come out of the boxes. Let me tell you, there's one person I'd like to give a couple extra-special chocolates to. Ones filled with real strychnine." Hanna's lip curled with disgust.

"Who are you talking about?"

"Kyle Allerton. He just texted me to say he'd be a few minutes late. You're lucky you haven't met him yet. That creep has been stalking me ever since I let him take me home from the Business Council meeting last month. He's the reason everyone is meeting here. His Highness said he didn't want to wait for someone to unlock the doors at the community center. I have to get the keys from the Village Office next door, and he thought it would be more convenient for the committee to meet at our shop and go over together. I know there are others who have keys, and I'm not even part of the decorating committee. It's just an excuse so he can come and harass me." Hanna shot a look at Alex. "David Copperfield's hands are easier to keep track of than Kyle's. He must have an octopus in his bloodline."

Alex hadn't met the man, but she'd heard plenty about him. And none of it was good. "If only you were dating someone. That might deter Kyle's amorous advances. It's a shame your romance last Christmas didn't work out."

"Kyle doesn't seem like the kind of person to worry whether someone is dating. Or married."

Hanna's last boyfriend had moved away just before Thanksgiving. She hadn't seemed upset about the breakup, but she'd been acting strangely ever since. The past week she'd been coming early and staying late. Working late wasn't unusual for Hanna, but she usually had to be pried out of bed with a crowbar. As far as sacrifices went, Hanna equated getting up early to donating an organ.

Maggie opened the kitchen door. "Ladies, we have visitors who would like to see you."

Hanna glanced at Alex. "I'll be right out. I just need to finish these last two trays."

Alex wiped her hands on her apron and followed Maggie. Their sales area consisted of two rooms, one on either side of the hall. The larger room had probably been the living room when the house was originally built.

Maggie's husband, Drew, and their son, Duncan, were waiting in the shop.

"Hi, Alex." Duncan, the tall, blue-eyed sheriff's deputy was speaking to Alex, but his gaze was searching the room for someone else. When no one else appeared behind Alex, Duncan lowered his soot-black lashes.

To hide his disappointment? Alex had noticed a marked change in the relationship between her sister and Duncan in recent weeks.

"What are you two up to?" Alex asked.

Drew puffed out his chest and pushed his wire-rimmed glasses further up his nose. The retired pharmacist was a few inches shorter than his son and had narrow, slightly stooped shoulders. "I've been doing a ride-along with Duncan today. He's been investigating a complaint about a scam targeted at seniors. Duncan got a report that a senior had given away a large sum of cash. When her adult son asked the senior about it, the senior said it was an investment. But it looks like it's bogus. When her son started asking questions, Mrs. Matthews told him to mind his own business."

"Dad! You can't disclose the names of people involved in the investigation when you go on a ride-along."

"Oops. Sorry. Alex, pretend you didn't hear that."

"My lips are sealed. I've seen that happen before, though. Seniors are embarrassed they got scammed, so they don't report it. The last thing they want is for their families to find out." As a former business banker, Alex had seen her fair share of scams.

"It's tough, because we have to respect the senior's right to privacy. If she won't report it, there's not much we can do." Duncan straightened up when he saw Hanna.

Hanna slipped into the room with a tray of chocolate samples. "I thought I heard your voice, Drew." She proffered the tray. "Would you care for a sample?"

"Don't mind if I do." Drew paused to select one of the treats. "Though I should probably be filling up with vitamin C. I feel a cold coming on."

Drew was known for becoming a bit of a hypochondriac since retiring, and Alex hid a small smile as Maggie rolled her eyes. Alex glanced at Hanna's reaction, but she and Duncan were locked in a stare as his hand hovered over the tray. Alex wondered if there was a new romance in the air. Duncan and Hanna had dated when the twins first moved to town four years ago, but after a couple of months Duncan had decided he wasn't ready to open himself up to those emotions. At the time, he had recently lost his wife to cancer and decided he needed a friend, not a romantic partner.

As far as Alex knew, he hadn't dated since. She wondered if anyone else had noticed the looks Duncan and Hanna gave each other.

Chapter Two

Once Duncan and Drew left to investigate further leads in the seniors scam, Alex donned a light jacket and headed to Cookies 'n Crumbs to get lunch for her crew.

Montana's Flathead Valley had been experiencing a warm spell for over a week, and there wasn't much snow left aside from where it had been piled high in parking lots. Thankfully, the Christmas festival caught the last of the cold weather, and they'd been able to hold all the events, including the snowman contest.

Alex stopped and gazed down Main Street. Harriston's founders had come from England, and their influence could still be felt in the architecture and traditions. Even calling itself a village was a nod to its English roots. The conservative, sleepy village was decked out for Christmas with fresh cedar garlands and white lights strung around the shop windows, big black planters filled with festive greenery, and red bows by its shops' front doors. There was a giant Christmas tree festooned with lights and giant ornaments in the middle of the village's main intersection.

The official tree lighting had been done on the first evening of the Christmas festival. The volunteer firemen had been in charge, and Santa had made a special appearance from the North Pole, to flip the switch. The whole town had counted down, and then the lights had flared briefly before the area was immersed in darkness. The electricity had been restored thirty seconds later, but it had caused a few snickers.

The bright and cheerful bakeshop, decorated with white shiplap and reclaimed wood walls, was on the next corner. Alex stepped through the door and inhaled the scent of fresh baking while she admired the strategically placed red, white, and silver decorations that reminded customers Christmas was fast approaching. The lineup was right to the door, and to Alex's delight, Isabelle Pearson, the mayor's wife, stood in front of her. The brunette always had a ready smile, and today was no exception.

Isabelle's hazel eyes lit up as she greeted Alex. "It's so hard to pass this place without stopping in."

"You know it. It's going to be a long day today. I have to help at the reunion dance tonight." Alex barely managed to squeeze the door shut behind her. The place was packed.

"Everett and I will see you there, then. I want to catch up with all my old school friends. Not to mention dance. I love country music and line dancing." Isabelle wiggled her curvy hips.

"Everett doesn't strike me as a line dancer."

"He's not. Everett wants to stay home and watch a 'very important basketball game.'" Isabelle held up her hands to make air quotes. But I went to his school reunion two years ago, so I told him if he wants to stay happily married, he'll be escorting me."

"Didn't Everett go to Harriston School?" Everett was tall, dark, and handsome, and had won the last election by a landslide. His business savvy and easygoing nature helped him successfully navigate the many personalities he had to deal with in the village. *And boy, were there some personalities.*

"Nope. He attended the high school in Swanson. We were rivals back in the day. I was a cheerleader for Harriston, and he played on his school's football team."

"Did you know each other then?"

"We knew of each other, but it was in college that we started dating. We got married after I graduated from the nursing program."

"As it happens, I was going to call you after lunch. I know it's short notice, but do you think you could teach a line dancing class before the dance?"

Isabelle was silent for a moment before a smile spread over her face. "I've never taught line dancing before, but I think I could do that. There are a couple of popular line dances that are simple enough that people can catch onto them quickly. When do you want me there?"

Alex gave Isabelle all the particulars and breathed a huge sigh of relief.

"Maybe it's none of my business, but I heard you're in a hot and heavy romance with Eddie Mills?"

Alex almost choked. "Hardly. We met in September for the first time. He attended one of the Business Council meetings in lieu of his boss, and we happened to sit together. I found out he was a jack-of-all-trades when he wasn't working his real job as manager of the farm equipment dealership, so I asked him to build a bench in the shop for Watson. I'd hardly call those interactions romantic. Besides I think he's a few years younger than me. The village gossips do get around. "

"Not 'the village gossips.' *The* village gossip, Miss T, mentioned it in her blog. And lots of women are going out with younger men these days. Have you gone out on a real date?"

"Why would that woman be talking about me on her blog? I'm not anyone important."

"Oh, she talks about everyone—assuming you're doing something interesting."

"Honestly, if my love life is the best Harriston's got to offer . . ." Alex shook her head. "Tom's the only person I've been trying to date. It's been tough with him gone so much this past year." Tom Kennedy lived next door to Alex.

"Didn't you and Tom start dating last Christmas?"

"We did, but then Tom's brother in Alaska got sick, and Tom went there to nurse him until he died. Then he had to deal with the estate. Tom's been away more in the past eleven months than he's been home." Alex and Tom had recently started to revive their fledgling relationship, but Tom seemed distant. Was the fifty-nine-year-old still as keen on dating her as he had been last January? He seemed to run hot and cold, and Alex didn't know what to think.

"There's no rule that says you can't date more than one man at a time. Keep your options open. You're not getting any younger, you know."

"Now you sound like my mother. She's been telling me a woman's best years end at thirty-nine." Alex's overbearing mother meant well, but she had some strong opinions. While Alex had thought middle age might be encroaching, it would appear everyone else believed it had arrived. "I might as well book a room at the senior's lodge. Hanna and I can get a spinster special."

Alex put in her order, and a few minutes later, with food in hand, she headed back to the store. Alex, Hanna, and Maggie munched on their sandwiches in the conference room while Watson looked at them as if she hadn't been fed in a week.

Alex told them about her conversation with Isabelle. "Is my situation really that desperate? Maybe Tom is my last hope. Should I be signing up for a convent in case it doesn't work out?"

Hanna and Maggie glanced at each other, and then Maggie looked at her watch. "Hanna, did you need to go get the key for the community center?"

"Shoot! Is it time already? Thanks for reminding me." Hanna rushed from the room as if the Grim Reaper were chasing her.

Maggie quickly got up. "I think I hear customers. I better go check." She was gone faster than a Formula One race car.

A Nutcracker Nightmare

What's going on? Alex wondered "Watson, we've been abandoned. Here's one of your favorite bacon-flavored snacks, just for sticking around." Alex grabbed a treat from a jar on the desk and handed the little strip to the dog. Watson loved the treats, and Alex figured they were the doggy equivalent of cupcakes.

Alex went to help Maggie straighten up the displays. "Why did you and Hanna take off like a couple of shopaholics late for a Neiman Marcus sale when I asked if my dating situation was desperate? Do you know something I don't?"

Maggie's hand paused as she was about to move one of M. C. Beaton's Agatha Raisin books. She pulled the copy of *Kissing Christmas Goodbye* off the shelf and moved it to a nearby display of Christmas gifts. "Hanna and I didn't want to say anything because it might not even be about you."

"What are you talking about?"

"I showed Hanna a blog post this morning that Miss T wrote. I better just show it to you." Maggie pulled her phone from her pocket and with a few taps and swipes brought up the blog.

A certain cougar in the village has been seen carrying on with a handsome, younger man who manages a local farm machine business, while her beau, a man of God, has been away, nursing a dying family member. How sad, but you know what they say: when the cat's away, the mice will play.

Alex could feel the heat rising up her neck. How dare this woman! Alex knew rumors in Harriston were more numerous than chocolate chips in a banana loaf, but this was unbelievable. If she ever found out the identity of Miss T, she'd have a few words with her.

"You know this isn't true." Alex looked Maggie in the eye.

Chapter Three

Alex worried that Maggie might believe Miss T's accusation that Alex was involved with another man. As Tom's sister, her loyalty would clearly lean toward her brother.

"I know you aren't catting around. But there are other people in the village more susceptible to believing anything in print. I wouldn't worry about it. It's just gossip and scandal mongering. People will forget all about it with the next thing Miss T posts."

"Do you think people are saying anything because of the age difference between Tom and me?" Even though Alex didn't care about the twelve-year difference in their ages, she knew there would always be some people who had an opinion about it.

"My momma used to say, 'It's better to be an old man's sweetheart than a young man's slave.' I wouldn't worry what other people are saying. It's more important that you stay true to what's right for you."

Hanna rushed in the front door. "The decorating committee will be here shortly. Alex, when they head over to the community center, will you help me bring the chocolates and table decorations? You can take your own car and come right back to the store. I'll probably be a bit longer."

"I can stay there and help you—that way it'll go faster."

A Nutcracker Nightmare

"We don't want Maggie to be alone too long. It might get busy. I think it's better if we take the two cars. I'll bring out the chocolate samples," Hanna called over her shoulder on her way to the kitchen.

Hanna brought out a tray of chocolates and had barely set it on the counter when the little brass bell on the door jingled, heralding the arrival of an elderly lady with wispy white hair worn in a bun, and the latest Stephen Curry kicks strapped to her feet. Some people said Eudora Harris had been the village postmistress since the days when mail was delivered by stagecoach, though not to her face. The postmistress's mind was sharp, her dark eyes were shrewd, and she considered eighty to be the new sixty. It was rumored Eudora had enough dirt on the local postal authorities to keep her job until she was ninety.

"Speak of the devil." Alex smiled as the scent of talcum powder trailed the woman into the shop.

"Did I hear my name mentioned?" Eudora had taken over the role of primary mover and shaker in the community volunteer world last year. The spinster had a network of spies the CIA would envy, and there wasn't much that happened in the village that she didn't know something about.

Alex gave her friend a hug. "No one calls you that." *Anymore.* As a former banker, Alex tended to be more comfortable with spreadsheets and PowerPoint presentations than hugs among friends and neighbors. But after living in Harriston for four years, she'd adapted. Even the Republicans and the Democrats hugged each other in the village.

"You two are beautiful, but when you put your hair in ponytails like that, it's almost impossible to tell you apart."

Alex smiled. "I'm pretty sure you know the difference, but Hanna's the one with chocolate on her shirt."

Eudora looked at Hanna's shirt. "So it seems." The postmistress turned back to Alex. "I wanted to give you these lists."

Alex took the sheets from Eudora. "What are they?"

"It's a list of all the people preregistered for the dance. There's also a list detailing everything to do with the food. Everything is color coded. You'll see when you go through it all."

Organization was Alex's middle name, but Eudora had taken it to epic levels for the dance. The octogenarian was in charge of the whole weekend, and Alex was sure no detail had been overlooked. The woman probably had the number of public bathrooms in Harriston on a spreadsheet.

"I found an instructor for the line dancing class."

Eudora looked at Alex over her glasses. "Thank heavens. I don't know who's idea speed dating was to begin with, but I think a more inclusive activity everyone can participate in is a better fit for this weekend."

The front door opened, and a tall brunette with horn-rimmed glasses strode in. Her long hair, parted in the middle, flowed over her shoulders and spilled onto a black turtleneck that topped tight black jeans. She wore a long silver necklace around her neck and carried a blazer over her arm.

"Hello." The newcomer gave everyone a big smile that bared her teeth. She reminded Alex of a shark, albeit an attractive one. "I believe the decorating committee is meeting here?"

Maggie hurried up to the woman, with her arms outstretched to give her a hug, but the woman recoiled and stuck her hand out at the last second. The aborted hug turned into more of an awkward pat on the arm. "Brooke Gibson." Maggie stepped back as her face turned light pink. "Look at you. Your mother never mentioned you were coming to town. I thought she and your dad went on a cruise?"

"Hello, Mrs. Fletcher." Brooke pressed her lips together. "Actually, my plans changed at the last minute. I wasn't supposed to be here until New Year's. My parent's left on their cruise last week, and their house is being renovated while they're away. I had to make arrangements to stay at the Heavenly Haven B&B."

"Call me Maggie. We're all adults now. I'm sure your parents are very disappointed they won't get to see you. They're always telling us about your latest accomplishments. They're so proud of you."

"It was always nice to go to your house after school until my parents finished for the day. I loved your famous triple-chocolate brownies. Do you still make those?"

Maggie smiled. "Occasionally. You know you were a delight to babysit. You were a great example to my own children. You always refused to go play until your homework was done."

"When your parents are both teachers, learning is instilled into you from birth. Success was always something to strive for. I'm up for a judgeship, you know. I'd be among the youngest to be appointed if I make it. I've worked so hard for this. I swear, nothing is going to stand in my way." Brooke took a bottle of pink liquid from her purse, removed the cap, and raised the bottle in the air. "Cheers." She took a swig.

Alex looked at the liquid curiously. She recognized it as an over-the-counter medication for the relief of various gastrointestinal discomforts.

"Stress." Brooke held up the medication as if in answer to the unspoken question from Alex. "Pink Bis has been my constant companion since high school."

"Since Drew retired, he's been concocting all kinds of home remedies for all his ailments. Have you seen a doctor, Brooke?" Maggie's voice was filled with concern.

Brooke snorted. "I'm supposed to learn to relax. That's not so easy when you usually work seventy hours a week and you're trying to get appointed as a judge. It also doesn't help that I ate at the Chinese restaurant last night." Brooke tapped her stomach with her fist. "You know, that place hasn't changed since high school. The food is as terrible as ever."

"How long are you in town for, dear?" Eudora peered closely at Brooke.

"I'll be here until Monday. Then I'm scheduled back for a few days at New Year's to see my parents."

"Do you have a hard time getting away from work?" Alex could imagine if you worked seventy-hour weeks, taking time off would be difficult.

"It's not easy, but there are some things you have to take care of in person, or they come back to haunt you." The lines around her mouth deepened, and Brooke took another swig of the pink liquid.

Hanna brought the sample tray to the ladies, and they all reached for the chocolates.

"These are very nice." Brooke savored a Strychnine Strawberry. "So they're named after poisons? Clever idea for a mystery bookshop." She reached for a Gingerbread Gelsemine truffle. "I can't resist chocolate."

Everyone's head turned to the door as it opened again.

"Start the party. The star of class of '99 is here!"

The man had to be well over six feet tall, and he swaggered into the room, flashing a few thousand dollars' worth of dental work with a thousand-kilowatt smile. Alex was afraid she'd be blinded if the light from his unnaturally white teeth hit her square in the eye. The cost of the caps on his teeth could have funded the school lunch program for five years. He'd probably had a muscular physique in high school, but it looked like gravity had had its way with him, and now much of his bulk was riding low over his belt.

He stared, open-mouthed, as he looked from Hanna to Alex. "Are you the double-mint gum twins? Nice. What's better than one pretty girl? Two! So which of you is Hanna?"

Hanna looked like she was grinding her teeth at the man's attempt at humor. "This is my sister, Alex. Chocolate?" Hanna shoved the tray in front of Kyle.

Alex could see the glint in Hanna's eyes and was fairly certain her sister was wishing the chocolates were filled with real strychnine.

"Ah, you want a professional's opinion. I guess it's not often you get the former vice president of a huge national chocolate company to try your chocolates. It's nice to see amateurs like yourselves trying to make a go of it with these cute candies." Kyle waggled his finger in Hanna's face.

Not a good idea, Alex thought. Hanna had been a biter as a child.

"You're not trying to bribe me for the Festive Foods Chocolates Competition, are you?" Kyle tried to put one arm around Hanna's shoulders, but she quickly moved out of range, leaving him to stumble a bit. "I'm sure you're well aware I've been asked to judge the handmade chocolates. It's not often they get someone of my caliber for an event like that."

Brooke's lip curled, and it looked like she was on the verge of saying something, but instead she shook her head.

Alex was prevented from commenting when the front door banged open and a short, stocky woman marched in.

"What the H is going on? I've been waiting at the community center for twenty minutes. I had to close the pharmacy early to help decorate." Her glare landed on Kyle. "I don't have time to wait around for has-been prima donnas. I've got a dinner date with my mom before the dance tonight. Let's get going." The newcomer pulsed with impatience and tapped her hand against her leg.

"I guess nothing's changed since high school. Your mom is still the only date you can get, Lucy." Kyle sneered at the dowdily dressed woman.

"Better a date with my mom than spending time with a crook." Lucy Dunn made a rude gesture to Kyle and marched straight for the tray in Hanna's hands and grabbed several of the chocolates. Kyle edged closer to Hanna, and Lucy hastily moved toward Alex.

"You better watch it. You don't want to be hit with a slander lawsuit." Kyle's eyes narrowed as he looked at Lucy.

"It's only slander if it's not true. My mother and I were discussing just that at the Chinese restaurant last night." Lucy glared at Kyle.

Silence choked the room and Kyle's confident look seemed to falter. In the awkward pause after the pair's remarks, Kyle leaned nearer to Hanna and whispered, "You better make nice to me, or I might not be inclined to vote for your chocolates at next week's competition."

Kyle's comment rang through the silent room. Hanna looked at the former exec with contempt and walked several feet away.

"You're such a pig," Lucy spat out.

Kyle looked down his nose at Lucy and followed after Hanna, telling her he'd only been joking.

Alex took a closer look at the woman beside her. Lucy was five feet tall on a good day and had full, heavy-lidded eyes and colorless lashes. Alex had never seen her wear makeup, but the woman came across as efficient and competent. She had gotten to know Lucy after Drew sold his pharmacy, and Alex had started purchasing prescriptions from Lucy's pharmacy around the corner. The single woman and her mother ran the old-fashioned shop in the same way it had been run since it was started over seventy years ago. The building still had original everything. The only upgrades had been those demanded by law and their profession. It was a window into the past.

"I don't think I've heard a single good thing about him." Alex wondered how Kyle had managed to become a high-powered CEO.

After a moment's hesitation Brooke said, "It's so like him. He's bullied and blackmailed people all his life. One of these days someone is going to get fed up and teach him a lesson."

"He was born bad." Lucy licked chocolate off her fingers. "It didn't help that he was an only child, and his parents indulged his every wish. I'm pretty sure they're regretting that now."

Watson trotted into the room and stopped in front of Alex. She barked twice, danced in a circle, and then moved a few paces away. When Alex didn't move, Watson barked again and then stepped back.

"She's trying to tell you to follow her. This is something new I've been teaching her." Hanna put the tray down on the counter, and everyone followed Watson back to the conference room. The dog padded over to the television and barked at it, and then looked expectantly at the group.

Hanna smiled like a proud parent. "The tape is over. Watson wants us to put in a new one. I've been teaching her how to get people to follow her."

Everyone except Kyle laughed and congratulated Hanna on Watson's new trick. Hanna changed the tape, and the group walked back to the sales floor. The main floor of the Victorian-styled bookshop was filled with dark wood and rich fabrics. In addition to the two front rooms used as a sales floor, there was a conference room, and a modern kitchen. A tall Christmas tree stood between the sales counter and the front window in their larger sales room. The tree was covered in hundreds of white twinkle lights and delicate vintage mercury ornaments Alex had inherited from a dear friend who had died last Christmas. This year they'd also strung lights across the ceiling, to give the room an even cozier feel.

Eudora, Lucy, and Brooke had gathered around the chocolates again. Kyle had tried to start a conversation with Brooke as they walked down the hall, but she had expertly maneuvered Eudora between them. Eudora had extricated herself from Kyle and joined the other women.

All heads turned when the brass bell heralded someone new. A nice-looking man with a jaw chiseled from stone, dressed in jeans and a denim jacket, walked in and joined their ranks. "Sorry, I'm late."

"Hi, Nate. Come on in. Why don't you try some of those chocolates?" Maggie gestured to the counter. She had obviously decided to take one for the team and had led Kyle into a corner, and it looked like she was keeping him corralled away from the others.

Alex wanted to shove a sock in Kyle's mouth so he couldn't make any other rude remarks. She and Hanna stood between the two groups as a physical barrier.

Nate Baxter was Watson's vet. The twins had had to limit the number of treats they fed Watson after Nate told them the dog was getting pudgy. He walked over to the three women manning the chocolates as he nodded to everyone in the room and grabbed one of the little confections.

His face hardened as he looked at Kyle. "I picked up the trailer with the decorations from the hardware store. I got a call from Zara that you never showed up."

"I decided to drive the Jag today, so couldn't do it. Sorry, dude. I guess I forgot to call and let her know."

Kyle tried to dart around Maggie, but she managed to step in front of him and halted his attempt to join the others.

Nate grabbed a second chocolate. "We should probably get going. A storm's coming, and we'll want to be done well before that." Nate popped the chocolate into his mouth.

"There's nothing in the forecast." Eudora scanned her cell phone.

Nate quickly swallowed his chocolate. "I've been working with farmers for years, and they and their animals can predict the weather better than the weather service. The farmers I talked to this morning swear there's something coming."

"Oh dear. That's not good news for our reunion activities this weekend." Eudora's brows knit together in worry. "Nate, do you know any farmers that need some rat killer? Eddie has been helping me around the house in his spare time, and he found a tin of strychnine-based rat poison in my shed. It looks like it's quite old."

"A few of the farmers around here employ that below ground for pocket gophers. They are a nuisance, but as a vet, I hate to see that stuff used. It's a nasty way to die. Strychnine is regulated now, so I don't imagine anyone would use anything that old." Nate put his hands in his pockets after starting to reach for another chocolate.

"That's a shame. I hate things going to waste. I'll let Eddie know he can get rid of it when he tears down the shed in the spring. Unless you girls need it?" Eudora looked at Alex and Hanna and winked.

The twins grinned. True or not, Alex had always considered poison a woman's weapon. She loved mysteries with killers that used poison to dispatch their victims. The idea for their poison-themed chocolates had been born of that love, though they definitely didn't use real poison.

"Besides poisoning them, a lot of the local ranchers and farmers like to use gophers for target practice. There'll be a contest to see who can shoot the most gophers in the spring," Nate said.

"That's awful." Hanna looked stricken. She couldn't stand the idea of hunting anything.

"I remember when my father and his friends would shoot gophers years ago. I'm afraid I don't care for blood sports," Eudora said. "When my father went into the retirement home, I wanted to get rid of the rifles, but father told me to hang on to them. He said you never know when you might have to shoot an intruder. Well, I don't think I could shoot at anyone, no matter the circumstances."

"I've got some rifles at home, but when we started having kids, I locked them up," Nate said. "I bought my wife a stun gun a few years ago, for personal protection, when they had that spate of break-and-enters. I'm often away on vet calls in the evenings, and we both felt better knowing she had it. You might consider getting yourself one of those if you don't like guns."

Lucy spoke around a chocolate she had in her mouth. "My mom and I have a stun gun at our house too. I've hidden it away, though. With my mom's dementia and all, I don't want her using it on me because she thinks I'm an intruder. Do you own a gun, Brooke?"

"I never give out that kind of information, or even my personal opinions on guns or any other weapons. I've been gearing up for a judgeship all my life. I don't want anything like that on record." Brooke folded her arms across her chest.

Alex had never thought of getting any kind of weapon. Hanna worried every time Alex picked up a knife, because Alex was prone to slicing her own fingers. Alex didn't think something more lethal was a good idea. She'd taken self-defense classes several years ago. One of her customers at the bank owned a martial arts studio, and she'd convinced Alex that as a single woman she needed to know the basics of defending herself.

Kyle finally maneuvered himself around Maggie and stood facing Nate. "We should go shoot gophers this spring. Maybe you'd like to come, Hanna? Let a real man teach you how to handle a gun."

"Does that mean you're going to have Nate teach Hanna how to shoot?" Lucy smirked at Kyle.

"Why don't you pop another chocolate in your mouth. You've only got two or three in there now."

Alex was shocked. These two were really getting in the digs. Everyone else looked embarrassed.

Kyle leered at Hanna. "Did you know I was the star quarterback during my senior year? I got a football scholarship to one of the top colleges. If it wasn't for getting married and my in-laws insisting I work for their company, I could have gone pro."

"No doubt. Lucky for your in-laws." Lucy made a face.

A Nutcracker Nightmare

Kyle obviously didn't catch the sarcasm in Lucy's voice. "Yeah. They've been struggling since I left the company. Sales increased by over five hundred percent while I was vice-president. They've been tanking since I left." A pained expression crossed his face. "I would have forgiven my ex for having an affair, but she was determined to end the marriage."

"This is all very nice, but I have a dinner with my mother to get to tonight. Can we go and get the community center decorated? Now." Lucy headed to the front door and stood there expectantly.

"It wouldn't hurt you to miss a meal, Lucy." Kyle laughed at his own cruel humor as he blew an air-kiss to Hanna.

Lucy ignored him and left, with most of the others following closely behind.

Eudora pressed her lips together and put her hands together in a prayer position. "Give me strength."

"I'll be over shortly with all the chocolate and table decorations," Hanna called out.

When the door had closed behind Eudora, Alex looked at Maggie and Hanna. "Can you believe that guy? What a jerk!"

"I spoke to Kyle's mother before Thanksgiving. They're in Palm Springs right now. It's been difficult for them having him live at home again. She said the reason Kyle left his wife's family's company is because he was involved in some kind of embezzlement. They offered him the choice of divorcing his wife voluntarily or they would have brought charges against him." Maggie shot a dark look at the door. "That tearful bit about his wife having an affair was phony-baloney."

Hanna was nodding. "Isabelle told me he was never offered a chance to play professionally. He just wasn't good enough. And you're right, Alex. He is a jerk. I wish we had some of that rat poison!"

27

Chapter Four

At the community center, Alex parked next to Hanna at the side of the building closest to the kitchen. When Hanna had the kitchen door unlocked, she waved for Alex to bring in the first box.

Once everything from their vehicles was in the kitchen, Hanna looked at her sister. "Can you help me carry this box down to the basement?" She kicked a large plastic tote filled with a variety of Christmas decorations.

"Why is it going down there? I thought all the festivities were upstairs." Alex was eyeing a beautiful wooden nutcracker sticking out of the box.

"These are for another event on Monday. I just want them out of the way. We can take the outside steps down to the basement. It's directly below us, and I've got keys." Hanna grabbed a set of keys off the counter. At the bottom of the stairs, she unlocked the door that led into the basement, where various meeting rooms were located.

They placed the box just inside the door.

"I'm going to leave this door unlocked for now, in case I have to come down again. It's quicker this way than going through the hall and down the interior stairs."

Alex pointed to the nutcracker. "Doesn't that remind you of the one Mom has?" Their parents and Oma had emigrated from

Germany in the seventies, and one of the things they'd brought with them was a collection of authentic nutcrackers made in the Erzgebirge region, where their family came from.

Hanna picked up the solid wood nutcracker, carved to look like an old-fashioned czar. "This looks like it could be handmade. It's beautiful."

Hanna and Alex had their own collection of nutcrackers they liked to bring out on November first, along with the rest of their vast array of Christmas decorations.

"I better get back to the shop. You didn't want me to leave Maggie alone too long." Alex gave the nutcracker one last look.

The twins went up the half flight of stairs to the parking lot, where Alex headed toward her car, and Hanna carried on up the second half flight of stairs to the kitchen. She waved to Alex before she went inside. Alex was about to get into her car when she heard shouting. Curious, she walked to the front of the building. Instead of unloading the trailer behind the truck, Nate and Kyle were squared off against each other. Nate's hands were clenched at his side, and Kyle seemed to be taunting him.

"This is your last chance, bud. Tomorrow I'll follow through," Kyle sneered. The sneer was wiped from his face as Nate's fist connected with Kyle's jaw.

"Don't ever threaten me again!" Nate shouted at Kyle.

Kyle had managed to stay on his feet, but he looked shaken. There was hatred in his eyes as he stared at Nate. "You'll pay for that."

Before more punches could be exchanged, a truck pulled into the parking lot and stopped beside the duo. Eddie, Eudora's odd-job person, got out and seemed to size up the situation. "Sorry, I'm late. Let's get these things moved." He pointed at the trailer behind the truck.

Alex decided to go back to her car before any of the trio noticed her standing there. *Wow. What was that all about?* Kyle certainly had a way of winding people up. That man was rotten to the core. Hopefully, he wouldn't cause any problems at the dance that night.

Chapter Five

Alex and Maggie closed the shop early after Hanna returned from the community center. Alex walked across the street and picked up some takeout from Hickory Smokehouse. The Southern barbecue restaurant was a favorite and had a following that stretched throughout the Flathead Valley and beyond for their authentic pit-style meats.

Since Hanna planned to go straight to the dance from work, Alex fed Watson after she changed and left the dog with a few guilt-induced treats. That dog had her wrapped around its paw.

Alex evaluated her reflection in the hall mirror one last time. She'd taken her thick blond hair out of its ponytail and touched up her makeup. She was wearing a new blouse, and it was a little more revealing than what she usually wore. The lady at the store had assured her it looked incredible, and Alex had to admit it did seem to flatter her pale complexion. Alex hoped Tom would find it attractive too. She grabbed the takeout containers as she headed next door.

Her neighbor had retired as the warden of the Kalispell Jail several years ago. He often quipped that he swapped inmates for congregation members, since there wasn't that much difference in looking after the spiritual and physical needs of the two groups. It had been a difficult couple of years for him. He'd lost his wife a year and a half ago, and less than a year later, his brother.

Last Christmas Alex had been surprised when Tom started showing a romantic interest in her. Initially, things had looked promising, but almost a year later things had stalled. Something seemed to be holding Tom back. He hadn't even kissed her yet.

As Alex was about to climb Tom's front stairs, a syrupy smooth drawl came from the dark several feet away. "I guess when you're not much of a cook, you have to rely on takeout."

"Better takeout than to be poisoned by your cooking, Penelope." Alex clenched her hands around the containers and turned to face her neighbor from across the street. What Penelope Shaw lacked in class, she more than made up for with gossip and spite. A few years ago, the fifty-something woman had given food poisoning to the better part of the ladies' auxiliary with a chicken pasta salad. While Alex hadn't lived in Harriston then and so had escaped the food poisoning, she had a rocky past with the woman.

"That incident was nothing more than unfortunate timing. It was purely coincidence that everyone with food poisoning also ate my dish. At least I'm not two-timing a recently widowed pastor. Not to mention wearing such an inappropriately low-cut blouse. What do you have to say about that?"

"What are you talking about? I'm not two-timing anyone. I'm barely *one*-timing. And this blouse looks like it's from the children's section compared to your wardrobe. As I recall, at the funeral reception for Tom's wife you were dressed like a madam from a brothel and stuck to him like fleas to a dog." Penelope's tendency to dress in revealing clothes made her look more like a hooker than a middle-aged retail merchant.

"I've never dressed in anything that wasn't appropriate to the occasion for a Southern lady of good breeding." Penelope, with her heavy perfume and high heels, scurried back to her house, sinking into the lawn with every other step.

Alex figured Penelope must have seen Miss T's blog post. The heavily mascaraed, man-hunting divorcée had been stalking Tom since she first got news of his wife's passing. There had been a few skirmishes when Tom started to show his interest in Alex, but Penelope had backed off recently. Maybe she was renewing her attacks.

Tom welcomed Alex into the house with a quick hug, and Alex's heart did a little somersault. He stepped back and eyed the meal Alex was holding. "I knew I made the right decision dating you instead of Mrs. Matthews." Mrs. Matthews was in her eighties and had been bringing Tom baked goods since he became a widower, but each delivery came with a recitation of her most recent health problem. And now she'd fallen victim to a scam.

"You look amazing." Tom stared at Alex, and her stomach did another one of its gymnastic moves. Tom's gaze flared and Alex held her breath. And the doorbell rang. *Rats!* Were they ever going to be alone?

Tom sighed and opened the door to find his sister offering a plate. "Dessert. Drew said he couldn't eat it because his throat is sore. He's sure he's coming down with something. You know how serious a man-cold is." She rolled her eyes.

"Thank you, Sis. Drew's loss is my gain."

"I can't stay. Drew made a special poultice and needs me to rub it on his chest and throat. He'll have to stay home, but you can still pick me up for the dance." Maggie closed the front door behind her while shaking her head.

Alex and Tom laughed as they headed to the kitchen. The romantic moment had passed. "I'll save this for later." Tom put the dessert into the fridge. "How was your day?"

That was all the invitation Alex needed to tell him about the gathering of the decorating committee. Alex loved that she and

Tom had developed a strong friendship. They sat at the kitchen table, eating the brisket and mac and cheese Alex had brought, as she let everything pour out about the afternoon's events.

"You've certainly had an interesting day. I don't know those kids all that well—they were several years ahead of mine in school."

Tom had two adult children in their thirties. Alex wasn't sure she'd call the group from her shop "kids." But it was funny how the terms *young* and *old* changed with perspective. Alex had turned forty-six on her last birthday, and she was starting to appreciate how young sixty seemed.

Tom was musing almost to himself. "I'd heard Kyle was back in town. He's not much of a churchgoer, though."

What a shock. Alex couldn't imagine Kyle would spend his time in a place that emphasized helping others.

"Of course, I know Lucy and Brooke. Brooke is a hotshot lawyer out east now. As I recall, she was a very academically minded young woman. Her parents both taught at the school, though they're retired now. It's too bad her parents are Catholic. I'd love to have them in my congregation."

Alex had hoped when she left that Tom might kiss her goodbye, but no such luck. He and Maggie would arrive at the dance after the line dancing lessons, but there wouldn't be any PDAs. Alex wasn't even sure if her lips worked any more.

As she walked home, she looked over at Penelope's house. Alex was almost certain her nemesis was standing behind the curtains of her living room, watching her. In Harriston, there was almost always someone watching you. It was a town filled with its share of secrets and gossip. Alex had learned early on that many of the village residents were related to each other by blood or by marriage, and news spread faster than chocolate syrup on a warm brownie.

Chapter Six

The line dancing class had gone off without a hitch. Well, almost without a hitch. Alex had gotten roped into participating. *Big mistake.* Dancing was not in her wheelhouse, and three minutes into the first song, she'd stepped left instead of right, and hopped and vined the wrong way, and then somehow tripped over her own foot and ended on her behind. In the process she'd managed to take down two other people. When she'd suggested she sit out the rest of the class, no one argued. Since Isabelle had everything under control, Alex went to help Hanna.

As people first arrived, Hanna had flitted in and out of the kitchen and managed to visit with several friends. She seemed to be having a blast. By seven the majority of alumni had packed the community center's ballroom, and the DJ started to play a mix of soft rock and nineties favorites. Alex was watching people, many of whom she'd never seen before, and wondered what it would be like to go to her own high school reunion. She'd never been to one before and found it fascinating how these people, ranging in age from their twenties to a few in their eighties, were behaving like teenagers. She'd heard several people comparing one another's achievements. Were they trying to decide who was the biggest loser, and were happy as long as it wasn't them? Was being a lawyer better than running a local car repair shop?

Hanna's lips were pressed together in a grim line as she hurried past Alex and waved her into the kitchen. "I'm not going out there again. I'll put the food on the counter, and you take care of keeping the tables stocked."

"Are you okay? You look angry."

"I'm fine!" her sister practically shouted.

"Okay, then. I'll leave you here in the kitchen, being fine." Something was obviously bothering Hanna, but Alex had learned to leave her sister alone when she was in a mood. Even though Hanna wasn't angry with Alex, it was best to stay out of the line of fire. That was the thing about being twins. You didn't read each other's minds, but you could definitely read each other's moods. And in this case a deaf, dumb, and blind man would know better than to go near Hanna. She was as grouchy as a reindeer demoted from Santa's sleigh team.

Round tables were set up throughout the ballroom, and people were milling about. Tom and Maggie had arrived just as Hanna had retreated to the kitchen. After saying hi, they'd headed into the throng to visit with their friends.

Alex worked fast to put food out by quarter to eight. In addition to a number of salads, Hickory Smokehouse brought brisket, mac and cheese, coleslaw, and corn bread. The restaurant made true Southern corn bread that had a rich, buttery finish and a cakelike texture, with a sweetness that just melted in your mouth.

Isabelle was in the buffet line, and Alex overheard Everett tell his wife that he was going to the washroom. Isabelle's eyebrows drew together, and she put a hand on his arm. "Again? Are you feeling okay? You've spent more time in the washroom tonight than at our table."

Everett kissed his wife on her cheek and shrugged as he walked away. "Nature calls."

On the other side of the buffet table, Kyle was swaying slightly as he stood in line behind a pretty woman with frosted blond hair.

He bent forward and whispered something in her ear, and she turned around and flashed him a death glare before switching position with the man in front of her. Alex shook her head. She hoped they'd get through the evening without a fight breaking out.

Brooke came and stood beside Alex. "I need a break. If I see one more picture of someone's ugly kids, I'll scream. Some woman younger than me was showing me pictures of her grandchildren. Don't these women know what the feminist movement was? There are options besides getting married and having children. Right? You obviously get that."

Was her marital status burned into her forehead? Why did Brooke assume she was single? Thankfully, there was a loud crash at the drinks table, and it saved Alex from answering. Someone had dropped a pitcher of water, and Alex rushed to the kitchen for paper towels to help clean up the mess before someone slipped.

After a quick marriage and an equally quick divorce, right after college, Alex had wanted to get her career moving before she walked down the aisle again. She just hadn't realized there would be so few viable choices by the time she hit her thirties. She desperately wanted to be satisfied being a career woman, to be content with her sister, dog, circle of friends, and her shop. But it was a sham. She had one failed marriage under her belt, and she secretly wanted to fall in love and have a happily ever after. Did her family and friends think of her as an old maid—or worse, a crone?

When a man was single, he was free, or a bachelor, something to be envied. Ugh. By the time Alex had cleaned up the water and took up her post again, Brooke had moved on to complain to someone else.

At eight thirty Alex started putting out the desserts from Cookies 'n Crumbs and trays of Killer Chocolates. She watched everyone drifting past the buffet tables and took a moment to relax as people happily chatted and ate their way through plates piled high with food. She absently fingered the gold charm on her necklace. It was in the shape of a yin, with her name engraved on it. Her mother had given the twins the yin and yang gold charms on their sixteenth birthday. Hanna had the yang half. When Alex left for college, she hadn't been able to find the necklace. She'd been devastated. Even after she'd enlisted everyone's help, they'd never been able to locate it. The necklace appeared to be lost forever.

Then last year her mother had been renovating Alex's old bedroom and had removed the baseboards when everything was being painted. Tucked between the baseboard and the wall, where her bed had been when she was a teen, was the necklace. It must have come off one night and fallen into the crack and stayed there all those years. Her mother and Hanna had conspired to get the necklace sent to Harriston without Alex finding out. It had been such a special Christmas present last year.

Alex watched Lucy come back for a second helping of dinner. As Lucy walked past Kyle's table with her fully loaded plate, he called out something to her. She responded with a lift of a finger in an obscene gesture. She must have said something as well, because everyone at the table laughed, and Kyle's face turned red.

When the DJ resumed playing, he started with a popular country and western line dance. The majority of people who weren't still eating headed to the dance floor. Alex took the opportunity to refill the food on the buffet tables and then went to the kitchen to help Hanna with dishes, but she was shooed away.

"Don't even think of helping. I want to make sure I have enough to do to keep me in the kitchen the rest of the night." Hanna scowled and cut into a chocolate sheet cake with such force Alex was surprised the knife didn't chip.

"What's wrong? Are you feeling okay?"

"I'm fine. I just don't want to have to go out there."

Alex didn't understand, but she left Hanna alone. Tom and Maggie were visiting with a couple she didn't recognize, on the far side of the room, and Alex decided to take a break and get herself a Coke at the bar.

Despite what she'd told Isabelle, Eddie had recently been showing a romantic interest in Alex, and she wasn't sure how she felt about it. The dark-haired bartender looked smoking hot dressed in a black shirt and pants, with a black apron around his waist. Eddie seemed to have more jobs than an actor in Hollywood. "You certainly get around: manager by day, bartender by night. I heard you were doing some work for Eudora as well." Alex melted just a little as she gazed into the pool of dark chocolate eyes that crinkled at the corners as he smiled at her.

"I bought a house a few months ago. It's a real fixer-upper, so I've been working odd jobs in my spare time to pay cash for the renos I'm doing."

Good-looking and fiscally responsible; was there no end to Eddie's charms? As she stood waiting for her drink, Alex felt an arm slide around her waist. The strong scent of liquor and body odor filled her nostrils as hot breath fanned her cheek.

"Save me a dance tonight, baby. You've got me all hot for you!"

Alex recognized the voice. She turned around and glared at Kyle. "I suggest you remove your arm from my waist. Perhaps you've confused me with my sister, Hanna. Though I doubt she'd be interested in dancing with you either. You should be ashamed of yourself."

Kyle held a wineglass in his hand and looked confused for a moment. He'd obviously had too much to drink. "Oh. Sorry. Thought you were your sister. You two sure do look alike."

Alex watched him stumble toward the dance floor. Lucy had been standing a few feet away, watching the scene. She sidled up to

Alex. "I've known him since kindergarten, and he's always been a moron."

Shocker. And here I thought he'd been Mr. Congeniality. "Why aren't you dancing? It seems like almost everyone is on the dance floor."

"I'm not much of a dancer. I prefer to keep Eddie company."

Who wouldn't? Movie-star good looks, a great work ethic, and charming, Eddie was the ideal catch.

"Honestly, I'm not sure why I even came tonight. I'd rather be at home with my cat." Lucy sipped at her drink.

Eddie handed Alex her Coke and wiped his hands on the black towel tucked into the waistband of his apron. "Are you okay? I saw Kyle put his arm around you. I was going to come to your rescue, but you took care of him pretty quick." Eddie had a crooked smile and a smooth, deep voice made for commercials.

Alex smiled her thanks. "We modern women have made knights in shining armor redundant." She stood with her drink in hand and watched the dancers for a moment. She noticed Duncan walking off the dance floor with his arm around a gorgeous redhead and sitting down beside her. The woman turned and looked up into his eyes and laughed at something he said. *That might explain Hanna's mood.*

Alex's gaze wandered over to the buffet tables, and she saw Kyle leaving the kitchen with a tissue pressed to his nose. Brooke was standing just outside the kitchen doorway watching him and guzzling her Pink Bis. Lucy followed Alex's gaze.

"I don't think I've seen her without a bottle of Pink in her hand since eleventh grade. Brooke is a type A personality on steroids."

Alex was about to respond when Isabelle and the pretty woman Alex had seen Kyle whisper to in the buffet line approached the bar and ordered four drinks.

"This is so great," Isabelle gushed. "I've been catching up with everyone. There are people here I haven't seen since graduation. Alex, have you met Zara Nichols?"

Alex shook her head. "I don't think we've met."

"Zara, this is Alex Wright, one of the owners of Murder and Mayhem. Zara and I were in the same class all through school. We were both cheerleaders. She and her husband own the hardware store in Swanson." Isabelle's gaze included Lucy. "The three of us went through school together."

Lucy glanced at the two women. "Though we didn't hang out in the same circles. Except for our study group. Hey, Zara."

Zara tugged at her form-fitting dress. She half smiled at Lucy and then craned her neck to see where their drinks were.

Alex looked around the room. It seemed as if most people were either on the dance floor or sitting in groups around the tables closest to the DJ. "It's certainly a good turnout. I would have thought, with the small class sizes, there would have been fewer people here, especially this close to Christmas."

"We were a pretty loyal group to the school. That was our world growing up. Football games, pep rallies, drinking milkshakes at the diner in the general store after school." Isabelle did a quick look around the room. "It was such an idyllic time." She glanced at Zara and Lucy. "I guess there was some bad stuff too. Life is never perfect."

"No kidding." Lucy made the comment quietly, and Alex didn't think anyone else had heard.

A glass shattered, and the four women swiveled their heads in the direction of the sound. Kyle stood in the middle of the room and stared blankly at the glass shards by his feet. He slowly looked up, and his gaze landed on Everett several feet away, headed to the hall. Kyle shouted at him. "You come back here and get me anudder drink." It sounded as if he was blaming Everett for knocking the glass out of his hand. Everett glanced back at Kyle and kept walking as he shook his head.

"I met Kyle for the first time yesterday. Apparently, he was some kind of football star in high school." Alex leaned in and whispered,

"He seems to be living in the past." And now he's slurring his words—not a good sign.

Isabelle nodded. "He and Everett were major rivals back in school. They have a history of violence on and off the field. When Kyle first moved back to Harriston last summer, he kept hitting on me. He got really aggressive about it. I finally said something to Everett, and he told Kyle if he didn't leave me alone, he'd file a restraining order against him."

"I think it's safe to say we all did things we regret in high school, but most of us learned from our mistakes." Zara paused for a moment. "Or maybe not as much as we should have. But Kyle definitely didn't. I was at the cash register, getting my takeout order at the Chinese restaurant last night, and I saw him and Brooke having dinner. He was being so rude to the waitress. It's bound to catch up with him."

Alex raised her eyebrows. Kyle better hope karma wasn't a real thing.

"I can't believe I dated him in high school." Isabelle twisted her mouth in a show of distaste.

Alex's jaw gaped open as she gawked at her friend for a moment.

Isabelle looked at Alex. "I know. It's one of my bigger regrets. It was only for about two weeks in our junior year. Even in that short time, there were moments when I could have killed him." Isabelle pursed her lips. "We'd better get back to the table with our drinks. Our husbands will wonder what's kept us. Though Everett seems to have gone to the washroom again."

As she finished her drink and headed back to the buffet area, Alex was still trying to wrap her head around Isabelle dating Kyle. She grabbed a tray of desserts in the kitchen, then paused and looked at Hanna. "I noticed Kyle coming out of the kitchen. It looked like he had a bloody nose."

"Oh, did he?" Hanna didn't look up from the food she was arranging, though Alex thought she saw a smile tugging at Hanna's lips.

"Once I get everything restocked, I'm going to chat with Eudora. Unless you need my help in here?"

"Nope. Everything is under control. You go ahead." Hanna had finished plating the Hot Chocolate cookies.

Alex grabbed one of the cookies dotted with mini marshmallows and drizzled with chocolate glaze and took a bite.

"Alex! Those are for the guests."

"What? I love those cookies, and this one was calling my name. '*Alex. Alex.*' Couldn't you hear it?" Alex laughed at her sister as she went to refill the buffet tables. With everything stocked, she grabbed a small plate and put a few mini cupcakes and cookies on it, then ambled over to Eudora, who was staffing the entrance and collecting tickets. Eudora wore a pink dress that was all lace and bows, and talked animatedly to Tom. The widower carried his tall, broad frame well. His nose had weathered a few breaks, which added character to his rugged face. Eudora's eyes sparkled as Alex put the plate of goodies in front of her. Alex had added some of the older woman's favorite Salted Brownie Crinkle cookies to the assortment. "I thought you might like a few sweets. I was afraid there wouldn't be any of these left by the time you're done. You've been sitting here for hours."

"I'm actually almost finished." Eudora looked at her watch. "I'm done in ten minutes, at nine thirty. I plan on having a few more goodies then. But thanks for bringing these over. You know how I love these cookies."

Maggie came up behind them and put her arm around Alex. "We need to head out."

Tom reached for Alex's hand and gave her fingers a squeeze. Her toes would have curled in her boots if they'd had room.

"We old folks need our sleep." Tom let Alex's hand go after only a second.

"Speak for yourself," Eudora piped up. "I'm going to party like it's 1999."

Everyone chuckled.

Alex looked through to the entryway and noticed the view from the front doors was white. It looked as if a blizzard was raging. "Have you seen the weather?"

Tom walked to the exit. He peered outside, then returned to the group. "Looks like we have an unexpected storm. It's not going to be pretty on the roads."

"Nate mentioned some farmers said there was bad weather coming. But the weather forecast never called for this," Alex said.

Eudora grimaced. "These squalls come up suddenly. Hopefully, the plows are out. I know some of these people have to drive to other towns tonight." She looked at Tom and Maggie. "You two drive carefully."

The pair smiled at Alex and Eudora, and after getting their coats, they headed into the storm. Alex looked around the hall. Kyle and Brooke stood close together near the bar. They seemed to be having a heated discussion. Brooke was poking Kyle in the chest with her finger. Kyle was still pressing a tissue to his nose.

"I'm going to wrap up now so I can enjoy the buffet and dance for the rest of the night. Will you be doing some dancing?" Eudora stood and did a little jig to demonstrate her ability.

"Unfortunately, I'm a menace on the dance floor. Besides, I should probably start putting away the dishes of hot food."

As she approached the kitchen, Alex could see Hanna standing in the doorway, slightly hidden by the doorframe. She seemed to be staring at the dance floor. Alex wondered if Hanna was wishing she could participate in the activities. Or was she watching Duncan?

A Nutcracker Nightmare

When Hanna saw Alex approaching, she moved back into her sanctum.

After clearing off all the dishes in heated serving trays, Alex poked her head into the kitchen. "Anything I can do to help? If you want a break to go and dance, I can take over in here for a bit."

"Just keep other people out of here, and I'll be happy. I've got everything under control. The last thing I want to do is go on the dance floor."

Alex was puzzled by Hanna's behavior. She usually loved being surrounded by her friends. This couldn't be about Duncan dancing with some of his old classmates. Alex found a quiet spot near the buffet tables and watched the dancers while keeping an eye on the desserts. Seeing the balloons, yearbooks, pictures, and trophies around the room reminded Alex of high school, but not in a good way. Unlike Hanna, she hadn't been popular, and she had been only too happy to move away for college.

At quarter after ten Alex started putting out the sandwich platters, when a woman stumbled to the drinks table and dropped the glass she'd just filled with punch. The contents spilled all over the table and floor. *Not again.* Alex quickly went into the kitchen to get some paper towels, but there was only one left on the roll. Hanna sent her to the utility closet on the other side of the ballroom for more. When that didn't yield any paper towels, Alex tried the ladies' washroom. As she entered, Brooke was emerging and held the door open for her. Alex smiled and went inside. She sniffed the air. It smelled like smoke.

No paper towels—just a forced-air dryer. As Alex turned away, she saw some black ash in the sink. Alex knew there was another utility closet in the basement and decided to check down there. At the bottom of the stairs, she saw a smooshed red velvet cupcake on the floor. Ugh! *What is wrong with people?* She picked up the cupcake and a candy wrapper beside it. She glanced down the hall and realized there wasn't a garbage can in sight. She put the candy wrapper in her pocket, and placed the cupcake back on the bottom stair. She'd grab it when she returned upstairs.

Alex's gaze moved from right to left as she walked down the hall. There were poster boards advertising all kinds of community activities. Did they really do doggy yoga on Mondays? Maybe Watson would like that. Alex paused and ripped off the phone number for the Weight Watchers group and stuffed it in her pocket. She might need it after Christmas.

Approaching the utility closet, she noticed a smear on the wall. *More of the red velvet cupcake? Gross.* She opened the closet door, took a step inside, and stopped short. Alex gasped and her stomach did a flip-flop, but in a very different way from when she'd been with Tom.

Lying on the floor, eyes partially open, staring blankly at the ceiling, was Kyle.

Chapter Seven

Alex was frozen in place, staring at the vacant expression on Kyle's face. Karma had finally caught up with the high school Grinch. There was blood matting his thinning hair, and lying on his chest, stained with blood, was the nutcracker that had been in the box by the door. Alex shook her head to clear her mind, then bent down and touched Kyle's wrist. No way was she putting her fingers on his neck.

He was warm, but there was no pulse. Alex stepped back. There on the shelf were several rolls of paper towels. She glanced at Kyle again. *Not much chance this was an accident.* His ashen face looked different than it had in life. He looked shrunken. She pulled the phone out of her pocket and called Duncan.

Alex's call hauled Duncan off the dance floor. He raced down to the basement while keeping her on the phone. After viewing the body, he told Alex to stay with it until he could find some support.

"Don't touch anything." Duncan looked sternly at Alex before heading back upstairs.

She couldn't believe he'd said that, as if she was a newbie to a crime scene. As she waited, she was careful not to disturb any potential evidence as her eyes and phone captured her surroundings.

She took a closer look at what she had assumed was cupcake icing on the wall outside the utility closet. It was fairly fresh, though it was drying in parts. Definitely not icing. She looked closely at the floor as well and could see some small drops of blood. There were also some smears, as if someone had tried to clean it up. Alex guessed Kyle had been killed in the hall and dragged into the utility closet.

When Duncan finally returned, he explained that he'd called in support from the sheriff's department and was told the sheriff was the only person available. There were two major accident scenes on the highway because of the sudden storm that had hit the area. That, plus a domestic incident in another community, had the entire sheriff's department tied up. He had enlisted Isabelle's help in dealing with the situation in the basement. "She'll be here in a second." He bent down to take a closer look at Kyle's body and to snap a few pictures with his camera.

A moment later Isabelle came down the stairs with a first aid kit in her hands. She scanned Alex from head to foot. "Are you okay? You're not feeling light-headed or anything? Last thing we want is to have you pass out. Of course, this isn't your first body, is it?"

Nope. This wasn't the first body Alex had dealt with. Alex wasn't sure what Isabelle planned to do with the first aid kit. A bandage slapped on that wound definitely wasn't going to fix Kyle. "I feel fine. I think he was killed out here and dragged into the closet." Alex pointed to the smear on the wall and the drops on the floor.

"I'll leave you two with the body for a few minutes. I've got some things I have to do upstairs." Duncan hurried away.

Isabelle was looking at Kyle's body from the hall while she took gloves out of the first aid kit. "I don't think I need to check for a pulse to make sure he's dead, but formalities. I assume you checked for a pulse?"

Alex nodded. "No pulse, but he was still warm."

Isabelle bent down and touched Kyle's neck. "He certainly hasn't been dead for very long." Isabelle examined the body. "I don't want to disturb any evidence, so I'm limited in how much I can do. Ah—Duncan is back." Isabelle straightened up.

Isabelle confirmed Kyle was dead, and she and Alex watched as Duncan took more pictures with his cell phone.

"Alex, you're free to go back upstairs. Please don't say anything about this for now." After Duncan dismissed her, Alex wandered away, ever so slowly.

Isabelle pointed at Kyle's head. "There's an obvious wound here, but it looks like there might be another wound to the back of the head. They'll be able to get a better look at that during the autopsy."

Alex couldn't hear any more of the conversation as she slowly trudged upstairs and stood at the back of the room. Duncan told her he'd asked a couple of volunteer firemen who had been on the dance floor all night to stand as sentries by the exits. No one was going in or out. Aside from the door sentries, no one seemed to be aware that anything was amiss yet.

Duncan came back up to the ballroom about fifteen minutes later. He headed to the DJ and spoke to him for a minute and then took a microphone the DJ gave him. After explaining there had been an accident, he told everyone they would have to stay in the ballroom until he'd had a chance to talk to them.

There was an immediate buzz in the room. Duncan shushed everyone and also warned them of the weather conditions and that roads were treacherous. He strongly suggested anyone from out of town make arrangements to spend the night in Harriston, if possible.

Almost immediately there was a scuffle by the exit hidden behind a balloon arch in the corner of the room. A moment later, a disgruntled senior Alex recognized as Fenton Carver was being led away from the exit by one of the burly firemen. It would appear at least one person had hoped to escape before the lockdown. After Duncan went back to the basement with another fireman, people in the ballroom gathered in groups. Eddie would continue serving nonalcoholic drinks, since Duncan had said there would be no more alcohol sold. Lucy was still standing near the bar, and she and Eddie were talking. Everett was with a group near the DJ. Alex walked straight to Hanna, who was standing alone outside the kitchen by the buffet tables.

"What's going on?" Hanna looked like it had been a long night. She'd worn a dark blue sparkly outfit of matching pants and top that had looked stunning earlier, but now her hair hung limply to her shoulders, and she had frosting on her shirt. "You'd think someone had been murdered, with the way Duncan is acting."

Alex looked at her sister pointedly and raised her eyebrows.

"No! You're not serious?"

Alex glanced around to see if anyone was within hearing. Only Brooke was nearby, but she seemed intent on stuffing as many of the red velvet cupcakes into her mouth as she could. Alex leaned closer to Hanna but still had to raise her voice to be heard over the music. "Kyle, I found him in the utility closet downstairs when I was looking for paper towels."

Hanna's eyes were round. "Murdered?"

"Unless he hit himself over the head with the nutcracker from the box we took down this afternoon." It was at that moment the music ended, and Alex's comment sounded loud to her ears.

She glanced behind them to see if anyone was paying attention. Zara was sitting a few feet away by herself, twirling a strand of hair around her finger. She had looked perfect earlier, gorgeous in a Christmas red, off-the-shoulder gown. The dress hugged her curves and flared out at the knee. Now she looked a little worse for wear. Her beachy waves were flat and glued to her forehead; her pale face made the mascara that dotted the area under her eyes stand out; and her gown, like its owner, had lost its perkiness.

Alex lowered her voice. "What happened in the kitchen earlier? It looked like Kyle had a bloody nose when I saw him coming out."

Hanna sucked in a deep breath and let it out slowly. "I hit him in the face."

"Why? I get the guy was a jerk, but what specifically prompted you to hit him?"

Hanna was looking at the now-empty dance floor. "He grabbed me from behind and tried to kiss me. He scared the bejeezus out of me, and I just swung around and whacked him with the wooden spoon in my hand. Honestly, I didn't even know it was him until it was too late. Kyle said I'd be sorry next week at the chocolates competition. He grabbed a piece of paper towel for his nose and left." Hanna swiped a cookie from a nearby table. "I thought I'd ruined my chances to win next week. Assuming he even remembered what happened. He was pretty drunk."

"With Kyle dead, I guess we'll never know." Alex watched the buffet tables. Brooke scarfed down the sweets she held in one hand while she clutched her pink bottle in the other. "Why would anyone kill Kyle?"

Hanna looked at Alex like she'd lost her mind. "Why *wouldn't* anyone kill him? He was rude and obnoxious to everyone he met. I don't know of anyone who liked him, except maybe his parents. And that's questionable. Maggie said they were spending an extra week in Palm Springs because Kyle was still living with them."

"I know he wasn't liked. Lots of people would have enjoyed decking him like you did. But that's a long way from murder."

"Maybe someone got tired of his rude jokes. Or maybe he tried forcing himself on someone."

"And why was he downstairs? The party was up here. Did he arrange to meet someone down there?"

"You can ask Duncan. It looks like he's coming over here."

Alex watched the deputy sheriff approach them. He had the same build and coloring as his Uncle Tom, and even in his civilian clothes he gave off calming vibes.

"Do you have any idea what Kyle was doing in the basement?" Alex asked.

"None that I'm going to share with you at this point." Duncan smiled. "Can I talk to you first? Hanna, I'll talk to you next."

Alex followed the deputy into the senior's room, where they'd had the line dancing lessons earlier. He asked her if she needed some water. Once she'd assured him she was fine, he started. "The sheriff will be here shortly. I've been told the roads are a mess. Travel is taking longer than usual." Duncan adjusted a notepad on the table. "Tell me what happened."

"I think you should know what went on earlier today. While we were setting up, I saw Nate punch Kyle. It sounded like Kyle was taunting him, but I really don't know what it was about. I should also mention Kyle and Lucy were pretty combative toward each other at the shop this afternoon." Alex told him about Kyle mistaking her for Hanna at the bar. She went through the remainder of the events that had led her to the basement. "When the spill happened, I went searching for paper towels. I couldn't find any up here, and I knew there was a utility closet downstairs. I felt like I was having déjà vu when I saw him in there. Why do I keep finding dead bodies?"

"You seem to have developed a sixth sense. Let's make sure this is your last."

"No argument there. What do you think happened?" Alex hoped his close relationship with Hanna would be an effective inducement to get him to tell her what was happening.

"Sorry, Alex. I can't share details of the investigation. I'll tell you what I can, but I'm not jeopardizing my career. I can confirm what you've probably assumed. I'm treating this as a suspicious death. I'm hoping someone saw something that will point us in the right direction."

"I don't think there will be any shortage of suspects if it comes down to who didn't like Kyle."

"Let's hope we have more to go on than that by the end of the night. Try to keep this to yourself for now. If you think of anything else, let me know. And Alex, don't get involved in this investigation. You aren't a suspect, so mind your own business." Duncan softened the last comment with a smile. "Please, send Hanna in."

As she walked out a tall woman with cropped salt-and-pepper hair strode toward Alex. The woman groaned as she approached. "Don't tell me you're involved. Sweet baby Moses, what have I done to deserve this?"

"It's nice to see you too, Sheriff Summers." Alex headed to the bar to get a drink while she waited for Hanna to give her statement. The DJ had stopped the dance music and had switched to Christmas tunes playing softly in the background. People were milling around, wondering what had happened. There was a line of people at the bar, waiting for their drinks.

When it was her turn, Eddie leaned a little closer to Alex and grinned. "Hey, gorgeous. Another Coke? Any idea what's going on?"

"A Coke would be great, but we'll have to wait and see if Miss T can fill everybody in on the excitement tonight."

"Who's Miss T?"

Eddie grabbed a glass and poured her soda. Alex studied him from under her lashes. He had a slender, wiry body, but he wasn't tall—maybe five feet nine. His dark hair, the color of espresso, was cut short at the back and sides but slightly longer on top. He had a strong jaw covered in a bit of stubble. His nose was unconventionally large, but it suited his face. "I can't believe you haven't heard about Harriston's very own gossip columnist. No one seems to know who she is, but she finds out about all the latest gossip from around the village." Alex wasn't going to mention that Alex and Eddie had been fodder for her blog posts recently.

"I guess I haven't had much time to spend online." Eddie slid the glass to Alex. "I saw you go in and talk to Duncan a minute ago. Now the sheriff is here. You must have some idea what's happening?" He glanced over at Alex and gave her another flash of his very sexy smile.

Alex's heart did a little two-step. Some men really were too attractive for their own good. "Sorry. I've been asked not to say anything for now." Alex glanced at the bar and motioned to a flier pinned there. "I see there's a new dog rescue shelter in the area?" Alex had a soft spot for dogs in need of homes. That was how she and Hanna had ended up with Miss Watson. Hanna had dragged Alex to a rescue, promising they would just look at the dogs. *Yeah, right.* Alex's heart had melted at the sight of the animals, and she'd wanted to take them all home.

"I know the owner. The rescue was started several months ago, and they're already at capacity. They need to find homes for some of the animals to make room at the shelter. I'm going to adopt one once the major renovations are done on my house."

"I wish I could adopt another dog, but one is definitely the limit that I can bring to the shop." Alex was drowning in the depths of Eddie's dark eyes. She tore her gaze away and looked back at the flier.

"I know they could use donations as well. The shelter is struggling to keep up with all the expenses. They were surprised at how much it costs to run a rescue. They ran into some major issues before it even opened, and had to spend a pile of money to fix them."

In her twenty years as a business banker, Alex had seen many businesses fail because they were undercapitalized. Getting a new business off the ground often took more money than many owners planned for. When Alex had traded her banker's hat for a business owner's, she'd understood the commitment required to start a new enterprise.

"I'll definitely make a donation." Alex snapped a picture of the flier.

With her drink in hand, Alex wandered over to Lucy, who was still hanging out near the bar. Alex tried to run her fingers through her hair, but they got stuck in all the knots. Alex glanced at her reflection in her glass. She'd been ogling Eddie, and all the while her hair looked like one of those matted faux fur rugs. She fluffed it as best she could.

Lucy's short hair was a little more bedraggled than usual as well, but Alex didn't think Lucy spent much time worrying about her appearance. The pharmacist had gone with a more casual look and wore black jeans with a billowing black shirt.

In contrast there were a few women, like Zara, in full evening dress. Alex was wearing black velvet jeans and had opted to put on a red sweater with pockets over her new blouse, after what Penelope had said.

"You've been standing here all night. Don't you want to go visit with your former classmates?" Alex hadn't really stayed in touch with anyone from school. She was friends with a few people from high school on social media, but their only contact was liking each other's pictures occasionally.

"I can't think of anyone I'm interested in talking to. Brooke was probably my closest friend, but we haven't kept in touch." Lucy nodded her head in the direction of the senior's room. "What's going on? Duncan didn't give a whole lot of information when he asked everyone to stay in here. You were just talking to Duncan— what gives?"

Chapter Eight

Alex wasn't sure what to say. She didn't want to lie outright. Eventually, everyone would know Kyle had been killed. "Someone's been hurt." *Murdered is hurt.* Alex knew Duncan didn't want the details of the murder circulating before he had a chance to speak to everyone. "Have you been watching people come and go?"

"Ooh. Mysterious. I've been here by the bar most of the night."

"Have you seen anyone you didn't recognize come in the last hour or two?"

"Fenton was the last person to arrive, as far as I can remember. He arrived shortly after ten, I think. He came to the bar, but Eddie was on a break, so I spoke to him. He was looking for Kyle." Lucy made a face. "I told him I hadn't seen Kyle in a while. Fenton wandered off, and now he's over there talking to Eudora." Lucy gestured to the pair sitting at a table in the middle of the room.

"But there have been people going in and out occasionally to have a cigarette. The designated smoking area is out the doors behind the balloon arch over there." Lucy pointed to the spot where Fenton had tried to escape earlier. The arch, made up of purple, gold, and white balloons, had been set up as a backdrop for people to take selfies. "They're not supposed to smoke on the veranda out front, but the weather's been getting nasty. I haven't seen anyone leave for a while." Lucy paused and looked over to the entryway. "Actually, that's not quite right. Shortly after Fenton came to the bar, I saw Nate standing in the entry. It looked like he was looking for someone, but he left right away."

"When was the last time you saw Kyle?"

"He headed out into the hall about the same time Eddie went on his break. Maybe Eddie saw where he went." Lucy looked for the bartender. "Hey, Eddie."

Eddie walked to the counter beside them. "What's up?"

"When you took your break, did you see where Kyle went? I think he was just ahead of you when you went into the hall."

"Sure. He was weaving in front of me. He headed toward the stairs to the basement. Either that or he was going to the women's washroom. He was drunk enough. I wouldn't be surprised."

Alex wondered if that was just before Kyle had been killed. "Did you see anyone else in the hall at that time?"

"No. I went into the storeroom. I had to make a call, and then I moved some boxes around, looking for a case of red wine. It was at the very bottom of the pile, so it took some shifting to get it out."

Before Eddie could say more, a couple lined up at the bar, waiting to order drinks. He excused himself and went back to work.

Lucy was nibbling on some chocolates and other desserts piled on a plate. "Where do you get your ideas for the chocolates? They're so good. Do you come up with your own recipes?"

"Actually, it's Hanna that comes up with the ideas for the chocolates and creates the recipes. I help in naming them and making them, but she's the master chocolatier. My family started making chocolates in Germany. They immigrated to Frankenmuth, Michigan, before I was born, and opened a restaurant and gift shop. Their chocolates are famous in the area.

"I see. Family business. That's how I ended up being a pharmacist." Lucy squinted at a chocolate in her hand. "I come from a long line of pharmacists. My parents expected one of us kids to take over the pharmacy when they got too old. That ended up being me." She pressed her lips together in a frown and then bit into the chocolate.

"You don't sound very happy about that."

"I'd planned on becoming a nurse and moving away from here. But that's the way things go sometimes. Now my mom has Alzheimer's, and all she does is help out with ringing in sales and stocking shelves. She can't be left alone in the store for long. I'm not sure how much longer she'll be able to help out at all. The shop will have to be sold when I'm too old to run it." She shrugged. "I don't have kids."

Alex could see Hanna emerge from her interview with Duncan, and Brooke tried to go in. She was stopped by the sheriff, who pointed at the chairs along the wall outside the door. She and Duncan closed the door and headed out of the ballroom. Alex thought Duncan was probably taking the sheriff to see the body. Hanna joined Alex and Lucy. "Duncan is going to interview Brooke in a minute, and then he wants to talk to you, Lucy."

Lucy took her plate of goodies and went to wait beside Brooke. Once she was out of earshot, Alex turned to Hanna. "Did Duncan tell you anything?"

Hanna shook her head. "He said he's just trying to figure out where everybody was and if anyone saw anything. So far he can't place anyone else in the basement before you. He said he saw you in the ballroom most of the night, so you're off the hook. I'm surprised he noticed anyone else with the way he was watching his former high school sweetheart all night."

Instantly, everything became clear for Alex. "You're jealous. That's what this is all about. Your sudden desire not to leave the kitchen. Is it the redhead?"

Hanna crossed her arms. "No. I'm not jealous. I don't have any claim on Duncan. If he wants to dance the night away with a middle-aged former beauty queen with a bad dye job, so be it."

"She was a beauty queen?"

"She was Miss Rodeo Montana right after high school."

"You searched her on the internet? This must be serious."

Before Alex could say any more, Isabelle reappeared in the ballroom. She approached the bar, and a moment later Everett joined her. She and Everett whispered furiously to each other while they waited for their drinks. With drinks in hand they approached Alex and Hanna. Everett was a lawyer, and as the mayor he'd been great at promoting businesses to the wider world while helping the village retain its cozy, small-town feel.

Isabelle and Hanna had become friends when the twins moved to the village and Hanna started attending Isabelle's twice weekly yoga class at the community center. Isabelle's eyes were wide as she looked at the twins. "I can't believe what happened. Everett says there's already a rumor that someone was killed."

Everett looked at Alex apologetically. "Someone said if you were here, a dead body couldn't be far behind."

Isabelle looked at Alex. "Sorry. He's just repeating gossip. No one else actually knows what happened."

Everett put an arm around his wife. "I'm sorry you got dragged into this. Why didn't they just call the coroner or a doctor?"

"Duncan is an assistant coroner. The sheriff is the county coroner, but Duncan wanted someone with medical training to check the body. Apparently, the next closest thing to a nurse here tonight is a dentist. Not a doctor in the house."

Alex tried to maintain a neutral expression. *It didn't take long for the gossips to hit on the right conclusion this time.* Everyone would eventually find out she'd found the body. Since she wasn't involved otherwise, she planned to stay out of this murder investigation. At least that's what she told herself.

Isabelle looked up at her husband. "How are you doing? You spent more time in the men's room tonight than in the ballroom with me. Did you see anything suspicious on your trips through the hallway?"

All eyes turned to Everett. Alex paid close attention, even though she kept reminding herself of Duncan's admonishment.

Everett gave his wife a look. "It wasn't that many trips. I didn't see anything suspicious. The hall and the men's washroom were empty."

"Not that many trips? I counted at least six, and the briefest was five minutes. I was beginning to wonder if you were having meetings in the council chambers." Isabelle took a sip of her drink. "Everett was hoping not to run into Kyle tonight. Ever since he threatened to slap a restraining order on him, the guy's been a bigger jerk than usual."

Everett put a hand in his pocket and shrugged. "Have you guys looked outside? It's a blizzard. I bet it's a sheet of ice under the snow. I wouldn't be surprised if some tree branches come down. Hopefully, we won't lose power anywhere in the village tonight."

Everett had looked distinctly uncomfortable when Isabelle brought up his frequent trips to the bathroom and their length. Maybe he was having prostate problems. Alex was no expert, but she thought that was more of an issue for older men, and Everett was only around forty.

"The village plow should be out," Everett said.

Hanna peered around the room. "Some of these people are from out of town. I hope the county plows are working too."

"I'll go check on that." Everett finished his drink in one swallow and headed to the stage, and Isabelle followed.

Alex saw Duncan and the sheriff go back to their interviews. Lucy and Brooke broke off their conversation as Brooke was ushered in immediately. Several minutes later, when Brooke came out, she joined a group of people milling around the dance floor.

Hanna asked what Alex was looking at. "I'm just watching people. Someone here could be a murderer."

"You don't think the killer would have stuck around?"

Alex shrugged. "Why not? Duncan put someone at each door, so no one's been able to leave since I found the body."

It was a long evening. Even though Alex and Hanna had been questioned first, they had to wait until they were given the okay to go home. What little food was left they'd put out.

Brooke approached Alex as she stood beside one of the buffet tables. Brooke snatched the last two cookies from a plate and ate the first one in two bites. "This is the worst reunion ever. I think I'd start drinking if it wasn't such a cliché. Then I could tell all my sorrows to a bartender. It's too bad those secrets aren't protected by attorney–client privilege. Do you know how many secrets I have locked up in here?" Brooke tapped her temple. "Even if I sat on the bench and I knew someone was guilty as sin, if I discovered that when I was their attorney, I'd have to completely disregard it."

"Doesn't that bother you?" Alex couldn't imagine representing someone who she knew was guilty of a crime.

"That's what our justice system is all about—innocent until proven guilty. I help guilty people or companies get off all the time. It's not about whether you're actually innocent; it's about the prosecution being able to prove you're guilty. I better get some more water before I head home."

Alex felt like she'd talked to almost everyone by the time the last few people were being interviewed. Most people had been allowed to leave immediately, but Duncan had come out and asked if Alex could stay. The sheriff wanted to talk to her.

When the last person left Duncan waved Alex into the room.

The sheriff began before Alex's butt touched the chair. "Tell me exactly what happened tonight from the time you got to the community center. And I'm not interested in theories, just give me the facts."

Alex had been through this before with the ex-marine. Her interviewing style resembled KGB techniques. Alex recited the facts as accurately as she could.

When Alex was done Sheriff Summers looked Alex in the eye. "Don't. Get. Involved. In. My. Investigation. Is that clear, Miss Wright?"

"Yes, ma'am." Alex got up to leave.

"I'll come with you. I need to talk to Hanna." Duncan looked exhausted. He had dark circles under his eyes.

Hanna was waiting just outside the room, and Duncan got right to the point. "Hanna, I need you to come to the station tomorrow morning. We need to get your fingerprints."

"Why do you need her fingerprints? She was in the kitchen all night. She didn't go near the basement." Alex looked at Hanna for confirmation.

"I was in the basement earlier this afternoon when we first got here, remember. You probably need them for elimination?" Hanna looked at Duncan. Even though she was being polite, her tone didn't have the warmth it had in recent weeks.

Duncan didn't answer Hanna's question, but instead looked at Alex. "Who can provide me with a list of people who were at the dance tonight?"

"I can do that. I've got a list of everyone who was registered to attend in my car. Though it was possible to buy a ticket at the door as well. Anyone who just dropped by won't be on my list. It was up to Eudora to take the money from them at the door. Knowing Eudora, I'm sure she has a list."

While Duncan waited with Hanna, Alex got her keys from her purse and went outside. There were about two inches of snow on the ground and a sheet of ice underneath. Alex almost slipped numerous times in the short distance to her vehicle. The wind was gusty, but at least it wasn't snowing anymore. Alex popped the trunk to her SUV and grabbed the bag with all the papers Eudora had given her for tonight. As she pressed the button on her key fob to close the trunk, she slipped on some ice.

In her effort to save herself, the bag in her hand went flying. *Close call.* She bent down to retrieve the bag while she held onto Kyle's Jaguar parked next to her vehicle. Before she straightened up, she saw something red and white behind the front tire of the Jag. She almost reached out to grab it when she realized what it was. It was a bloody rag.

Chapter Nine

A lex had been reaching out to grab the cloth sitting behind the Jag's driver-side front wheel when she'd realized it was actually a white rag stained with patches of what looked like blood. She'd snatched her hand back as if she'd been burned. Alex took her cell phone from her pocket and texted Duncan, letting him know what she'd found. He'd texted her right back, instructing her not to touch anything.

After Duncan and the sheriff came out and took pictures, they put the cloth into an evidence bag and told Hanna and Alex to go home. Duncan didn't say much with the sheriff there, but Alex wondered if the rag was what had been used to clean up the blood she'd seen smeared in the hall outside the basement utility room. At the end of the hall in the basement was the door that led to the parking lot that she and Hanna had used that afternoon. It was usually kept locked from the outside. Hanna had unlocked it that afternoon. Had she relocked it? The kitchen entrance was almost directly above it. Maybe whoever killed Kyle had left via the basement back door. It was possible the killer hadn't even been one of the guests at the dance. Kyle could have met with someone who hadn't been at the dance, and after killing Kyle the murderer could have exited that way and tossed the bloody rag under the car.

The twins drove home on the treacherous streets, the few blocks to their house. They decided to have some chamomile tea before heading to bed for a few hours' sleep. Alex carefully set her tea on the coffee table and pulled her feet up on the sofa. "We should be at the sheriff's office at seven thirty. That way we can be back in time to help open the store. It shouldn't take long to provide your fingerprints."

Hanna took a sip of her tea and put the mug down. "I need to tell you something. Please don't judge me. I'm already feeling terrible enough."

The pit of her stomach felt hollow. What could Hanna need to tell Alex that would prompt that kind of warning? In fairness, Alex was prone to blurt out whatever first came to mind. Alex nodded to Hanna.

Hanna ran her hands through her hair. "Tomorrow"—Hanna looked at her watch—"nope, today is Duncan's birthday. I made a special cake to surprise him at the dance at midnight. I've been working on it in the past few evenings at Murder and Mayhem. When we went to the community center in the afternoon, I waited until you left to bring it to a spare room in the basement."

Alex tried her best to keep her expression neutral.

"When I heard about Duncan being all chummy with his old girlfriend, I took a peek at the dance floor. I saw the two of them together, and I got so mad, I decided to scrap the whole cake idea. I was going to go down and get it and take it to my car, but then everything happened. I don't want him to find out about the cake."

"You know he's bound to see it when the forensics team goes through the basement. I assume it's still in the basement?"

Hanna nodded. She looked so miserable, Alex's heart went out to her.

"I thought maybe we could sneak into the basement and get the cake before the whole sheriff's department descends on the area. I still have the keys to the community center. We could be in and out in a couple of minutes."

"We could also get caught and be in huge trouble."

"I know. But I just want to get the cake so I'm not totally humiliated."

Alex did not have a good feeling about this. Her head was screaming at her, *No way. Come clean to Duncan, and everything will be fine.* But when she looked at her sister's pleading eyes, she couldn't say no. "Fine. We'll go at about four. That's in two hours. Hopefully no one will be around by then."

* * *

At the appointed time, after almost no sleep, Alex woke up. The twins debated whether they should walk but decided to drive over. Alex decided they should park in the alley alongside Hickory Smokehouse to keep the car away from prying eyes. It was a short walk through the alley to the back of the community center. Alex hoped no one would ever need to know about their break and enter. As Hanna had pointed out, technically it wasn't breaking and entering if they had keys. Alex wasn't sure that's how the sheriff would see it if she ever found out.

Alex kept to the side of the building. No point in letting their boot prints advertise they'd been there. The area immediately around the community center had so many prints in the snow theirs wouldn't be noticed. Dressed all in black, and wearing gloves, the sisters went to the back door, where they'd taken the bin of Christmas decorations the previous afternoon.

"What if we get caught?" The thought kept running through Alex's mind.

A Nutcracker Nightmare

Hanna shushed Alex. "We won't. Focus."

Once they had the door open Alex looked Hanna in the eyes. "You stay here and keep a lookout. I'll go grab the cake." Alex used her phone as a flashlight in the dark basement hallway. At the door of the room Hanna said the cake was in, Alex tried to turn the handle. The door was locked. She quickly walked back to her twin. The exterior door was around a jog in the wall, and she couldn't actually see Hanna from the hallway where the doors to the rooms were located. "The door is locked. I need the keys."

"Crap. It wasn't locked before. Let me see. Maybe you're at the wrong room."

The two quickly went back down the hall, following the small beam of light from Alex's flashlight in her phone. Hanna went straight to the door Alex had just tried to enter. When the handle didn't turn, Hanna pulled the key ring with all the community center keys from her pocket. "Hold the light on the key ring." She fiddled with them for a moment. "I'm not sure which key it is." She tried two before hitting on the right one.

Alex and Hanna entered the small room. Hanna's amazing creation sat where she'd left it on a table against the far wall. It was a gorgeous two-tier buttercream cake in blue and white. Hanna had made little blue uniforms and tiny gold handcuffs that she'd decorated the cake with. It had mountains layered on the side of the bottom tier and was covered in flowers and other swirls. Hanna shuffled to the table. "I'll get the cake. You hold the door open for me.

As Alex turned to hold the door, she ran into a solid object. She gasped and let out a cry at the same time she instinctively kicked at the thing blocking her way.

"Hey. Cut that out. It's me." Duncan grabbed Alex by the arm and shone a light into her eyes.

"Duncan? What are you doing here?" Alex had stopped kicking when she heard his voice.

"Me? What are you two doing here?" As he said it, he shone the flashlight across the room, illuminating Hanna holding the buttercream birthday cake in her hands. "This is a crime scene."

"Um. We came to get the cake Hanna made. Things obviously didn't work out last night, so we wanted to set up a surprise for later today. Surprise! Happy Birthday!"

Hanna chimed in. "Yeah. Happy Birthday."

"I should arrest you two for breaking and entering."

Alex chirped up. "We didn't break. We just entered. Hanna had keys, legitimately procured. And there wasn't any crime scene tape over the door. How were we supposed to know this room was off limits?"

Duncan found the light switch and flipped it on. Bright light illuminated the room, and Alex had to shield her eyes for a moment. She hoped Duncan would buy her lame excuse.

"I know. Only the front has crime scene tape so far. That will change shortly. Since it is a cake for me, I won't haul you to the department this time. But the cake has to stay here until the techs have gone over everything. I promise I'll let you know as soon as you can pick it up. It looks delicious, by the way." Duncan smiled at Hanna.

Alex looked at Hanna and could tell her sister's return smile was as fake as the beard on a department store Santa.

As Duncan led the way back to the exit Alex asked him how he'd found them.

"I was driving by and saw your car in the alley. It didn't take me long to figure out where you'd gone. Then I just followed the wet tracks to this room."

"What are you doing out at this hour?" Alex had hoped no one would be around this early in the morning.

"I just got a call that the crime scene techs are on their way. It's been a long night." Duncan rubbed the back of his neck. "How about you guys get out of here before I have to explain why you're here. Especially under the circumstances."

"What circumstances?" Alex stopped walking and turned around to face Duncan.

"I shouldn't have said that." Duncan cringed.

"Well, you did. What do you mean?" Hanna put her hands on her hips as she faced him.

The deputy hung his head. "During one of the interviews last night, someone mentioned they overheard you threaten Kyle after you hit him."

Hanna laughed. "Oh, is that all? He frightened me when he snuck up behind me and grabbed me. I just swung. I had no idea it was him, and when I realized who it was, I told him he'd regret it if he scared me like that again. I didn't mean it literally."

Duncan's mouth pinched. "Did he do that often? Grab you?"

"He's been a pain for the last month. He's been making suggestive remarks and harassing me to go out with him. He even threatened to give me poor marks for my chocolates in the competition next weekend if I didn't reconsider."

"Why didn't you mention any of this when you gave your statement last night?"

"You didn't ask. When you asked if I knew of anyone with a grudge against him, I told you almost everyone who'd met him thought he was a jerk. But I don't know anyone who disliked him enough to kill him."

Alex felt like she was at a tennis match with her head turning back and forth between Duncan and Hanna.

"When you come in to provide your fingerprints you'll need to revise your statement."

"Fine."

"Ladies." Duncan gestured for them to head through the exit as he held the door open. He stayed behind.

* * *

Alex and Hanna decided to nap in the living room until they needed to head to the sheriff's office. Alex would pursue the conversation Hanna and Duncan had had later. She was so tired she didn't think she could process anything else until she'd had a bit more sleep.

Upon waking, Alex splashed some water on her face and changed clothes. She grabbed a Coke from the fridge for the drive. Hanna raised an eyebrow.

"What? I need some caffeine if I'm going to get through this day." Alex popped the top and took a long swig from the can.

Hanna yawned. "No judgment. I'm debating whether to grab one myself. Let's go before my willpower dies completely."

"It's warmed up in the past few hours. The snow and ice are already turning to slush. I hope the plows have been out."

Chapter Ten

A lex drove her car in silence. Hanna must have nodded off.
As she navigated the slippery roads, Alex thought about
everything that had happened. There were a few details Hanna
had left out when she'd described her encounter with Kyle last
night. Alex was beginning to wonder if there were any other details
Hanna had neglected to mention. While the sisters didn't usually
keep secrets from each other, their relationship wasn't quite as open
as Alex had thought it was. She realized she hadn't been telling
Hanna everything either.

She'd been worrying that Tom didn't want to pursue their relationship. Alex had been flattered when Eddie started showing her
some interest, but she hadn't wanted to admit it to anyone, including to herself. It seemed Hanna also hadn't been sharing her feelings about Duncan with her twin.

Growing up, Alex and Hanna had always been extraordinarily
close. Alex felt a certain responsibility for her sister and brother, as she
was the oldest, if only by several minutes. When Alex had moved away
to go to college and then taken a job far from home, the twins had
remained close, but the relationship had changed. Alex hadn't realized
her sister was on the cusp of divorce until Hanna had called her days
before she and her ex-husband announced it to the rest of the family.

Alex knew she would need to tread lightly, something she wasn't particularly good at, in respecting Hanna's privacy while trying to get her to open up about what had been going on lately. Especially to get the details of what had happened the previous evening.

As Alex pulled into a parking spot a block down the street from the sheriff's office, Hanna sat up.

"Sorry. I must have nodded off. How were the roads?"

"Messy. Things are warming up fast, and the ice is melting. Are you ready to go in?"

Hanna sighed. "Let's get it over with. We've still got a ton of work today at the shop. Plus, the alumni dinner is tonight."

The sisters walked along the sidewalk of the picturesque town that hugged the sparkling blue bay where the Swan River flowed into Flathead Lake. The main street was lined with art galleries, shops, and a live theater. Swanson showcased the best of Montana, from cowboys to the latest cuisine. The town pulled out all the stops each year, to deck its halls. There were dazzling lights lining the street, and each business was fully decked out in holiday decor. A few doors down from the theater was the sheriff's department. Alex reached for the door to go into the building just as Eddie opened it from the other side, on his way out. The heartthrob held the door for Fenton to exit and continued to hold it open for Alex and Hanna. Last night's bartender had bags under his eyes but still looked as handsome as ever.

"Hey. Did you have to provide fingerprints too?" Alex wasn't surprised that others had been asked to provide elimination prints.

Eddie grimaced. "Yeah. Since I helped with some of the setting up, they wanted to be able to eliminate me. Though with the number of people at the community center in the last couple of days, I'm not sure that's going to be helpful. Maybe I'll see you later?" Eddie looked at Alex hopefully.

"I'll be at the alumni dinner tonight. How about you?" Alex felt giddy. Was it too much to hope that a younger man really was interested in her?

"I wasn't planning to go, but if you'll be there, I'm changing my plans. See you later." Eddie's boyish grin lit up the dreary entry as he let the door handle go.

Alex headed to the hard plastic chairs in the waiting area. Hanna had already gone to the front desk and was talking to a deputy. She was led to another room almost immediately. As Alex waited, Nate walked in. He spoke to the person attending to the desk and then joined Alex in the waiting area.

"Are you getting your fingerprints taken too?" she asked.

Nate looked surprised. "No. Someone vandalized my car overnight. Actually, it's my wife's car, but it's in my name. The idiot keyed along the entire driver's side."

"Oh, that's terrible. Crime has definitely been worse this past year in the village."

"Do you think? Multiple murders in twelve months." There was sarcasm in Nate's tone.

Alex tilted her head and sighed. "I was actually thinking about thefts. Now there's someone scamming seniors. But murder is definitely on the rise. Hopefully, we don't become another Cabot Cove." Alex laughed, but Nate just looked at her a little strangely. He obviously wasn't a *Murder She Wrote* fan. "I heard you were at the dance last night? Did you see anything suspicious?"

"I wasn't at the dance." Nate shifted in his seat and looked over at the desk.

"Oh. Someone told me they saw you at the entrance to the hall. Maybe they made a mistake, though I'm sure they told the deputy last night as well," Alex challenged him.

"Yeah. I forgot. I did stop by briefly. The snow was really starting to come down, and I was only there a minute." Nate's face was flushed. "I'd better see how much longer this is going to take." He hurried to the counter.

Ten minutes later the twins were headed back to Alex's car. As they strolled down the street, Alex told Hanna about Nate's unusual behavior. "That was odd, right?"

"No question. But we're not getting involved, remember." Hanna seemed distracted.

A few yards before they reached the car, they approached an alley and Alex could overhear someone speaking in a soothing tone.

"Don't worry. I'll take care of it now that Kyle is gone."

She knew that smooth voice: Eddie.

As they came level with the alley, a very disheveled Fenton Carver replied, "I never thought I'd say this, but he got what he deserved." Both men looked at Alex and Hanna as they passed. Hanna hadn't been paying attention, but Alex stared directly at both men. She nodded, and Eddie motioned in acknowledgment. Fenton just glared.

Alex didn't catch anything else, but those were certainly curious comments. She reminded herself she was not investigating this murder. The police were. So whatever that conversation was about was none of her business. *Yeah right. And you're still the same size you were in college. Oh, the lies we tell ourselves.*

Alex stopped at the house to pick up Watson, and the three ladies headed straight to the shop. Once they were inside and Watson was set up on her bench with her favorite tape, Alex sat Hanna down in the kitchen. "Okay. Spill. I told myself you're an adult and deserve your privacy, but let's be realistic. When have I ever minded my own business? Tell me what's going on."

Hanna looked miserable. Alex was afraid her sister might start to cry, so she turned on the kettle, grabbed a tin of cookies, and shoved it in her sister's direction.

Hanna took a cookie and it all tumbled out. "The only reason I've been dating is to make Duncan jealous. And it seemed to be working. After my little romance earlier this year, Duncan's been giving me so much more attention. I know we've been friends, but he seemed to be showing more romantic interest. The truth is, I haven't stopped caring for Duncan since we broke up. I thought if I played it really cool, we'd get together again when he was ready. Lately, I thought we were headed in the right direction, and then last night he was spending all that time dancing and flirting with his old girlfriend." Hanna took a sip from the cup of tea Alex had set in front of her. "I got mad and decided I'd take the cake home and throw it in the garbage."

"You already told me that. I know you're upset with Duncan, but it'll work out."

"You don't understand. Around the time of the murder, I was at the basement door. I lied to Duncan. My statement says I didn't leave the kitchen the whole night."

"How can that be a lie? I had my eyes on the kitchen entrance most of the night, and I never saw you leave once."

"I left by the door that goes directly to the parking lot." Hanna clasped her hands in front of her chest. "Earlier, I told you part of the truth, but I may have implied I didn't go down to get the cake. The fact is, I did. I went down to the basement to get the cake so I could put it in my car. My hand was on the door handle when I heard voices. I went back up to the kitchen because I didn't want to run into anyone. I planned to go down again later, but then everything happened."

"Then anyone could have gone in that door without being seen all night."

Hanna shrugged. "I guess so. Aside from some of the volunteers, no one knew the door was unlocked, though. Anyway, when

Duncan asked me if I'd been in the basement at any point, I just got all nervous and blurted out that I hadn't been in the basement since the afternoon. I didn't want him to find out about the cake."

"Maybe that's how the killer came and went." Alex would bet all their Strychnine Strawberry chocolates on it. "Could you tell who was speaking?"

Hanna shook her head. "It could have been anyone."

"You know this means you could be considered a suspect? You were near the scene of the crime. And you lied to Duncan."

"I know and I'm not sure what to do."

"Well, you need to tell Duncan the whole truth. That means telling him you were at the basement door around the time of the murder. Think back. Did you see anything?"

Hanna shook her head. "It was only a few seconds before I headed right back upstairs. But I've been thinking about it, and there may have been tracks in the snow on the stairs leading down to the back exit. I was so angry at the time, it didn't really register what I was seeing."

Before Alex could question her sister any further, Maggie walked into the kitchen and handed Alex a container. "My special triple-chocolate brownies. After Brooke mentioned them yesterday, I decided to make some. Drew doesn't feel like eating them. He says his throat is too raw. All he wants is gelatin and juice."

Alex eagerly opened the container and grabbed one and took a bite. "Duncan doesn't eat them? These are divine." The brownies were a chocolate lover's dream, made with three types of chips and rich chocolate icing.

"He has a container too. I was looking for any excuse to be in the kitchen after I got home. Drew is unbearable when he's got a cold. Today he thinks he's getting pneumonia."

"Does that mean he's going to miss the alumni dinner tonight?"

"Probably. I haven't decided whether I'll go. We should get set up for opening. I imagine we'll be busy later today after the pancake breakfast at the school."

"*Dang.* I forgot about that. Tom and I were going to have breakfast together."

"Duncan is here. He wants to talk to Hanna. I think it's about the murder. He told me about Kyle on the way here."

Alex and Hanna looked at each other. Alex mouthed, "Tell him."

"You come with me. I'm not talking to him alone." Hanna put her hands together as if she was praying.

"Maggie can you get things ready? We'll be out as soon as we can."

"Of course." Maggie looked concerned as Alex and Hanna filed out of the kitchen.

Duncan was seated at the conference room table. Watson was happily watching her show, but the volume had been turned off. On the table in front of Duncan was a folder. "I only need to speak to Hanna." Duncan focused on Alex.

"I want Alex here." Hanna grabbed Alex by the arm.

Duncan gestured to the chairs across from him. "Fine. Have a seat. Both of you."

Before Duncan could speak, Hanna came straight to the point. "I have something I need to tell you." She spilled out everything she'd already told Alex—though she left out the part about making Duncan jealous and the part about Miss Rodeo.

"Well, I'm glad you clarified that because someone came forward this morning and amended their statement as well. They said they went to the kitchen around ten last night, and it was empty." Duncan pulled a photo from the folder in front of him and placed it directly in front of Hanna. "Do you recognize this?"

"It looks like the nutcracker that was in the box Alex and I took downstairs at the community center."

"This nutcracker is what killed Kyle. It has one fingerprint on it. Yours." Duncan stared at Hanna. "It's been wiped clean except for the crown, where we found your fingerprint."

"That makes sense. I picked it up and looked at it. Alex was there when I did it. There should be more than just one print on it. Why would I wipe most of it, leave one print, and then tell you I touched it?"

"Killers make mistakes all the time. It could be argued you just confessed to touching it because you were worried someone may have noticed your absence in the kitchen last night. I really wish you'd been straight with me from the start."

The meeting went downhill after that. Hanna amended her statement, and Duncan warned her that she was a person of interest.

After Duncan left, Alex and Hanna retuned to the kitchen. Hanna looked like she was ready to cry. Alex gave her a hug. "Are you okay?"

Maggie had joined them and her gaze drifted between the twins. "What's the matter?"

"Someone came forward this morning with information that I wasn't in the kitchen the whole night."

"Do you want to tell Maggie about last night?"

Hanna nodded and spilled out the events that had led her to leave the kitchen the night before. "I'm officially a person of interest in Kyle's death. Duncan said I was heard threatening the victim, my fingerprint is on the murder weapon, and I was at the scene of the crime. Means. Motive. Opportunity. A perfect trifecta."

Maggie gave Hanna a hug. "He can't possibly think you did it."

"He says his personal opinion has to stay out of the investigation. He's following the evidence. Right now, they don't have any other leads."

Maggie eyed Alex. "I think you need to put on your sleuthing hat again. Not that I don't have confidence in my son to solve this, but I know he's going to be under extra scrutiny because he knows Hanna. The sheriff thought about taking him off the case, but a few deputies are off with the flu, and they had a rash of incidents last night. The department is stretched pretty thin. The sheriff would prefer not to call in the State if she can help it. Duncan thinks she wants to show how well she runs our county. I think a little unofficial help might be in order."

"I'm not sure that's a good idea after what happened last year. Plus, I promised Duncan I'd stay out of it, and the sheriff was very specific in telling me not to get involved." Alex had every intention of doing some sleuthing, but she felt she should put up a little resistance.

"Well, too bad for the sheriff. I'm Duncan's mother and I supersede her authority. He needs your help. He just doesn't know it. Please. People talk to you in a way they won't when they're being interviewed officially."

Alex's shoulders slumped. *Better to make a really good show of it.* There was no way she could resist Maggie's plea after all the woman had done for them, even if Alex wanted to. "All right then. Let's set up our murder board."

Maggie handed Alex a brochure. "I thought this might come in handy." It was a brochure showing all the events for the weekend as well as a picture of all the alumni who had donated to the high school renovation fund.

Hanna propped open the kitchen door so they would see anyone coming into the store. "Ladies, I hope you don't mind if I get to work while you start. I have a lot of chocolates to make. I started a batch of gingerbread truffles last night. I need to roll them now."

Alex erased most of the board. She left a corner that had a list of what Hanna had to make today. She wrote Kyle's name at the top. "This is our victim. We know how he was killed, though there were two injuries. I overheard Isabelle say he also had a wound to the back of his head." Alex showed Maggie and Hanna the pictures she'd taken at the scene. "The problem is the number of potential suspects. Not only could it be someone who was at the dance, but thanks to the basement door being unlocked, it could be anyone who was in town."

"Why don't you start with the people we know didn't like Kyle." Maggie was flipping through the brochure.

"I saw Nate punch Kyle yesterday in the community center parking lot. I think Kyle was threatening Nate in some way." Alex wrote his name down.

"Kyle was pretty mean to Lucy yesterday at the store," Hanna added as she prepped her ingredients.

"True. But I think she was in the ballroom all night. Every time I looked, she was standing beside the bar." Alex tapped the chalk against her palm. "I'll write her name down anyway. Maybe I can find out why they have so much animosity between them."

"If she was at the bar all night, she might be able to tell us who was going in and out of the ballroom," Maggie said.

"Yes. I know she mentioned Fenton came in, asking if Kyle was around. And this morning I heard him talking to Eddie outside the sheriff's department. Eddie said he was going to take care of something now that Kyle was gone. I'm adding Eddie and Fenton to the list."

Maggie looked perplexed. "I can't imagine Fenton having anything to do with Kyle's death. He's my age—though I suppose that doesn't rule him out."

"What about Everett? He was in and out of the ballroom to use the washroom more often than a woman in her last trimester. He also had a history with Kyle, and he just threatened to take a restraining order out on him." Alex wrote his name down as the other two agreed it was possible. "Any other suspects?"

"None come to mind. I think you need to go over to the school for that pancake breakfast. While you and Tom eat, maybe you can get a feel for what people are saying. And do you think you could bring some of those huckleberry pancakes back for us?" Hanna gave a small smile.

Chapter Eleven

Tom was waiting at the entrance to the school. His gaze lingered on Alex as she approached. He gave her hand a squeeze, and it felt like an electrical current shot up her arm, leaving a wake of goose bumps. He let go as they went into the gym to get in line for the huckleberry pancakes.

"You look like you're bursting to tell me something." Tom watched Alex with his gorgeous forget-me-not blue eyes.

Alex glanced around to see if anyone nearby was paying attention. She saw Penelope up ahead, serving pancakes. Their eyes met briefly, and Penelope looked away with a scowl on her face. The woman was wearing a Mrs. Claus outfit that should have been R-rated. "I don't want to get into all the specifics, but Duncan has declared Hanna a person of interest in Kyle's murder."

"You're kidding? Why on earth would he think that?"

"Unfortunately, I'm not joking. Hanna went down to the basement exit on the outside of the building around the time of the murder. Her fingerprint is on the murder weapon. Plus, someone overheard her threaten Kyle earlier in the evening. As of right now, she's their only suspect."

"Please tell me you aren't planning to start questioning people again."

"I could tell you that, but I'd be lying. Duncan is too close to this case. He has to be careful not to show any bias, so he's going to have to strictly follow the evidence. And right now the circumstantial evidence is pointing to Hanna. Maggie insisted I help Duncan."

Tom's brow creased.

She hoped another cease-and-desist request wasn't coming. "All I'm going to do is ask a few questions. What harm can that do?"

"As I recall, that almost caused you to become a victim this time last year."

Alex waved her hand. "That's in the past. I'll be much more discreet this time." She pushed aside thoughts of last year.

"Famous last words," Tom whispered as they came level with Penelope. He gave the woman a warm smile. "Hi, neighbor."

Alex watched as Tom's gaze seemed to hover around the level of Penelope's forehead. No doubt he was trying not to look at her neckline that plunged deeper than the Grand Canyon.

Penelope's face lit up as she smiled back at Tom. "I'm glad you made it out this morning. These pancakes are divine. Here's an extra one for you." She put four of the biggest pancakes on Tom's plate.

"Hi, Penelope. It's so nice of you to volunteer." Alex greeted the woman with a tone oozing sweetness.

Penelope's smile was gone in an instant. It was like the sun being covered after a volcanic eruption. The scantily dressed woman slapped two of the tiniest pancakes on Alex's plate and stared at her with eyes like chips of ice, daring her to complain.

"Could I have another plate of pancakes? I'm taking them back for Hanna and Maggie."

Penelope put several larger pancakes on another two plates and handed them to Alex without a word.

Brooke was beside Penelope, handing out juice to go with the pancakes. She beamed at each person as if she were on the campaign trail. When Alex got to Brooke, the wannabe judge glanced to her left and rolled her eyes at Alex as she handed her a cup.

The school had five long rows of tables pushed together, end to end, to accommodate the large crowd of current and past students, teachers, and their families. Alex and Tom found seats near the stage.

Tom smiled at the two seniors sitting across from them. "It's nice to see you ladies enjoying some of the festivities."

Both women had their mouths stuffed with pancake. The faster chewer, a round butterball of a woman replied first. "At our age we need to get out to every event that offers free food. Pensions just don't keep up with inflation these days. Poor Rose here hardly gets any Social Security. Don't get me started on how the government expects seniors to survive. I went to the dance last night. Goodness knows I wasn't going to miss it, even though they were charging twenty dollars. But poor Rose had to stay home."

Alex didn't think it would take much to get Vicky Potts started on anything. There was nothing she loved better than to complain about the government and the problems plaguing seniors.

Rose had finally finished chewing and added her own two cents. "Now, Vicky, don't get all excited. I'm still working at the pharmacy, and Lucy will take care of me. Things are just a bit tight at the moment. Even if the dance had been free, I wouldn't have gone."

"Well, it just isn't right. Seniors shouldn't be expected to work into their seventies." Miss Vicky, as she liked to be called, was getting worked up. "You're lucky to have Lucy. Not every daughter would live at home to take care of her mother. Miss T just put out another bulletin." Miss Vicky wore a smug expression. "She's an influencer. She said a certain forty-something young man who'd recently moved back in with his parents was more of a burden then a help, God rest his soul. So don't get me started on young people today. They're either running off and leaving their families, or coming back as adults to sponge off them. No social responsibility. Thank goodness I never had any children. They only disappoint you in the end."

The woman's short hair was an unnatural shade of ebony black, courtesy of drugstore hair dye, and contrasted sharply with her more salt than pepper eyebrows. Alex stared, partly because of Miss Vicky's hair but also because she was keeping an eye on where the food was landing as the woman spoke with her mouth full.

"Not like in our day, when family took care of their own. Your Lucy is one of the good ones, Rose. The way she stepped up in high school." She patted Rose's arm. "Nowadays they just stick you in a cheap senior's home so it doesn't deplete their inheritance."

Thankfully, Miss Vicky stuffed another bite of pancake into her mouth, overloading her capacity to eat and speak, and they were spared any further rambling on the neglect seniors suffered these days. Alex already had her meager meal eaten and thought she saw Fenton heading into the hall near the stage entrance. "Is that Fenton heading out of the gym?"

Rose swiveled her head around faster than an owl honing in on a mouse. "It certainly is. Such a handsome man."

Alex silently acknowledged that beauty was in the eye of the beholder, but Fenton looked like he'd been run over, stomped on, and hung out in the rain for a few days. He must have had a rough night.

"Tom, I'll be right back. I just want to catch Fenton before he leaves."

Before Tom could respond, Alex was halfway to the door of the gym, where she'd seen Fenton go out. Before she could get out the door, Everett stopped her. "Alex, I'm glad I ran into you."

Alex wasn't glad at all. She was wondering how she could politely sprint off without offending Everett.

"This will only take a second."

Alex reluctantly turned her attention to Everett.

"Would you mind donating a couple of your deluxe boxes of chocolates for our silent auction this afternoon? We had a snafu and realized we were a couple prizes short of what we had hoped for."

"No problem. Someone can pick them up any time before the auction. Say, are you sure you didn't see or hear anything at all on your many trips to the washroom last night?"

"I wouldn't say *many*, but like I told Duncan, the last time I was in there before you found Kyle, I didn't hear anything."

Alex interrupted. "Are you sure about the time?"

"Within a few minutes. I looked at my watch before I headed to the bar from my table. It was ten minutes to ten. When Lucy said Eddie had gone on a break to get some more booze from the storeroom, I decided to head to the washroom. The men's washroom is right beside the storeroom, and I heard Eddie talking to someone. He seemed to be talking about some renovations. Apparently he was still in there when I went to the bar a few minutes later to try and get a drink again. Lucy said he'd be back soon, but I didn't want to leave Isabelle any longer, so I went back to our table. Though I could have waited for a drink. Isabelle was still up dancing."

"Was there anyone else in the washroom with you?"

"No. Just me. But I do remember Fenton walking toward the bar just ahead of me when I went back into the ballroom. I overheard him ask Lucy if she'd seen Kyle. He looked a little damp, so he must have been outside."

By the time Alex was done talking to Everett, she had limited hope of still finding Fenton. Alex continued out the door of the gym and was in a little alcove off the main hallway. She could hear voices nearby. She peered around the corner and saw Nate and Fenton in a heated discussion. She paused out of sight and listened, but all she heard was, "I'm not lying for anyone," before Nate banged out the door at the end of the hall that led to the parking lot.

As Fenton came parallel to her, she called out, "Hello, Mr. Carver. How are you?"

The man seemed startled to see her there. "Why? What do you want?"

Alex had heard about Fenton from Maggie and Drew so often, she felt like she knew the cantankerous old man, but she'd actually never been introduced to him, though she'd seen him around the village. This morning's meeting in Swanson didn't exactly count as an introduction. The man had bristly gray hair that looked like it had been cut with a weed whacker, and eyebrows so bushy they looked like he'd pasted a squirrel's tail above his eyes. They warred with the tops of his ears for hairiest body part.

"I just wanted to introduce myself. I don't think we've officially met, but I've heard so much about you from Drew Fletcher. He's told me how you're the spark in the engine that keeps the historical society running." Alex had to think fast, and she hoped flattery would soften up the old curmudgeon. What Drew had actually said was that there wasn't a spark of creativity in the old goat. *But, hey, he did use the word* spark.

"Well, that's probably true. Who did you say you were?"

"I'm Alex Wright. My sister and I own Murder and Mayhem."

"I'm not much of a fiction reader. Mostly manuals and farming magazines is all I have time for these days. I'm not interested in whatever you're selling."

"I promise I'm not selling anything. I'm just trying to get to know people in town. I saw you coming out of the sheriff's department with Eddie this morning. I notice you still have a bit of the fingerprint ink on your hand." Alex was looking at Fenton's right hand.

"I ran into Eddie at the station. Last night they asked me to provide my fingerprints for elimination purposes. Waste of time. But I suppose if it helps find Kyle's killer, then it's the least I can do."

"I heard you arrived at the dance quite late and wanted to talk to Kyle. Did you get to talk to him, by any chance?"

Fenton pulled a bag of cough drops out of his pocket and fished one from the bag. He squinted at Alex all the while he unwrapped the candy and popped it in his mouth. "I've heard about you. You're pretty nosy." Fenton shrugged. "I wasn't going to the dance. I'm too old to be doing stuff like that. Changed my mind at the last minute. Had some things to discuss with Kyle. Not sure why you're interested. I taught him in school, and now I buy my farm equipment from the dealership his dad owns."

"Did you have a chance to talk to Kyle?" Alex wanted an answer.

"Naw. Couldn't find him."

"I heard you coached the football team back in the day. Was Kyle one of your players?"

"He played for me, alright. The kid had real potential. I encouraged him, same as I did for a few boys over the years who looked like they could get football scholarships. What of it? I didn't see Kyle last night."

Alex was prepared for Fenton's surly attitude. She wasn't about to give up in the face of some crankiness.

"I was just curious. I saw him arguing with Nate yesterday before the dance. Nate actually punched Kyle. It made me wonder if there were other people that might have had a disagreement with Kyle recently."

"How's that any of your business?" Fenton took a step toward Alex, invading her personal space.

She was sure he meant to intimidate her, but she stood her ground and lifted her chin a fraction. No one was going to scare her. *In a public place with no weapon in sight.*

"Kyle may have rubbed some people the wrong way, but that doesn't mean he should have been killed. You should mind your own business." He peered at Alex for a second, then turned and left.

That went well. At least he'd talked to her. Alex felt bad for abandoning Tom, and hurried back to their table. Miss Vicky was in the middle of a diatribe about the sad state of affairs with the national healthcare system. At least she'd finished her food.

As soon as Alex sat down, Tom interrupted Miss Vicky. "I'm sorry, we've got to go. I have an appointment in ten minutes. It's been nice talking with you." Tom got up and pulled Alex by the hand and practically ran from the table. Alex struggled to reach for the plates of pancakes for Hanna and Maggie. As they walked out of the gym doors Alex had just come through after talking to Fenton, Tom leaned in and said, "I hope you got whatever information you were angling for."

Tom was walking forward but looking at Alex as he spoke. He veered too close to the wall and bumped into Isabelle. "Sorry. Didn't see you there."

Isabelle had been peeking into a classroom window. "No harm done."

Alex tried to hide her smile. "Since we've run into you. I have a question about last night. I overheard you mention a cut on the back of Kyle's head when you spoke to Duncan. Do you think he could have hit his head against the wall before he was bludgeoned? Could that factor into Kyle's death?"

Isabelle thought for a moment. "I'm not a doctor, but hypothetically speaking, a wound like that could have been caused by a person striking their head against a wall, or even the floor. I'm not sure if it factored into Kyle's death. But the autopsy will reveal far more than what I can tell you.

Tom took Alex's hand as they headed toward the school's front doors. "I'm glad I was able to help you with your inquiries by our meeting up with Isabelle. I wish I could help you grill your suspects this afternoon, but Eudora called me this morning. Since the community center is locked down as a crime scene, she's asked if they can hold the alumni dinner at the church tonight. I need to go over and help set up the tables and chairs." Tom stopped on the sidewalk across the street from the church and looked at Alex. "Please be careful." He brushed a lock of hair away from her cheek.

Alex's stomach suddenly had butterflies careening around. "I promise I'll be careful. Besides, at this point my suspect list is pretty short. Or long, depending on how you look at it. Almost everyone who knew Kyle disliked him, but there has to be more to why he was killed than his generally rude and obnoxious behavior. The hard part is knowing whether there's someone who hated him who wasn't even at the dance."

"There's probably more to it than Kyle's generally poor behavior, and I know you're going to investigate, but I really would be devastated if something happened to you." Tom brought Alex's hand up and brushed his lips against her fingers. He gave Alex a half smile and strode across the street to the church.

Alex was rooted to the concrete. A rush of heat warmed her face. Her mind warred with her heart. Her heart wanted to focus on the moment she'd had with Tom, but her head insisted she figure out why someone wanted Kyle dead. This time her head won out. She headed north to walk the short distance back to the shop.

Chapter Twelve

When Alex returned to the shop, she gave Maggie the pancakes and suggested she take a break and go eat in the kitchen with Hanna. There were a few customers browsing, and Alex ensured they were looked after before sitting down at the computer. It was time to learn a little more about their victim. Before she could lay a finger on the keyboard, a skinny, gray-haired man with a Brylcreem comb-over and prominent front teeth approached the counter. Alex smiled at the man expectantly.

"Excuse me. I need some help finding a mystery for my wife. She's laid up in bed and needs something to keep her busy."

"I'm sorry to hear that." Alex came around the counter. "What type of mysteries does your wife like?"

The man fiddled with the bow tie he wore. "She said to get something set in England. In fact, you better make it two books."

"In that case, why don't you get her a couple of Agatha Raisin mysteries by M. C. Beaton. I'd suggest *The Quiche of Death* and *The Vicious Vet*—they're the first two books in the series." Alex pulled the books off the shelf and walked back to the counter.

"I'll take anything that will keep her busy for a while. She's had me fetching and carrying for two days. We came for the reunion, but her gout flared up as soon as we got to my parent's place. She had me driving to Kalispell last night to get her some painkillers. I got caught in that sudden storm, and it took forever to get home. There was a bad accident on the highway."

"I'm glad you made it back safe. I was at the reunion dance last night, and I heard there were a couple of accidents on the roads."

"Actually, I drove by the community center on the way home and couldn't believe how many cars were parked there. I was tempted to go in and see some old friends. I saw the vet—what's his name?" The man snapped his fingers. "Baxter. I think he's a few years younger than me. He was running around the side of the building to his truck, I think. Nasty weather. I hope I can get to the alumni dinner tonight."

A few years? I'd peg you as mid-fifties at a minimum. Why is it that we all think we look younger than we are? "What time did you drive by the community center?"

"About ten. Well, I better go. The barracuda—I mean wife—is waiting."

Alex was at the computer again, and Watson trotted behind the counter and plopped onto Alex's feet. She reached down to give the dog a scratch behind the ears. "You must be tired of watching television." Within seconds the dog was quietly snoring.

The man's account of seeing Nate around ten tallied with what Lucy had told Alex the night before. It also meant Nate had had the opportunity to kill Kyle. When she typed in Kyle's name, a long list of hits came up, including his social media. Alex looked at some articles that were connected to his former in-law's company. Unfortunately, there was very little new information. There was an announcement naming the new vice president of the company, and it simply said Kyle had gone on to pursue other interests. Yeah—like not going to jail.

Alex finally decided to scroll through Kyle's social media. All his accounts were public. Surprise, surprise. This was someone who had enjoyed being seen by others. There were pictures of Kyle at parties, restaurants, behind the wheel of his Jaguar, and as Alex looked more closely at multiple pictures, though the backgrounds were blurred, she realized they must have been taken at a casino. She could see the corner of what must be a roulette wheel and poker tables. She started to scroll through the comments.

One user, Nightingale_91, commented, "Still haven't learned your lesson. Quit while you're ahead."

Alex looked at some other posts more carefully and realized they were also at casinos or gambling establishments. As she went through the comments, she found more from Nightingale_91. Some were nastier, calling him a "loser" and making fun of his thinning hair.

Kyle had responded to some of the comments with his usual witty charm. "Bite me" seemed to be a favorite.

Despite scrolling quite a ways, she didn't find anything that enlightened her about who might have a reason to kill Kyle. A group of seniors came in the shop led by Eudora. The postmistress gathered them like a general with her troops and instructed them to find some books and to try the chocolate samples. Once her orders were being carried out, she went directly to Alex.

"I'm glad I found you here. I heard Hanna is a person of interest in Kyle's death."

"How did you . . . never mind. I should just assume you know everything as it happens here in the village."

"Perhaps not everything, but I do seem to hear quite a bit. Though this Miss T seems to have an even better network than mine. That's why I thought it prudent to come see you, especially since you found the body."

"Dang. I was hoping that wouldn't get out right away."

"Dear, you know what this town is like. There are forces at work that even I don't understand."

"What do you know about Kyle's past? Is there anything that would make him a target for murder?" Alex could use any help she could get right now. She didn't seem to be going anywhere in her singular pursuit.

"Kyle was not a nice youngster. Spoiled, I should think. He was an only child and overindulged, in my opinion. Being a spinster, and childless, I'm not sure if my opinion is worth much, but there it is. His parents gave him everything and didn't hold him accountable for the mischief he got himself into. They just kept bailing him out."

"I'm not a parent either, but that does sound like a recipe for disaster."

"When he was still in elementary, he was routinely bullying other children. By high school he was breaking into the summer cottages that had been closed up for the winter, to have wild parties. I heard he'd charge admission and make a pile of money. Of course, he was never caught, but one hears things. The worst thing I remember had to do with an accident he was involved in. A student, a couple of years older than Kyle, was in the car with him. The poor dear had been offered a football scholarship, but the accident injured his back so severely he was never able to play football again. There was talk Kyle had been drinking, but his parents hushed it all up."

"Wow. It sounds like he just carried that type of behavior into his adult life. Someone mentioned he embezzled from his in-laws and got away with it by giving his wife an easy divorce."

"Yes. I've heard that as well. There were also other incidents in high school. It was always suspected he was involved in some cheating in his senior year, but it was never proven."

"That figures. He came across as such a jerk, I assumed he wasn't that bright."

"An understandable assumption, but not at all correct. A jerk may be an apt description, but he was quite smart—just lazy. He had a master's in business and from all accounts, did a good job at his previous company—aside from the embezzlement, of course."

Eudora moved out of the way as some of her friends came to the counter to pay for their purchases. Maggie joined Alex and relayed the message that Hanna needed help in the kitchen.

Hanna had coated multiple molds with milk chocolate. Alex picked up a piping bag and started adding the ganache to the molds on the counter. It was important to move quickly before the mixture cooled too much. As they worked, Alex filled her twin in on what she'd discovered. "Do you think Kyle could have had a gambling problem?"

"That seems possible." Hanna's hands were a blur as she worked.

"If he owed a lot of money, he might have gotten desperate. Maybe that's why he embezzled from the company—to pay off his gambling debts," Alex mused.

"Maggie mentioned that Kyle's in-laws wanted him to pay back the money he embezzled, but he said it was gone. He ended up walking away with almost nothing in the divorce. Kyle's mom said he'd come home with a sob story of how he couldn't bear to leave his wife with nothing. Unfortunately for him, his mother-in-law called Kyle's mom and told her everything. She didn't want them to think they'd treated Kyle badly."

"Wow." Alex was at a loss for words.

When they were done, Hanna leaned against the counter and looked at her sister. "The more I find out about Kyle, the more I wonder why someone didn't try and knock him off sooner. What are the chances he changed in the past year?"

"Do men or leopards ever change their spots? Maybe I'm being too cynical."

"We're probably just bitter from our divorces." Hanna laughed. "But I say love 'em the way you find 'em, because they're not likely to change. I'd say it's a good bet he had a gambling problem." Hanna nodded.

Alex agreed. "Exactly. He has a history of dishonesty. Maybe he tried to cheat the wrong person?"

Hanna started spreading chocolate over the molds that were ready to be finished. They'd be scraped and tapped to get the air bubbles out. Then they'd go into the fridge and be unmolded after they were set. "That might be a motive for murder."

Maggie came into the kitchen. "Duncan is here and wants to talk to you, Hanna. He's in the office. It looks official. Alex, you'd better go with her."

Alex and Hanna both walked into the office-cum–conference room and sat down at the table, across from Duncan.

Hanna spoke up first. "Alex might as well hear whatever you have to say because I'm just going to tell her anyway."

"That's fine. I wanted to talk to you both. This is on the QT. I'd be in trouble if the sheriff knew I shared this with you. We have the preliminary results from the autopsy. Kyle had a high blood alcohol content—no surprise there. Blunt force trauma to his head is what killed him—also no surprise. But there were a couple of surprises. Kyle had five thousand dollars in the pocket of his jacket."

"That's interesting. Have you checked to see if he had a corresponding withdrawal from his bank account?" Alex asked.

"It'll take time to access his bank records. His fingerprints were on the money, as well as multiple others. It's all going to take time." Duncan paused and seemed to be deciding whether to continue.

Alex encouraged the deputy. "You said two surprises."

"Yes. Something unexpected. That rag you found under Kyle's Jag had blood on it, all right. But it wasn't human blood. It was animal blood."

Alex's jaw dropped. "What! That doesn't make any sense."

Duncan shrugged. "I don't know where it came from or how it ended up under Kyle's vehicle, but it doesn't seem connected to his death."

Alex looked at Hanna. She seemed as surprised as her sister.

"What about the cut on the back of his head?" Alex spoke up quickly.

"How do you know about that?" Duncan's eyes narrowed as he looked at Alex.

"I overheard Isabelle mention it to you while I was still in the basement. I also saw what looked like blood on the wall. I wondered if he might have hit his head."

"You wondered right, but please keep it to yourselves. We always like to withhold a couple things from the public. The blood on the wall was Kyle's, but that happened shortly before he died. It wasn't the cause of death. The nutcracker killed him. There were multiple prints on the banister leading down to the basement, including yours, Alex. The only fingerprints on the door handle of the utility room were also yours. Whoever was there before you wiped everything. There weren't any prints on either side of the back door that goes to the parking lot. And according to you, Hanna, your prints should have been there."

"That's right. I went in and out of that door earlier yesterday. Alex and I were careful not to leave any fingerprints when we went back this morning."

"Exactly. There should have been prints, but there were none. Personally, Hanna, I know you didn't do this, but there are others who may not share my views. I have to follow the evidence. I have to be careful not to appear to be swayed by our personal relationship. You threatened Kyle, and your print is on the murder weapon. You also had the opportunity, in the time frame Kyle was killed, to go down to the basement. I have to bring you to the station for official questioning. Alex, before you say anything, I don't have a choice. And I'm telling you again, officially, don't get involved in this. I'll find the truth. If the sheriff finds out you're snooping, she'll lose her mind."

Alex decided to interpret what Duncan said as *"If you snoop, don't get caught."* Alex wasn't going to sit idly by while her sister was practically accused of killing Kyle. She'd have more faith in the system if there weren't people being released from prison after it was discovered they were innocent. The justice system might work most of the time, but it didn't work all of the time. And Alex wasn't taking any chances with her sister's freedom at stake.

After Duncan and Hanna left, Alex explained to Maggie what had happened.

"I love my son and he's good at his job, but I'm sure he's under pressure considering he and Hanna are friends. That's why it's so important that you figure this thing out."

Alex agreed and went to finish the chocolates Hanna had started. When that was done, she'd head out to make some inquiries.

A half hour later Alex finished the chocolates. She washed her hands and went to the front of the house to find Maggie.

Maggie was straightening a display and paused to look at Alex. "You should know people have been coming in and asking for you. I think they're hoping to ask you about Kyle's death. I've just been telling them you're busy making chocolates and can't be interrupted."

"Thank you. Hopefully, with all the reunion activities I can ask questions without seeming too nosy."

"Several of the school's current and former teachers were just here. I overheard them talking about Kyle. A couple taught him in school, and they were telling the others that he was a bright student, but cocky. One of them mentioned he'd become particularly aggressive in his senior year. If it hadn't been for Nate intervening, Kyle would have been in numerous fights."

"Kyle and Nate were friends in high school? They didn't seem all that close when I saw them together."

"They were both on the football team. I'm not sure how close those friendships were. I think a lot of them hung out together because they played on the same team. Keep in mind, classes then were even smaller than they are now, and you usually grew up with the kids in your class."

"I went to a high school with about five hundred students. Not huge, but it's hard to imagine a graduating class of twenty. Everyone must have known each other quite well."

"Much like today, I think everybody knew everybody else's business. Despite that, there are always some secrets. Kids here in town were forced together by geographic requirement. Whether you were a cheerleader, or a drama club or debate team member, you were familiar with all your classmates."

"Maggie, can I ask you something? It's not really my business, but I think Duncan and Hanna really belong together. They're having a hard time communicating, and I think there are some misunderstandings between them. I'm not sure how, but will you help me get them to talk to each other?

"I've noticed the same thing, but I hate to interfere. It's a delicate balance being Duncan's mom and Hanna's friend, not to mention employee."

"I have no such inhibitions. If the chance presents itself, will you support me in whatever I do?"

"As long as it won't get me in trouble with either of them, you bet."

"I'll be heading over to the school. Text me if you need me to come back."

Alex wanted to track down some of the alumni who had gone to school with Kyle. Maybe there were old grudges that had resurfaced with this weekend's gathering. Alex grabbed her jacket and was walking toward the front door when she saw the Wicked Witch of the West come out of the east-side salesroom.

Chapter Thirteen

"I'm surprised you aren't in your shop, Penelope. Things are bound to be busy today."

The antique shop owner had shed her R-rated Mrs. Claus dress and was wearing a pair of tight red satin pants topped with a low-cut red sweater that had little Santa heads embroidered all over it. She wore red spike-heeled boots that made her look like she was ready for a role in a Christmas spoof of *Grease, Post Menopause.*

"I needed a new book. Besides, I was able to get someone to look after things while I helped decorate the church for tonight's dinner. Tom asked for volunteers, and some of us have a sense of community bred into us. I could tell Tom appreciated that I made time to help him. He and I worked side by side."

Alex knew Penelope wanted to bait her, and Alex refused to bite. She had far more important things to do today than to let Penelope annoy her. "That's wonderful you were able to help. I'm sure your presence helped lift everyone's Christmas spirits. It's been nice chatting, but I must go."

"I heard you were the one to find the latest body. You do seem to be making a habit of it. It's very unseemly, you know, to be involved in a murder."

"I'll keep that in mind if I run across any more victims. Maybe next time I'll just sneak away so someone else can find the body."

Penelope looked at Alex skeptically. "That deputy should be looking for the killer elsewhere. Not at dear Hanna."

"Duncan doesn't think Hanna did anything."

Penelope cocked her head. "This is Harriston. Every volunteer in the church knew Duncan just took Hanna away in his squad car, practically in handcuffs."

Alex couldn't believe that information was out already.

She left the shop and walked to the school. Off to the east her gaze lingered momentarily on the majestic Swan Mountain Range covered in snow. Alex wasn't much of a hiker, but there were a few easier trails she'd tried last summer. She loved the clean mountain air. In front of the Village Office, a couple of deer were snacking on some bushes. They barely glanced at Alex as she walked by. She'd only had about two hours of sleep last night, and Alex felt like she was on autopilot.

There was a concession, just inside the school's front doors, selling a variety of home-baked goods and hotdogs to raise money for a band fieldtrip to Seattle. On the counter was a collection jar for the new animal shelter Eddie had told her about. Alex purchased a Coke to revive her flagging energy, and dropped a five-dollar bill in the jar.

Once she'd guzzled half the can, she looked around, trying to decide where to go first. In the end she didn't need to go anywhere. One of Kyle's former classmates came to her. Brooke was purchasing a brownie from the concession, and as soon as she turned around, Alex called to her.

"That brownie looks delicious, but I need more caffeine than what I'd get in baked goods." Alex held up her can of soda.

"I have such a sweet tooth, I can't resist." Brooke unwrapped the treat and devoured it in a few bites. "Brownie with a Pink Bis chaser." The future judge reached into her purse and pulled out her bottle of Pink. "Not as good as Maggie's brownies, but it will do."

"This must be such a difficult day for you. Losing Kyle."

Brooke wrinkled her brows. "We weren't close. I hadn't seen him in years until this weekend."

"Huh. I thought you two were good friends. I saw you in a—I guess you could say—heated discussion at the dance. I just assumed you were fairly close."

"Ah. No, we were just talking about politics. You know how it is." Brooke was chewing on her bottom lip, and cast a glance at the exit.

"Did you see him again after that?"

"No." Brooke was scanning the entryway openly now. "I had something to eat after Kyle and I talked, and it didn't agree with me. I went to the bathroom soon after. In fact, I think I passed you when I was coming out."

"You were in the bathroom the entire time?"

"I'm afraid so. I should really go to the doctor when I get home."

"Do you smoke?"

"No. Vile habit. I was sorry to hear that your sister is being questioned. I'm sure she didn't have anything to do with Kyle's death. They should be talking to Coach Carver. He's the one who wanted to meet with Kyle just before he died. If I'd realized Hanna would be suspected, I never would have told them about her hitting Kyle and threatening him."

"You were the one who told Duncan about that?"

"I was standing just outside the kitchen door, eating, when he went in. I couldn't help seeing what happened. I told Duncan she had every right to hit him."

Alex was feeling the urge to hit Brooke. She reminded herself Brooke was obliged to tell Duncan what she knew. It was just so frustrating that Hanna was being questioned when other suspects were being ignored.

"Oh, there's Everett. I need to dash over and talk to him. It was nice to see you again."

Alex wanted to corner Everett as well. While she didn't honestly suspect him any more than she did Hanna in Kyle's murder, he'd had the opportunity, and there had been animosity between the two of them.

Alex wandered down the hall, past pictures of Santas with cotton-ball beards, to a poster-board display that had been erected with the pictures of each graduate from 1965 to 2015. Zara was standing in front of the display.

Alex stopped beside the attractive woman. "Not a very big class for each year. Some of those early years only had six graduates. You must have known everyone in your class quite well."

Zara nodded. "Most of us grew up together. Kyle is the first from my graduating class to die." She was winding a few strands of hair around her finger.

"It's always sad to see someone as young as Kyle pass away."

"I suppose. To be honest, I wasn't a huge fan of the guy."

"Why is that?"

"Mostly because he was cruel. He loved to humiliate people. But he was also a liar and a cheat."

"How so?"

Zara gave herself a little shake. "Sorry. I've got to go." The former cheerleader practically sprinted down the hall.

Alex had seen how Kyle could be cruel. What did Zara mean when she said Kyle had been a liar and a cheat? Was she referring to high school or something more recent?

After a walk through the school, without running into anyone else she recognized from Kyle's class, Alex decided to head back to the shop. She wasn't sure whether to add Zara to her suspect list. Did the woman have a personal history with Kyle, or had she just seen what he'd done to others?

When she walked into Murder and Mayhem, Drew, bundled in a scarf and hat, stood at the counter, talking to Maggie. This had to be important to drag Drew from his sickbed.

Alex patted Drew's back as she approached. "How are you feeling?"

"Don't get too close. I wouldn't want you to catch this bug. If you feel yourself getting sick, I'll send Maggie over with my special poultice. As I was just telling Maggie, this information is too important to text. She's been keeping me up to date on your investigation. I think I'm beginning to feel better, but you never know. I could relapse."

"I'm so glad you're on the mend. Even if it's only temporarily." Alex took off her jacket and rested it over a chair behind the counter.

"A little while ago—it must have been just before Duncan took Hanna with him to the station—sorry, I know he's just doing his job, but I can't believe he's actually considering Hanna at all—I was on the sofa with my eyes closed, and he must have thought I was asleep. He went into the kitchen to make himself a sandwich and put his phone on speaker while he spoke to another deputy. They were able to get into Kyle's phone and check all his texts and see who he's called and who has called him. Kyle received a text last night at 9:53 from Fenton, telling Kyle to meet him in the basement of the hall at ten. Duncan told the deputy to find Fenton and bring him in for an interview."

"Now, that's interesting. Fenton told me he didn't see Kyle last night." The front door opened and banged shut quickly. Alex turned to the door as Hanna walked in and headed straight to the kitchen. "I'd better go check on her."

Alex had only caught a glimpse of her sister's face as she'd stormed through the hall, but she didn't look happy. Alex approached the kitchen door with caution. She could hear Hanna on the other side, banging things onto the counter and muttering.

"Stupid, arrogant . . ." Hanna throttled a bag of dark chocolate callets. "Men!"

"You can't live with 'em. I know. How are you doing with the chocolates? Do you need my help? And I don't mean killing that bag—just making them the usual way."

Hanna stopped choking the chocolate for a moment and looked around. "After the ones in the molds are boxed, I just need to dip the Gingerbread Gelsemine truffles. Then we're all set for the dinner. After that I'll be working to fill our regular stock and what we need for the Festive Foods event next weekend. I think I've got it all under control. Assuming Duncan doesn't come back and throw me in jail." Hanna gave the bag one final shake before putting it down.

"It's not going to come to that. They have another suspect." Alex told Hanna what Drew had come to the shop to tell them.

"Hallelujah! What about you? Do you have any new suspects?"

"Fenton has moved up on my list. Everett saw him come into the hall at around ten. Though I'm not sure why he would want Kyle dead. I also ran into Zara at the school. She said she wasn't upset about Kyle's death. Though, to be fair, I have yet to run into anyone that is grief-stricken about his passing. She called him a liar and a cheat. When I asked her to elaborate, she took off."

"That's definitely worth looking into. If you don't mind, I'm going to skip the dinner tonight. I'm not feeling very festive. We're getting behind on chocolates for the store. We have several orders I need to get started on."

"I'll just stay and help. Four hands are better than two."

"No. Please go. I'll feel guilty if you stay behind. Besides, with our new tempering machine I can work almost as fast on my own. Please. I need some time alone."

How could Alex argue with that? The new wheel tempering chocolate machine had been an early Christmas present the twins had bought for the store. It allowed them to scale up production without sacrificing quality. "Alright. Promise if you change your mind, you'll tell me."

"I promise, but I won't change my mind. Besides, this will be your chance to talk to all your suspects. I think practically everyone will be there tonight."

"You know there's something that's been niggling at the back of my mind. I think it's something someone said, or maybe something I overheard. I hate that feeling."

Hanna was pouring more chocolate into the tempering machine. "It'll come to you."

Alex scrunched up her forehead. "You're right. I'll try not to think about it." As Alex said that, her phone pinged. Those dang butterflies were dancing around her stomach again. She wasn't sure if it was anticipation or dread. She had a text from Eddie.

Chapter Fourteen

Alex read the text from Eddie: Just wondering if you'd like to go for coffee after the alumni dinner tonight?

What to say? Was this supposed to be a date or just a friendly outing? Alex wasn't sure how to navigate this type of thing. Despite Isabelle's suggestion, Alex wasn't about to play the field. She would see where things went with Tom before she even considered dating anyone else. But was this a date? Maybe he knew something.

"Who's your text from?" Hanna was looking at Alex curiously. "You're making the most hilarious facial expressions."

Alex read Hanna the text. "Is he asking me out on a date?"

"It sounds like it to me. But we've already discovered I'm not the world's best authority on dating or reading cues from the opposite sex."

"I'll just tell him I didn't get much sleep last night and I'm heading to bed early." Alex wasn't sure why she didn't just tell Eddie she was dating someone.

Alex left the store early. Maggie said she would work until closing and take Watson home with her, since she and Drew wouldn't be going to tonight's alumni dinner. That would give Hanna the chance to work uninterrupted. Alex was looking forward to the opportunity to have a quick shower and to change before she headed to the church. She loved driving down her street, past the school with its children's artwork in the windows, and the houses all lit up for Christmas. One of their neighbors did a different theme in his yard each year. This year he had put up giant dinosaurs helping Santa with his gifts. The house and yard were lit up like Times Square.

She had barely put a foot out of the car when a dark shape appeared suddenly. Alex put her hand over her heart. "Penelope, I really wish you'd stop doing that." Alex's least favorite neighbor had appeared out of nowhere.

"Stop doing what?" Penelope snapped.

"Never mind." Alex didn't have the time or the energy to get into an argument with her nemesis. Penelope's mouth was pinched so tight she looked like a fish trying to drink from a straw.

"I just wanted to give you this parcel. The delivery driver was going to leave it on your doorstep yesterday, but I knew you and Hanna would be at the dance, and I didn't want it left out. It's for Hanna." Penelope handed Alex a parcel the size of a box of tissues from that ubiquitous online firm. Penelope started to walk away and then paused. "You know you should really let the sheriff's office handle this murder investigation. After what happened to you last year, I would have thought you'd know better."

"What are you talking about? I'm not investigating anything."

Penelope pursed her lips again. "You're not fooling anyone. You've been asking a lot of questions. You found another body. It doesn't take a rocket scientist to figure it out." Penelope flounced in the direction of her house and threw over her shoulder, "In fact, Miss T alluded to it in her blog today."

"Thank you for your advice." Alex tried to keep her tone even.

"Just so you understand, I'm doing this for Hanna. She'd be upset if something happened to you. God knows why."

"I absolutely understand. I'd never assume you'd do anything nice for me," Alex called out.

It looked like Alex was going to be late for the alumni dinner. She'd definitely miss the hors d'oeuvres, but hopefully she'd make it for the main course. Penelope's words were still running through her mind. Was she really that obvious in her questioning? Hopefully, the sheriff didn't become aware of her actions.

As the hot water flowed over her in the shower, Alex wondered what was in the parcel Hanna had ordered, and she realized what had been niggling at her. It's funny how when your mind is thinking about something completely different, it can recall a buried memory. At the school concession Brooke had said that Duncan should be looking at Fenton as a suspect because he wanted to meet with Kyle just before he died. How had Brooke known that? Duncan had only found out about that text on Kyle's phone, a very short time before Alex went to the school. There was no way the gossips had gotten hold of that little tidbit so quickly.

The only way Brooke could have known about it is if she was with Kyle when he got the text. And if that was the case, she wasn't in the ladies' bathroom the whole time, as she'd said. Which meant she could very well be the killer.

Alex rushed to dry off after spending longer in the shower than she'd intended. Duncan had told Maggie he was planning to be at the dinner to keep an eye on everyone. Should she tell Duncan what she'd remembered? Alex thought back to the ash she'd seen in the sink. What could that have been? Kyle had been carrying five thousand dollars in his pocket. Had he been blackmailed, or was he the blackmailer? If Alex had to gamble, she'd put her money on Kyle being the blackmailer. So was Brooke his victim? As a potential judge, any skeletons in her closet would be a real problem, especially if Kyle knew about them.

A Nutcracker Nightmare

When Alex got to her car, she saw a piece of paper under her windshield wiper. Ugh. She grabbed the paper, then got in and started the car. Once she had the heat turned up, she glanced at the note. *MIND YOUR OWN BUSINESS* had been written in block letters on the paper. Nothing else. It would appear she'd ruffled someone's feathers. *You'd think people could be a little more creative in their messages.*

Alex drove the short distance to the church parking lot, but it looked like every space was taken. She could just drive home and walk back. She circled the lot. *Oh, lucky day.* There were a few spots left at the back of the parking lot. She checked her watch. Six o'clock. Dinner should be starting any second. Even in the dark, Alex could see Brooke's rental car several spaces over. It had a distinctive ochre-yellow shimmer. She'd seen Brooke driving it yesterday. *Good. She's here.*

The church had a large gym that was used for everything from basketball games to wedding receptions, to dinners like tonight. Tom waved to Alex when she entered the gym. He was sitting with Eudora. They had done a lovely job of decorating the gym on short notice. Tall, narrow banners in purple with gold lettering were at every entrance, announcing the Harriston High Reunion. Giant purple, gold, and white balls, and stars, hung from the ceiling. They had another purple, gold, and white balloon arch—or maybe they'd been able to get the one from the community center—set up in a corner near the stage. People were busy sucking in stomachs and giving their Spanx a good workout as they had their pictures snapped in front of the arch. There were little purple and gold sparkly stars and confetti on each table, with a tall vase filled with purple and gold ornaments in the center.

Alex had decided to wear her high-heeled boots with a figure-hugging gray wool dress, and halfway to the table her heel slipped

111

from under her, and she almost went down. She managed to save herself a full fall, but her dignity was gone. Penelope was watching her and snickering. Once she was safely seated and had greeted everyone at the table, Alex looked around the room to see if anyone else had seen her less than graceful moment.

"Are you okay? You look distracted." Tom had his arm around the back of her chair.

Alex felt the heat creep up her neck. *Dang boots.* She finally faced Tom. "I'm fine. Have you seen Brooke? I was hoping to talk to her." Alex glanced over Tom's shoulder and spied Duncan a few tables away, sitting with Miss Rodeo. *It's a good thing Hanna isn't here.*

"No. I don't think so. It's been a little crazy. They had to bring some of the decorations from the community center at the last moment. It's still a crime scene, and nothing is supposed to be removed. Let me tell you, Duncan got an earful from Eudora about that, and he ended up letting her grab a few things under strict supervision."

"I saw Brooke's car in the parking lot, so she must be here." Alex stood up and took a quick look around. Sure enough, there was no sign of Brooke. But Miss Vicky, Rose, and Lucy were bearing down on them.

"Are these chairs taken?" Miss Vicky had already plunked herself down beside Eudora, so the question seemed superfluous. Eudora immediately grabbed a cream cheese–filled tomato from her plate and put it in her mouth.

"We didn't think we'd be able to find a table with three chairs together," Miss Vicky addressed everyone at the table. "We'd planned to get to the dinner early to get good seats, but Lucy had to work a little later than expected. Say, Eudora, do you mind if I finish that canapé on your plate? It looks like you might be finished with it."

Eudora's eyes bulged as she saw Miss Vicky reaching for her appetizer, but her mouth was too full to respond.

Lucy helped her mother settle into a chair next to Miss Vicky and then sat beside Alex. "I told you both I could have sat by myself."

"Nonsense, dear. I'm sure this is much nicer with all of us seated together."

Miss Vicky spoke to Eudora again. "These sort of affairs bring back so many memories, don't they? I was at the school today, looking at all the displays. It was nice they had a picture up of Olive. It happened around Valentine's Day in 1999 as I recall. Such a tragic accident."

Eudora glanced at Lucy. "It certainly was."

"Of course, they had a picture of Jack as well. Only right. I mean, he didn't die, but still. His life was practically ruined because of that accident. Such a shame when he couldn't play football anymore."

Rose almost knocked over her water glass. Lucy managed to catch it. "Be careful, Mom. When's dinner coming? I'm starving," Lucy said.

Alex hadn't seen him approach, but Eddie was suddenly seated beside Lucy. "Hi." Eddie glanced around the table. "This seat isn't taken, is it?"

Eudora spoke up first. "It's all yours. I didn't think you'd planned to attend tonight?"

"Alex made it sound like it would be fun, so I decided to come." Eddie looked at Alex and gave her a wink.

Alex was afraid to look at Tom. Eddie had made it seem like she'd invited him. As the catering staff walked into the gym with the first meals, Alex darted a quick glance at Tom. He was glaring in Eddie's direction. Eddie, on the other hand, seemed to be entranced in a conversation with Rose.

Their table was among the first to be served the main course, and Alex dug into her meal of roast beef, mashed potatoes, vegetables, and gravy, with gusto, once everyone had a plate in front of them. There were buns from the bakeshop on the table, as well. She wasn't about to let the tension between the two males ruin her meal.

Alex leaned closer to Lucy. "Last night, you were standing by the bar most of the night, right?"

"I only left to get food from the buffet tables."

"That's not quite accurate, Lucy, dear." Miss Vicky sat directly across from Lucy, and she'd interrupted her conversation with Eudora to lean across the table. "I came to the bar at about ten to say goodbye, and you weren't there."

That woman must have the hearing of a bat, Alex thought. She looked at Lucy.

Lucy didn't miss a beat. "That must have been when I was in the utility closet behind the bar. Kyle dropped a drink earlier, and someone mentioned the spot was sticky. I got some paper towels and cleaner to wipe it up."

Miss Vicky seemed satisfied, and she turned back to Eudora, stuffing a piece of meat into her mouth as she continued their conversation. She was chewing with her mouth open, and Eudora had to duck more than once to avoid a chunk of roast beef shot her way. Alex saw Miss Vicky pointing at Eudora's roast beef, and Eudora was quick to move her plate a couple of inches away from the woman.

Alex took a sip of her water. "I'm just curious. Why did you and Kyle have such a strong dislike for each other?"

Lucy dabbed at her mouth and took a drink from her water glass. "Funny story. Kyle and I were in the same class, starting in kindergarten. He's always been a bully, and in third grade he was pushing around some poor kid in our class. I guess I'd had enough, and I hauled off and punched him. He ran off sniffling, kids laughed, and Kyle never touched another kid—at least not when I was around. But after that we had an undeclared war between us. Silly, but that's really what started it."

"You guys never resolved your dislike for each other over the years?"

"He became nastier as he got older and bigger. By high school he was intolerable, and I didn't want anything to do with him. I didn't see him again after graduation until we were prepping for the dance on Friday, so it really wasn't an issue."

Miss Vicky's voice rose above everyone else's. "Tom, you look positively irritated. Is something wrong? I'd think you'd be thrilled tonight. Two eligible bachelors surrounded by five attractive, single women. You and Eddie could have your pick." Miss Vicky fluttered her lashes at the men.

Eudora rolled her eyes and got up to check on dessert. She returned fifteen minutes later with a clipboard under her arm and sat down as the first desserts were being served to diners at several tables. "There was a small snafu in the kitchen. The caterer just realized one of their staff accidentally put whipped cream on the dairy-free options for tonight."

Alex was still trying to find Brooke in the gym. She kept craning her neck to see if the future judge was sitting somewhere in the room.

Eudora watched Alex and finally stopped her monologue of the caterer's problems. "Are you looking for someone, Alex?"

"Sorry. I was hoping to talk to Brooke. I saw her car in the parking lot when I arrived, but I can't see her anywhere."

Miss Vicky leaned across Eudora. "I saw her when we arrived. She was sitting in her car, talking on her phone."

"Thanks, Miss Vicky. I'm just going to see if her car is still here." Alex walked out of the gym, focused on not tripping or having her heels slip on the shiny floor. Out in the hall there was a flurry of activity as servers hustled from the kitchen to the gym and back again to try and serve the two hundred and fifty guests waiting to eat dessert.

Pushing open the washroom door on a hunch, Alex caught the tail end of a conversation. She recognized her quarry's voice. "You'd better stop, if you know what's good for you." Then there was an abrupt silence.

Alex walked around the privacy wall and smiled at the two women facing each other in front of the sinks. Zara looked pale, and Brooke turned to the mirror and examined her reflection.

"Hi." Zara plastered a smile on her face that didn't reach her eyes. "Well, I'd better get back to my table, or my husband will think I got lost." She flashed a quick glance in Brooke's direction before heading out the door into the noisy hall.

Brooke rummaged through her designer bag until she produced a lipstick case. Brooke let the bag go, and it fell on its side. Alex could see a half-empty bottle of the ever-present pink bottle peeking out of the handsome shoulder bag.

Brooke looked at Alex's reflection in the mirror as she applied her lipstick. "I don't know why I even came tonight. I've spent most of the time on the phone. Hopefully, they haven't finished dinner yet."

"I'm afraid you've missed it. They're about to serve dessert. You can probably still go to the kitchen and get some dinner. I was actually looking for you."

Brooke glanced at Alex again as she pressed her lips together to distribute the lipstick.

"You mentioned something earlier today that got me wondering. I wanted to ask you about it."

Brooke turned away from the mirror and put the cap back on her lipstick. "Okay. Go ahead."

Now that the time was upon her, Alex's mouth had gone dry. What if she was wrong? Would this powerful woman think she was crazy? "Earlier today you mentioned that the sheriff's office should be considering Fenton as a suspect. You said Fenton had asked to meet Kyle shortly before his death."

Brooke tossed the lipstick back in her bag and scooped it over her shoulder. "Yes. I think Fenton is a far more likely suspect than Hanna."

"Well, the thing is, the only way you could have known about that message, is if you were with Kyle shortly before he was killed. I found out that Fenton texted Kyle at about five minutes before ten. Eddie watched Kyle head toward the basement stairs just before that time. You seem to have known about it even before the sheriff's department. How did you find out about Fenton's text?"

Alex could see the gears turning in Brooke's head as she worked out the time line. There was no getting around the fact that Brooke knew something she shouldn't have, assuming she'd been in the washroom during the time she claimed.

Brooke's eyes widened, and a vein in her forehead throbbed. The woman opened her mouth as if she was about to say something. Instead, she clamped her lips together again and paused for a moment. "That's a really good question. I must have overheard someone mention it. That's obviously the only way I could have known. So many people have been talking about the murder. That's really amazing how you picked up on that detail." Brooke walked toward the exit and paused. "I heard you were quite the sleuth last

Christmas. You should be careful. The village has ears everywhere. You wouldn't want the killer to find out you're after them." Brooke walked out.

Alex stood staring at the spot where Brooke had just been. Had Brooke just threatened Alex?

Chapter Fifteen

Alex sat beside Tom and stared at her dessert. It looked delicious, but Alex kept replaying what Brooke had said. Was she the killer? Every time Alex looked up, Eddie was staring at her, even though he was chatting with the other women at the table. He had an easygoing way about him and drew everyone into the conversation.

Everyone, that is, except Tom, who was glowering at the heartthrob.

"Dig in. That dessert is on my radar if you don't want it," Miss Vicky urged Alex.

Alex looked over at her table companion. She already had her dessert plate scraped clean. The woman ran her finger across an errant crumb and sucked it off her finger. Alex picked up her fork and had some of the triple-layer eggnog cake. There had been a choice of apple pie or cake, and for Alex there was no contest. The more icing, the better; and this cake had gobs of it.

"Did you find Brooke? I noticed she's sitting over there with Zara, if you need to talk to her." Eudora glanced in the direction of Brooke's table.

"Thanks. I ran into her in the washroom."

Eddie stared at Alex, and she could feel Tom watching her as well. Were they waiting for her to tell them why she wanted to find Brooke?

"Brooke was always such a nice girl, wasn't she, Lucy?" Rose smiled at her daughter.

"She was great. Finish your dessert, Mom."

"Oh, look. There's the mayor." Miss Vicky was waving at Everett on his way to the door. Everett waved back before he ducked out. "I'm sure that's already the third time he's headed out to the hall. It must be a strain on his family with him being so busy. Do you think their marriage is solid?"

"Miss Vicky, don't you start any rumors. I'm sure the mayor's marriage is just fine," Tom said.

Alex was nibbling on her dessert as she watched everyone in the room. Duncan stood near the doors with a phone pressed to his ear. His eyes scanned the room and came to rest on Alex. Was he talking about the investigation?

Eudora pushed her chair away from the table. "I'd better go tell our MC to get the show on the road. We're doing a brief memorial for Kyle tonight before we start the rest of the program."

"I think I should take you home now." Lucy reached for her mother's purse under the table.

"Nonsense. Your mother and I aren't children who need to be in bed by eight." Miss Vicky eyed the last couple bites of cake on the plate Alex had pushed away. "If you're not going to finish that, I'll take it off your hands."

The dessert was whisked away before Alex had a chance to reply. *I'd hate to have grown up with her. I would have starved to death.*

After swallowing her first bite, Miss Vicky said, "I heard that Kyle was conked on the head. Seems like a nasty way to die, but you know—karma. I feel sorry for whoever has to come up with something nice to say about him tonight."

Before Miss Vicky could continue, the MC tapped the microphone on the stage. Alex decided to go out to the lobby since she wasn't that interested in the program. She was also tired of the tug-of-war between Tom and Eddie. She felt like each of them was trying to get her attention. After excusing herself, Alex headed to the washroom first.

The men's washroom was next to the women's, and she couldn't help hearing someone cheering inside. Alex stood with her ear pressed against the door. Someone inside was listening to some kind of sports game and cheering or cursing as the game progressed. Unexpectedly, the sounds ended; the bathroom door was flung open, and Alex was nose to nose with Everett, who had his phone clutched in his hand.

"Oh, sorry." Everett gave Alex a funny look.

"Actually, I should be the one apologizing. I was about to go into the women's, and I heard cheering coming from your washroom. I was curious. It sounded like someone was listening to sports."

Everett shuffled his feet and swallowed hard. "Please don't tell Isabelle. There are some incredibly important basketball games being played this weekend, but I promised Isabelle I'd attend all the reunion activities."

"Let me guess. You've been sneaking off to the washroom to watch the games on your phone."

Everett nodded and held up his phone and showed Alex the screen. "They're in halftime right now. I've got to get back to the table so I can come back here when the game starts again."

"That's why you were constantly going to the washroom at the dance—to watch a game."

Everett nodded again. "I've really gotta go. Please don't tell Izzy."

"Your secret is safe with me."

Alex realized she now had one less suspect. Not, she reminded herself, that she ever truly considered Everett a suspect.

After she'd used the washroom, she headed to the lobby's sofa, sat down, and pulled her phone out of her purse. Alex glanced out the main doors and saw a pickup truck stopped in the parking lot, with its engine running. It had a logo on the door that seemed vaguely familiar. The passenger window was down, and a woman stood there, gesturing wildly. Alex couldn't see anyone in the passenger seat. The woman must be talking to the driver.

Alex got up and wandered closer to the doors so she could see who was outside, but the truck sped off before she could see the driver. The woman was left standing alone and gave the universal finger of displeasure to the driver. There seemed to be a lot of that going around this weekend. When the woman wheeled around, she saw Alex staring at her through the double doors.

Zara.

The petite beauty put her head down as she came inside. There were tears in her eyes she tried to wipe away. She looked up at Alex with a watery smile. "Have they started announcing the alumni donors?"

"They just started to thank donors a few minutes ago."

"I'd better get in there. The hardware store is getting a certificate."

She ran into the gym before Alex had a chance to ask Zara if she was okay. *Hmm. What was that all about, and who was in the truck?*

Alex decided it was time to get some input from her friends. She sent a text to Maggie. She had a reply within a minute. Then Alex texted Hanna and Tom to see if they could meet at Maggie's house at eight.

Alex looked up from her phone and saw Tom coming down the hall in her direction. When he got to her, he enveloped her in a hug. "How are you doing?"

"I'm fine. It was so noisy in there, I just wanted some quiet."

Tom led her to the sofa. "I'm sorry I haven't really been there for you this weekend." He leaned forward and kissed Alex on the forehead just as Penelope turned the corner and looked right at them. Steam practically shot from her ears. Tom turned red and pulled away from Alex faster than a politician caught with an underage model.

"Hi, Penelope. Were you looking for someone?" Alex basked in Penelope's angry gaze, though she wondered about Tom's obvious discomfort.

"I'm looking for Zara. Eudora sent me. She and her husband are about to get their certificate, and they couldn't find her." Penelope ground out the words through clenched teeth.

"Zara just headed into the gym a moment ago." Alex pointed at the door to the gym and gave her neighbor a giant smile.

"I must have missed her. I'll leave you to your activities." Penelope didn't wait for a response. She turned on her heel and headed back up the hall.

Tom looked at Alex. Was he blushing? Did he have feelings for Penelope? Is that why things were stalled between them? Maybe he just didn't know how to tell Alex he wasn't interested anymore.

They'd gone on their first real date on New Year's Eve to a restaurant in Kalispell. Alex had said she didn't mind going to Hickory Smokehouse, and Tom had jokingly said he didn't need the added stress of being watched by everyone in the village on his first date in thirty-five years. They had gone on several more dates in January, but they'd never done anything in Harriston. Then Tom had gone off to look after his brother. There hadn't been any more real dates until he'd wound up the estate last month. In fact, now that she thought about it, yesterday was the first time they'd actually held hands in public in Harriston, and there'd barely been a soul around to witness it.

Until now, Tom had either taken her out of town or they'd been in a private residence on their handful of real dates. Alex wasn't sure what to make of all her thoughts.

Tom heaved a sigh. "I'm sorry. It's been difficult getting used to the idea of people seeing me with a young and beautiful woman."

"Are you embarrassed to be seen with me?" Alex was trying to understand.

"No. Definitely not. The opposite, in fact. I'm worried you're embarrassed to be seen with me. I keep thinking people are wondering what we're doing together. The old guy and the dazzling beauty."

Alex was fighting the urge to utter a sharp retort. She took a calming breath. "I enjoy spending time with you. Can't we just enjoy being together without worrying what anyone else thinks?"

"Easier said than done. I'm afraid once you see how boring I really am, you'll drop me like a hot potato."

In almost a year, she and Tom hadn't even kissed on the lips. At this rate she'd be heading down the aisle pushing a walker if Tom ever proposed. Not, she reminded herself, that marriage was even on the table at this point. They were only just getting to know each other in a romantic sense, but realistically, at her age most relationships were headed in that direction. Alex was about to reply, when the doors to the gym opened and several people came out.

Tom got up and reached for Alex's hand. "Let's go. I don't need to be here. The committee is in charge of cleaning up and locking the building."

Alex decided to put thoughts of their relationship aside. Right now she needed to focus on finding out who had killed Kyle, because it certainly wasn't her sister.

Chapter Sixteen

After leaving the church, Alex and Tom drove to Maggie's house. Tom had walked to the church, so he went in Alex's car. They needed to fill Maggie and Drew in on the evening's events. Alex texted Hanna and asked where she was.

As they stepped into the house, Watson looked up from her spot on the sofa. She stretched and slowly made her way over to Alex for a pat on the head. Then she headed to the kitchen.

"Are you feeling well enough to have visitors, Drew?" Alex didn't want him to be overtaxed tonight. He was sitting on his La-Z-Boy sofa with a blanket draped over his lap and ministering to himself with nose drops. There was a thermometer, a box of tissues, several bottles of medication, and a mug of something steaming sitting on the table beside him.

"The old coot is perfectly fine. He had a bit of a sore throat, that's all," Maggie called out from the kitchen, where she'd headed after answering the door.

"My speedy recovery is likely thanks to my quick action drinking my special tea and applying the poultice overnight."

"That poultice stank to high heaven. I couldn't sleep most of the night because of the fumes." Maggie brought in a tray of cookies, a pitcher of apple cider, and glasses. There were also a couple of special dog cookies on the tray.

Watson was certainly being spoiled tonight. Maggie was dressed in one of her famous Christmas sweaters. This one was pink and had a reindeer applique, with little jingle bells sewn on in place of eyes.

Maggie looked at Alex. "Drew is a treasure. And sometimes I'd like to bury him."

"You'd be lost without me, dear."

There was a quiet knock on the door. "That's probably Hanna. I'll get it." Alex was grateful for the distraction and answered the door to let her sister in, then resumed her seat beside Tom. The entry opened directly to the living room, and everyone greeted the chocolatier.

Hanna held a box of chocolates in her hand. "You guys are probably sick of chocolates."

Tom reached out and took them from Hanna. "Not me. I wouldn't mind a few of those. Miss Vicky took the chocolates from my plate at dinner. She said men my age shouldn't be eating too much sugar. I almost had to beat her off with a stick to keep my apple pie."

"What's up?" Hanna looked from Alex to Tom. "You said you had news."

Alex hoped she wasn't leading them down the wrong path with her theory. "Earlier tonight, I realized Brooke knew about Fenton texting Kyle. She and I were talking at the school this afternoon, and she mentioned that Fenton should be a top suspect in Kyle's murder, not Hanna. She said Fenton asked to meet with Kyle that night. But Drew only overheard Duncan find out about that text a little while before I spoke to Brooke. There's no way she could have known about that unless she was there when Kyle got the text. I think she's the killer."

"Have you told Duncan?" Drew interrupted. "He needs to know."

"No. Until I have something more concrete, I don't want to say anything to Duncan. I confronted Brooke with it, though."

Hanna looked shocked.

Maggie and Drew both said, "No!"

Tom spoke up. "Do you think that was wise?"

"It was at the church when I went to look for Brooke. Zara was in the bathroom with Brooke when I got there. I was quite safe."

"I can't believe Brooke could have had anything to do with Kyle's death. She was always such a sweet girl when she was young." Maggie looked at the pictures of her children on the wall.

Hanna took off her coat and sat on a bench by the door. "What did she say?"

"She said she must have overheard it somewhere. I suppose there's a remote possibility that could be true, but I got the feeling she was going to say something else and then changed her mind." Alex looked down at her hands and rubbed at an imaginary spec of dirt. "Then she sort of threatened me."

"That's exactly what I was talking about. You can't go around questioning people and making accusations." Tom had covered her hand with his.

Hanna held up her hand to calm Tom down. "Before we get too excited, what exactly did she say?"

"She said I'd better be careful and that I wouldn't want the killer to find out I was after them. It' was pretty vague."

"You're right about not going to Duncan," Drew said.

"Drew! What are you saying?" Maggie looked at her husband in shock.

"Hear me out. Duncan has to follow evidence. This is just Alex's word against Brooke's. Plus, there's no proof that Brooke's explanation isn't true. Remember, she's a lawyer—she's not going to allow herself to be bullied by the sheriff's deputies."

"There was one other thing. When I went into the washroom, Brooke and Zara were talking. I overheard Brooke say, 'You'd better stop, if you know what's good for you.' What do you think she meant?"

"Could Zara be blackmailing Brooke?" Hanna asked.

"Maybe Zara saw something at the dance," Tom said.

"Or maybe Zara knows something from back in high school." Alex thought over the evening and remembered something else. "Later, I saw Zara in the parking lot. It looked like she was arguing with someone in a truck. It drove away before I could get a better look at it. She was crying when she came in, but tried to hide it."

"Her husband drives a truck. Maybe she was arguing with him." Drew reached for a chocolate. "I've heard they've had some trouble in their marriage."

Alex was struggling to keep her eyes open. "I don't think so. Penelope came looking for Zara a few minutes later and said Zara's husband was in the gym. I think I need to go home and get to bed. My brain is starting to shut down. There are too many things to remember."

Everyone agreed and gathered at the door to leave. As Hanna opened the door, Duncan was about to come in. "I just came home to grab a drink. Hi, Hanna. If I didn't know better, I'd say this was a meeting of your sleuthing club. But I know it can't be because I expressly told Alex to stay out of this investigation, and you know that applies to the rest of you."

"Of course, dear. You know we would never interfere." Maggie was jabbing a finger into Drew's shoulder.

"Ow! What was that for?" Drew looked up at his wife.

"Come on, Tom—you can walk me home. Hanna I'll see you soon. Come, Watson." Alex grabbed Tom and practically dragged him out of the house, with the dog following.

Once they were out on the road, Tom asked, "What was that all about?"

"I just thought Hanna should have a moment with Duncan. Alone."

"Maggie and Drew were both there."

"Maggie was signaling for Drew to get up from the sofa while I was getting you out the door. Duncan and Hanna are working under a few misconceptions, I think. They need a chance to communicate with each other."

After Alex had explained things to Tom about Hanna and Duncan, she'd realized Watson hadn't had her walk yet. Alex wasn't up to the usual route to the beach and back and decided twice around the block would have to suffice.

Alex could barely function when she went to bed at eleven. She was lying in bed with Watson snuggled up to her, thinking about who wanted Kyle dead. Everyone disliked Kyle, but who hated him enough to bump him off?

If Brooke had been in the basement with Kyle when he got the text from Fenton, had she killed him? If Kyle had been blackmailing Brooke when she was up for a judgeship, that would be a strong motive. Did this go back to something that had happened during high school?

Alex drifted to sleep with a kaleidoscope of thoughts running through her brain.

Chapter Seventeen

The next morning Alex could hear Hanna in the kitchen. Watson had left Alex's room at some point during the night, and Hanna must have closed Alex's door this morning. Grabbing her robe off the end of the bed, she headed downstairs. There were Christmas decorations in every nook and cranny of the house. Alex was careful not to let her robe get caught in a nutcracker display on the landing as she went downstairs. The nutcrackers, surrounded by Christmas trees and sitting on a bed of fake snow, seemed to be guarding the entryway they looked down on.

There were holiday tunes playing quietly, and the sweet aroma of fresh muffins and sharp refreshing scent of evergreen boughs and wreaths hanging on the walls made Alex smile.

Hanna poured water into a mug, threw in a tea bag, and handed it to her sister. "You look like you could use this."

Alex sat at the island. "Who are you and where is my sister?"

"What do you mean? Isn't it a beautiful morning?"

It was only eight, and it was still dark outside. "I suspect the beauty you're seeing has something to do with a conversation you had last night."

"Well, maybe. Duncan did explain that Miss Rodeo is happily married and pregnant with her third child. They were just having a good time remembering their years at school. I guess I may have overreacted when I saw them together."

"You think? But I'm very happy for you. Especially if it means you can focus a little more on figuring out who killed Kyle. Even if Duncan doesn't believe you killed him, he's still bound by the evidence."

"I know. I asked him about the case, but he said he'd already told us more than he should have. But I can pick up the birthday cake this morning. The community center is no longer a crime scene." The buzzer went off and Hanna removed another pan of muffins from the oven. A dish of butter and a jar of their wild huckleberry jam were on the island. The twins had made a trek into the mountains last summer to gather the plump, purple, wild berries. There was nothing like the intense flavor of the sweet fruit in the middle of a Montana winter.

"It seems to stretch the imagination to suppose Brooke doesn't know something, even if she isn't the killer." Alex was drooling as she looked at the muffins Hanna had baked.

Hanna got plates and knives, and put them in front of Alex. "Could she have been blackmailing Kyle?"

"I've been thinking about that." Alex sipped her tea. "Kyle is a washed-up former CEO. He left under a cloud of scandal and probably couldn't get a similar job again, as a result. What has he got to lose from having a secret exposed? Brooke, on the other hand, is hoping to become a judge. She'd have a lot to lose if something disreputable came out. And it would have to be something more than the usual stuff kids do when they're teens. Potential judges are scrutinized very carefully. If she had a secret, it was buried deep." Alex slathered butter and jam on her warm muffin. She bit into it, and the jam oozed down her fingers.

Hanna picked up the parcel Penelope had given Alex the night before. "I'm so glad this arrived in time."

"What is it? A present for me?" Alex took another bite of her muffin.

"Sorry. It's not a gift. It's special colors for the bonbons." Hanna slit open the box and showed Alex the contents. "I want to use these to differentiate some of our chocolates. They'll look gorgeous for the contest next week."

Bonbon was simply another way to refer to their filled chocolates. Alex had always loved bonbons more than truffles or solid chocolate. She loved the way the ganache or other filling oozed out when it was bitten into.

"I assume we're skipping church today?" Hanna was holding one of their giant Christmas mugs. This one was red and had "PEACE" written across it.

"I hate to do it, but there's a final cake-and-coffee farewell at the school this morning, as well as another impromptu memorial for Kyle. Doors open at nine. I think we should be there." Alex checked her reflection in the back of a teaspoon. "I think I need a shower. I'm looking a little rough."

Shortly after nine, as Alex and Hanna walked out the front door, Hanna was looking at her phone. "Miss T has a new post out this morning. Listen to this.

Miss T doesn't know everything that's happening in Harriston. For instance, she is not yet aware of who killed Kyle Allerton. Will our own local celebrity sleuth solve that mystery sometime soon? In the meantime, Miss T has heard there is no longer any happiness to be found between one couple that have been stepping out. Do their spouses know? They say the key to a happy marriage is communication. Miss T wonders if there is a key to a happy breakup.

"Do you know who she's talking about?"

"I have no idea. I'd like to know where she's getting her information. Assuming Miss T is a she. I suppose it could be a man."

Alex had been wondering who might be behind the name. Unfortunately, she didn't know everyone in the village. That would be something to ask Eudora.

At the corner Alex looked down the street both ways. The only vehicle in sight was a truck inching up the street to the south, more than a block away. Many people in the area would be at church right now. The walk was short. The school was only a half block from their house, directly across the street from their church, and while it was a little chilly, the day promised to be beautiful. The sun had risen above the nearby Rockies and filtered through a few clouds, making everything sparkle. There were already people streaming into the school. Ahead of them, Alex could see Zara lingering on the sidewalk near the walkway to the school. Across the street, Nate got out of a car that had a long, ugly gouge through the paint on the driver side. He strode toward the building at a good clip. When he saw Zara lingering by the walkway, he slowed down as he approached.

Alex had grabbed Hanna's hand and kept her at a crawl so they could see what happened. As Nate passed Zara, she joined the people heading to the entrance and reached out her hand and slipped something to Nate. Nate took it and put it into his pocket with no more than a quick sideways glance at Zara. They continued in through the doors without speaking a word, and Alex lost sight of them.

"What do you think that was all about?" Hanna whispered. "Was that a note?"

"I'm not sure. It could've been a note. I don't think anyone else noticed. I'll have to see if I can corner one of them and ask about it if I get the chance."

In the middle of the entry hall, where the concession had been yesterday, was a small table with several pictures of Kyle and a stack of leaflets.

Alex took one of the leaflets and perused it. There was a picture of Kyle with a small write-up telling of his accomplishments. That must have taken some real creative writing talent. While the actual accomplishments were real, the embellishments that mentioned his being devoted to his family seemed a bit much.

"Loving husband," Hanna read. "From what I hear, he loved a whole bunch of his wife's friends before she divorced him."

The twins headed to the gym where the gathering was to take place. The room was decorated with balloons in purple, gold, and white. Some were starting to look a little withered, much like the alumni. Alex spied Eudora near the stage. She was dispatching teenagers, to and fro, to put cookies, muffins, cakes, and thermoses of coffee and tea on a long table along the front of the room. She reminded Alex of a general orchestrating a military campaign.

"Let's chat with Eudora. She might have some insight on a few things I'm curious about."

"Put the gluten-free options on that table down there." Eudora was talking to a pimply-faced teenager and pointing to a small table separate from the rest. When the teen had headed off with a tray of muffins, the spinster turned to the twins. "These kids get extra credit for helping out today. It's nice, but they don't seem to be able to think for themselves."

"I didn't think kids today were supposed to do that. Maybe I'm being overly cynical. I know you're busy, but I just wanted to ask you a couple of things."

"Ask away, my dear."

"Have you read Miss T's most recent post?"

Eudora pointed another teenager in the direction of the coffee thermoses. "I have. I'm afraid it suggests you're looking into Kyle's death. So if you were hoping to keep that under wraps, I'm afraid you've been ousted."

"Surely, not that many people read that blog," Hanna said.

"Probably not many outside of Harriston, but she has quite a following locally. Have you looked at her social media page? She posts something every time she puts out a new article and links it."

"Are most of her blogs just gossip?"

"They're all gossip. And most of them are on the nose. Though she doesn't always name the individuals she's talking about. Sometimes she disguises their identities, but she often uses vague descriptions that most locals can figure out. For instance, you are referred to as the 'infamous local sleuth who likes to find dead bodies almost as much as eating chocolate.' That is not much of a disguise."

Hanna held up her phone to Alex. "She posted about it on Facebook this morning and it already has forty-seven likes."

"Do you have any idea who it could be?" Alex looked at Eudora hopefully. If anyone had an inkling, it would be her.

Eudora shook her head. "If I knew, I'd tell you. It could be anyone, even a man, though I'm confident it's someone who lives in the village. Whoever it is has been able to uncover quite a few secrets. People love to read those posts as long as they aren't about themselves."

"I know I've already asked, but can you think of anyone who might have had a grudge against Kyle? Maybe something from long ago?"

"Kyle might have had more than a few people carrying grudges against him. He was rather famous for being a bully. During his senior year he was intolerable. I know there were teachers who wanted to have him suspended for some of his behavior, but Fenton always defended him and pointed out that he was the star of the football team and maintained excellent grades." Eudora wrinkled her nose. "He got away with murder in those days. Sorry—poor choice of words."

"What about more recently? Is there anything that would make someone want to kill him now?" Alex asked.

"He only moved back six months ago. I heard he had a humdinger of a fight with Eddie in his office a couple days ago. Something about money. Kyle was alienating a few of the dealership's customers." Eudora saved a plate of shortbread cookies from hitting the floor when a youth tripped over his jeans that were dragging on the ground.

Alex and Hanna realized Eudora was too busy for their questions and went to wander along the stage, past the gluten-free baked goods. Hanna pointed out Penelope sitting with Miss Vicky. The two had their heads close together and were whispering and nodding. They looked like two birds at a bird feeder.

Lucy came into the gym and scanned the room. She looked over to where Miss Vicky was sitting and then hurried toward Alex and Hanna. "Have you seen my mother? I dropped her off out front and then had to drive a ways down the street to find a place to park. Now I don't see her anywhere."

The twins shook their head. Hanna spoke up. "She can't be far. Maybe she went to the washroom."

"Yeah, maybe. She doesn't always make smart decisions when she's on her own, so I try to stay close. I've even installed cameras at the pharmacy so I can keep an eye on her when I need to leave her alone in the store for a bit."

"I know Kyle wasn't exactly your favorite person, but I'm sorry he died." Hanna put her hand on Lucy's arm. "This hasn't been a good weekend for the reunion."

"It's too bad Kyle moved back to town. He was bad news in high school, and nothing had changed. He was the worst in senior year, but he was always intolerably self-centered."

"What made him so bad in his senior year?" Alex looked at Lucy curiously.

Lucy took a deep breath. "I could be wrong, so please don't repeat this, but I think Kyle was using steroids that year."

Alex was surprised. This was something new. "What makes you say that?"

"In senior year he became really aggressive and had huge mood swings. He also looked a little jaundiced. There were a few other things, but I never really gave it any thought at the time. Later, when I was in the pharmacology program and I learned about steroids, I started thinking about it. He had a lot of the classic symptoms of steroid use. I've never mentioned it to anyone, but it would explain why he was a bigger jerk than normal that year."

Hanna looked surprised. "Where would he have gotten the steroids?"

"I have no idea. They aren't actually that difficult to come by these days. I'm not sure how hard it would have been for him to get them back then. The person to ask would be Fenton. He spent more time with Kyle than his parents. Fenton really bent over backward for his team. But please don't mention my name. I'm just making a guess."

"No worries. Your name won't be mentioned."

"I'd better try and track down my mom."

Alex and Hanna looked at each other with raised eyebrows. Alex finally spoke. "I would never have guessed that Kyle might have used steroids."

"I'd like to know where he got them."

"Me too. Let's see if we can locate Fenton or Nate. Either of them should have noticed Kyle's behavior change. Maybe they even knew what he was doing?" Alex looked around the room as she said it. "Let's take a look through the halls."

Hanna suggested they split up. Alex went out the door by the stage while Hanna went out the doors at the other end of the gym.

As Alex contemplated where to look, she could hear voices coming from a room off the alcove, used by actors in stage productions. The door was leaned shut, but not closed all the way. When a tall teen bumped into her because she was blocking the doorway to the gym, Alex casually moved next to the door. With her ear pressed as close to the opening as she could without being too obvious, she listened to the conversation in the room. With all the noise surrounding her, it was hard to make everything out.

"I can't leave. It wouldn't be fair… Besides you might not want to take care of me eventually." It was a woman's voice, but Alex couldn't identify it.

"Nonsense. I've been waiting all these years…You're the only woman I've ever . . . after what you did for me . . . the risks . . ." A man's voice—was that Fenton?

". . . regret that. No one can ever find out. I wish . . .Kyle . . .I've got to go." The woman was speaking quietly and it was getting harder to hear.

"No… I'll protect you…Wait!" The man's voice rose.

"No. I need to go, now."

Alex quickly moved across the hall and pretended to stare at a bulletin board covered with pictures made of tissue paper to look like stained glass windows. She threw a quick glance over her shoulder and saw Rose enter the gym. Alex waited a few seconds and then turned around. Fenton was standing in the hall behind her, and his gaze locked with hers.

Chapter Eighteen

Alex silently gulped. "Oh. Hello, Mr. Carver. I was hoping to run into you today." She prayed he didn't realize she'd overheard parts of his conversation with Rose.

"Really. Why is that?" Fenton took several steps toward Alex and gave her a level stare.

"I have a question about Kyle I thought you might be able to answer. Someone mentioned that he was quite aggressive in his senior year, and suggested it might have been from steroid use. I was wondering if you knew anything about that? Would it have been difficult for him to get steroids?"

Fenton leaned in until she could smell the body odor lingering on him like a moldy carpet. "The guy just died. Are you trying to start a smear campaign? Even if he did use steroids, what does it matter now? Leave it alone." Fenton pushed past Alex and marched down the hall.

If looks could kill, Alex would be dead on the ground. Thankfully, it was just a couple of students in the hall, bringing more food to the gym, who had heard him. They'd given him the side-eye. Alex peeked back in the gym.

Lucy was hurrying across the room and scolding her mother loud enough that Alex could hear. "Where have you been? I've been so worried. Let's sit down with Miss Vicky, and I'll get you some cake."

Hanna was not far behind Lucy. Her brow was wrinkled, and she was biting her lip. When she reached Alex, she blurted out, "I just got a call from Duncan, and I have to go back to the sheriff's office this afternoon. They want to talk to me again."

"I'll come with you."

"No. You need to figure out who did this. Maybe we should try and track down Brooke and question her some more. She must be hiding something."

Alex knew her sister was right. Brooke had to be involved in some way, or she knew something she wasn't sharing."

Alex didn't want to mention her run-in with Fenton while Hanna was already stressing about another interview with Duncan and the sheriff. They could discuss everything when Hanna got back.

"Why don't you search the school, and I'll take a peek outside to see if Brooke's car is nearby." Alex couldn't imagine her not coming to the final event of the reunion.

"Sounds good. I'll text you if I find her." Hanna threaded her way back through the gym.

Alex walked out the school's front doors and wandered through the parking lot as she scanned the cars there and on the street. When she arrived at the far side of the lot, which was tucked up against the back of the gym where the stage was, she could see the back of Brooke's distinctive rental tucked into the last stall. Alex saw something on the ground on the driver's side of the car. She walked closer and realized it was a bottle of Pink Bis. Brooke must have dropped it. As she approached the car, the back door of the school opened and Hanna came out.

Hanna caught sight of Alex and called, "I didn't see her inside."

"This is her car over here." Alex was about to bend down to pick up the bottle, when she jumped back as if a rattlesnake had crossed her path. There was a set of boots only several inches away from the bottle of Pink. She gazed at the legs clad in a pair of stylish black leather boots. Alex was sure they must have cost a mint; the leather looked buttery soft. Alex gazed up further, and there was no mistaking the long mane of dark hair and the face. Alex could smell what she assumed was vomit, and tried to ensure she didn't step in it as she bent down closer to the woman to check for a pulse.

Hanna came up behind Alex and sucked in a lungful of air. "Holy Christmas tree! Is she dead?"

Brooke was lying face up with her arms at her side. Her body was slightly arched, almost as if there were a pillow under her back. No pulse, and Brooke's skin was cold and rigid. No surprise, as she'd obviously been lying on the ground for more than a few minutes. Was it too much to hope that whatever was wrong with her digestive system had killed her.

"Oh, yes." Alex scanned the area. Brooke's purse was within an arm's length of her body. The ever-present pink bottle must have rolled out onto the asphalt, where it caught Alex's attention. Brooke's cell phone and glasses were beside the purse. There was a set of keys on the pavement, inches away from the body, on the other side.

"I'll call Duncan." Alex got her phone out and pushed a button; she'd put Duncan on speed dial. He answered on the second ring. "I'm sorry. I can't talk right now, Alex—"

"Stop and listen. While you were preparing to question my sister again, another graduate of the Class of '99 has died in the school parking lot. The rest of that class might want to up their life insurance. They're dropping faster than freshmen at a frat party."

Duncan paused and was silent a moment. "What are you talking about?"

Alex explained how she'd found Brooke's body in the parking lot. "I checked for a pulse. Nada. Hanna is here with me."

She could hear Duncan moving as he spoke. "Stay where you are, and don't let anyone near the body. I'm calling the medical examiner as soon as I hang up. Hopefully, he can meet me at the scene. I'll be there as fast as I can."

Hanna looked a little green. "I guess this puts a twist on things. If Brooke killed Kyle, who killed Brooke?"

Fifteen minutes later a bald, middle-aged man came rushing through the parking lot. He introduced himself as the medical examiner. "I was nearby when I got the call about a body. What have you got?"

Alex silently pointed to Brooke, hidden between the cars. Hanna had sidled a few yards away to where she couldn't see the body. Her color was almost back to normal.

The ME stood beside Alex and took in the grisly scene. It looked like she'd been sick and then collapsed. Her red face looked up to the sky. Maybe she'd felt sick and gotten out of the car, intending to go the washroom in the school, but hadn't made it.

The doctor made a cursory examination of the body without actually touching much. He checked her pulse as Alex had. "I don't want to do anything more until pictures of the scene can be taken. She's been dead awhile—a few more minutes won't kill her."

Alex laughed, then thought better of it and stopped. "Sorry. It struck me as funny."

The doctor gave her a smile. "Don't worry. A little humor in my business is necessary. After all, my day starts when your day ends."

Alex tried to hide her smile as Duncan's cruiser pulled into the parking lot with his lights flashing. He walked over to Hanna. "You look a bit pale. Are you okay?"

Hanna nodded. "It's my first body. Not what I expected, but I'll be fine."

Duncan nodded to Alex and took a look at Brooke and pulled the ME aside. Alex strained to hear what they were saying.

A minute later the ME stayed put, and Duncan came over to stand with Alex and Hanna. "There's another car right behind me, and the forensic people should be here fairly quickly." As he spoke, he slipped rubber gloves onto his hands. "It's been a quiet morning everywhere else. Tell me what happened."

Alex described how she'd ended up in the parking lot. Alex tried to gloss over the part about wanting to grill Brooke on her possible involvement in Kyle's death. But Alex realized she may have made a mistake in thinking Brooke was the killer.

Duncan turned to Hanna, who had regained her color. His tone softened as he gazed at her. "How did you end up here?"

Hanna explained her part in the search. "I came out of that door"—Hanna pointed to the door Nate had exited from yesterday after his argument with Fenton—"just as Alex found Brooke."

"Oh, and you should check the feed for that camera." Alex pointed at a camera mounted at the corner of the parking lot, not far from Brooke's car.

As they stood there, Brooke's cell phone rang.

Duncan reached down and picked up the phone and answered it as he placed a coin in its place. He turned his back and took a couple of steps away as he spoke to the caller. Alex glanced at Hanna and inclined her head in Duncan's direction as she mouthed the word *you*.

Hanna's eyes widened, and she shook her head no.

So Alex did her best to edge closer while she listened in. Unfortunately, she could only hear Duncan's side of the conversation. From what he said, it sounded as if Brooke had been talking to the caller while she drove to the school. She'd hung up abruptly. When the person hadn't heard back, they were concerned and were calling back to see how Brooke was.

Duncan thanked the individual and took their contact information. He said goodbye so suddenly, Alex didn't have a chance to back up, and he almost fell over her when he turned around.

"Oh. Sorry, I was just moving out of the way."

Duncan stared at her shrewdly. "You two can go. We'll get your official statements later. You know the drill: don't say anything about this to anyone. We probably won't release all the details of her death, so I don't want the whole village to know exactly what happened." He'd dismissed them.

Alex walked as slowly as she possibly could in the direction of the school's front doors while Hanna moved ahead at a faster clip.

There wasn't anyone outside yet, and in the stillness Alex heard the ME's voice. "You'll need tox results to confirm this, but at first glance I'd say she died of strychnine poisoning."

"Seriously?" Duncan sounded shocked.

"Do you see the way her body is arched?"

The ME was cut off by Duncan before he could say more. "Alex, is there anything else we can do for you?" Duncan must have noticed Alex wasn't going anywhere fast.

"No. I'm good. Just being careful not to slip on any ice." *Rats! Caught.* Alex walked at a somewhat faster pace until she caught up to Hanna and they were out of sight. Hopefully, she could cajole some information from Duncan tomorrow.

Alex turned to Hanna. "Why don't you see if you can track down Doc Hansen? Brooke's been staying at his B&B. See what you can find out."

Hanna glanced at her watch. "He's probably at church. I'll head over there and try to find him."

Alex lingered at the corner of the building, where she was mostly out of sight. Soon the sheriff arrived with more deputies, and the parking lot swarmed with activity. They roped off that section with crime scene tape. A few people wouldn't be driving home for a while.

Alex didn't have fond memories of Sheriff Summers, from last Christmas. The woman hadn't been too pleased when Alex toppled her theories. Alex watched as the hard-as-nails sheriff took command of the crime scene. She and another deputy headed toward the spot where Alex was standing. Alex quickly turned and sprinted toward the school.

The sheriff had seen her and called out. "Miss Wright, it seems you've found yourself another body. Is this a new Christmas tradition for you?" The sheriff's long strides quickly caught up to Alex. "Where might my deputy find a person in charge?"

After Alex explained where Eudora and the principal were, the sheriff crooked her finger and had Alex join her as they walked into the school. They found a nearby classroom as the deputy headed to the gym. "Why don't we sit down and have a nice chat? You can tell me what it is about you that has people dropping dead whenever you're near."

Alex decided this wasn't the time to withhold information, and explained her suspicions and how she'd been looking for Brooke when she and Hanna came upon the body.

"Let me make sure I have this straight. You and your sister made an assumption that Brooke Gibson might have killed Kyle

Allerton, and instead of telling Deputy Fletcher of your suspicions, you instead sought out a potential killer?"

"Well, when you put it that way, it does sound a little foolish."

"There is no other way to put it. After what happened last Christmas, I would have thought you'd learned your lesson."

Why do people keep saying that?

"The sheriff's office may not be there to save you next time. In fact, there had better not be a next time. You and your sister are to stay out of our investigation. She is still a person of interest. And if either of you should happen to chance by some information pertinent to this case, you are to provide that information to one of our deputies. Is that clear?"

"Yes, ma'am." Alex wasn't about to argue with the woman, even though the sheriff's office had had nothing to do with getting her out of a sticky situation last Christmas. She meekly agreed to come to the station later to sign her statement, and left the room just as the sheriff's phone rang. Alex contemplated standing outside the door to listen in, but the deputy was heading her way with the principal.

Chapter Nineteen

Alex wandered back to the gym where the program was continuing. Eudora was up on stage and had obviously taken over when the principal was called away. She called Fenton up to talk about Kyle.

Alex looked for a place to sit and saw Eddie by himself nearby. She started to back away to go to another door, but he'd already caught her eye and motioned her over.

"Come sit here." Eddie flashed his warm smile as he indicated the seat beside him. "I've been meaning to call you and see if you'd like to go for that coffee another time."

Fenton was sharing a brief synopsis of Kyle's time as the star quarterback at Harriston School. As he droned on, Eddie leaned closer. He smelled of citrus, soap, and a hint of sawdust. The combination was intoxicating, and Alex was intensely aware of him.

There was no denying how attractive Eddie was, but Alex was uncomfortable having him so close. She could feel people's eyes watching them. She took off her coat and managed to create a bit more space between them. "I'm surprised they're doing another memorial today. I didn't think Kyle was that well liked."

"He's not going to be missed at the dealership. I've worked hard to have solid relationships with our customers, and he was undoing that work faster than I could make repairs. I hate to say it, but this is the best thing that could have happened for the company, though not for me personally."

"Yesterday, I overheard you talking to Fenton outside the sheriff's department. Was he one of the customers who had a problem with Kyle?"

"You overheard that?" Eddie looked a bit sheepish. "Yeah, Kyle was giving Fenton a hard time about renegotiating the terms of a loan. After everything that man did for Kyle. I couldn't believe it. I would have stepped in either way, but I can't lie. It's easier without having to fight Kyle on every issue."

"I heard you had a knock-down, drag-out fight with him a couple days ago?"

"News does travel around here. It was just another fight about our customers. We had them every week."

"How did everyone else feel about him at the dealership?"

"About the same as me. Even his father was unhappy about his return."

"Did you know him in high school?"

"Barely. I was a couple of years ahead of him, and I wasn't on the football team. By the time I started working for Mr. Allerton at the dealership, Kyle was already off at college. I think his dad had hoped Kyle would return and run the company after he graduated, but Kyle had bigger plans than working at a farm equipment dealership in a part of the country most people haven't even heard of."

"From the little I knew of him, that makes sense. How did his return impact you, aside from him alienating your customers?"

"About ten years ago Mr. Allerton and I formed an agreement for me to start taking on ownership of the company. I get between one and two percent ownership each year in lieu of a bonus. It threw everyone for a loop when Kyle came back unexpectedly last summer."

"That must have been awkward. What position was Kyle given at the company?"

"It was darn awkward. Kyle wasn't impressed that I own a significant percentage of the business now. His dad told him he could work in either sales or accounting, for a significantly smaller salary than he was used to. So Kyle called himself the CFO. But he was just a glorified accounts clerk who spent most of his time messing up the deals our salesman made. Mr. Allerton offered me an additional hefty cash bonus for putting up with Kyle. It was in my interest to keep the idiot alive."

Alex could imagine how Kyle would alienate customers with his abrasive personality. "He can't have wanted to stay here forever. Harriston doesn't strike me as Kyle's style."

"Kyle always talked about this or that company making him offers, but I think it was all talk. I'm not sure he had anywhere to go. At least not with a salary he felt he was worth."

Eudora was back on stage, looking flustered. "I'm afraid we haven't been able to locate Brooke Gibson, who was going to make some final remarks, but Zara Nichols has kindly volunteered to stand in at the last second.

Alex watched as Zara took the stage. No one here knew about Brooke lying in the parking lot. That was going to be a stunner. Zara spoke briefly about the importance of a school teaching more than just academics. She said schools help foster children's development in relationships, emotional skills, identity, and overall well-being. Alex was impressed with the off-the-cuff remarks the former cheerleader made.

"I'm guessing she isn't wasting much time crying for Kyle either," Eddie said as he watched Zara.

"Why do you say that?"

"She and Kyle were standing near the bar on Friday night. It was earlier in the evening, before Kyle was really drunk. She looked pretty angry and tried to slap him. He caught her hand and held it, and whispered something in her ear and then laughed as she stormed away."

"Did you hear what they'd been talking about?"

Eddie shook his head. "It was too noisy to hear much. I did hear her say, 'After what you did to my brother!' She said that loud enough for everyone to hear."

"Do you know what she meant by that?"

Eddie made a snort. "Oh yeah. Her brother was in my graduating class. Jack Hobbs was the best football player Harriston has ever produced, probably the whole state. He was going to college on a football scholarship. People said he was going to be the next Peyton Manning. He was an amazing quarterback. Unfortunately, Kyle insisted on driving back from a football strategy session they'd been to, and he flipped the car. Kyle walked away with barely a scratch, but Jack wasn't so lucky. It took him months to fully recover, and his football career was over. I talked to Jack afterward. He said Kyle purposely caused the accident. Kyle was buckled up, but Jack hadn't had a chance. Kyle gunned the engine and raced down the driveway of the place where they'd been. He couldn't make the turn at the road and flipped the car. Of course, Kyle denied it was anything but an accident, and there was no proof. Either way, Jack's future changed dramatically.

Eudora was back on stage, giving her final remarks and thanks to everyone who helped support the school, whether by donation or by helping out that weekend. She finished with an invitation for everyone to have a final look at the displays that had been set up in the hallways.

"Let's go look at some of those displays?" Eddie held out his hand to help Alex stand up.

She took his hand and then quickly let go once she was on her feet. As she walked out of the gym, she glanced back one more time to see everyone in the room. Nate was staring at her. She nodded to him, and he finally wrestled a half smile to his lips.

Eddie led the way into the hall, past the room where Alex had overheard part of the conversation between Fenton and Rose. They wandered down the corridor to a display of yearbooks that had been set up on a table. Eddie picked up one from the year he graduated. He flipped it open to his picture and showed it to Alex. "The hair and the clothes scream nineties. We thought we all looked so cool back then."

The pictures triggered a memory for Alex. "I looked like such a nerd in high school. Hanna had all the fashion sense." As Alex talked, she'd picked up the yearbook from Kyle's graduation year. She started flipping through the pages. There were lots of pictures of Kyle on and off the field. He had frosted hair with long curtain bangs and undercut at the sides. He reminded Alex of one of those boy band singers. Alex just wanted to reach into the picture and push the hair out of his face. Alex saw pictures of Brooke as head of the various groups she was part of. There was a picture of her from behind, giving the valedictorian speech. Kyle could be seen in the crowd, sneering.

Eddie had come to stand slightly behind Alex and was looking at the book over her shoulder. He reached around her with one hand, so it was almost as if he was hugging her. Alex's mouth went dry, and her skin tingled. He pointed to a picture of Fenton on the field with one of his football players. "Coach could be really tough. Even in his science classes he was known to throw chalk at students if they were messing around. I heard once he made the whole football team help him tear down an outbuilding on his property because they'd lost a game he thought they should have won."

Alex was having a hard time focusing on the picture, with Eddie standing so close to her. The picture had captured Fenton yelling at a kid. Alex was more interested in what was in the background. Off by the bleachers were several other kids. She recognized Kyle in his uniform with his nineties hair. He was shoving something into his gym bag that was lying on the ground. Alex looked more closely at the picture. It looked like it was a folder. Brooke, Zara, Nate (also in his football uniform), another boy wearing a hippie-style outfit, and a person partially turned away from the camera—all had similar folders in their hands. The person turned away was bent over a backpack resting on the bottom bench of the bleachers they were standing beside. It looked like they were putting the folder into their backpack. Alex put the yearbook on the table and moved slightly so she wasn't quite so close to Eddie. She pointed at the two kids in the photograph she didn't know. "Do you know who they are?"

"I'm not sure of his name, but I recognize him. I don't think his family live in town anymore." Eddie pointed to the hippie-style boy.

Alex pointed to the person turned away from the camera. "Do you recognize that person?"

Eddie picked up the yearbook and held it closer to his face. "I really can't tell who that is. It's not a very good angle. It could be a guy or a girl. Sorry."

Alex scanned the pictures of the graduating class, but there was no way to pinpoint who it was.

"I've got to go and finish some projects that need to be dealt with today. Maybe we could go grab dinner midweek?" Eddie was looking at Alex with a hopeful expression.

Whoa. Is he asking me on a date? Alex sucked in a breath. She didn't want to assume it was a date. What if she was wrong? That would be embarrassing. But she and Tom were dating. Either way it would be awkward. "Next weekend we've got the Festive Foods event, where we're running a display, plus our chocolates will be in the competition. It'll be a bit crazy until that's over. Maybe another time." *Why did I say that?* Now, if he asks again, it will be even more awkward.

"No problem. You take care." Eddie gave her a lopsided grin and strolled down the hall.

Alex let out her breath. That was so uncomfortable. She wasn't sure if she'd enjoyed it or was embarrassed by it. *Shake it off.* She pulled her phone out of her pocket and took a picture of the photo she'd been looking at.

Alex wandered around the school, looking at all the displays. There was no point in hurrying home. Hanna would have texted her if she was done at the church. She found herself staring at a tall glass case. In the center was an impressive trophy with brass plates on the front. Alex's gaze wandered over the miniature plaques for each year the football team had won. It looked like Coach Carver had led the Harriston Hawks to numerous championships. Alex shivered. She raised her eyes and saw Fenton's reflection staring at her from across the hall.

Chapter Twenty

Seeing Fenton staring at her had unnerved Alex, and she quickly made her way out of the school. Unsure what to do next, Alex went home and decided to create a new murder board to help organize her thoughts. After cuddling with Miss Watson for a few minutes, she found a large poster board and pulled different colored markers from a drawer. She wrote down the names of her suspects, or at least the ones she knew had some kind of history with Kyle. Except for Everett, that mystery seemed to be resolved.

Hanna came in the front door as Alex was writing down every scrap of information she could remember. Her twin looked disappointed.

"Did you find out something?"

"Not a thing." Hanna sat down on the couch beside Watson and scratched her ears. The dog began her pseudo purring. "I couldn't find Doc, so I asked someone where he was. Turns out all the B&B guests checked out early this morning except for Brooke. She didn't want the big breakfast they usually cook, so they went to Whitefish to have brunch with some friends of theirs."

Alex was disappointed. "What took you so long?"

"I was going to come straight back, but Tom saw me, and I felt guilty leaving, so I went to class."

Alex looked at the large farmhouse clock hanging on the wall. "Maggie should be home from church by now." Alex was still feeling some of her own guilt over her nonattendance that morning. Guilt was something she donned as easily as a raincoat in Seattle. Years of listening to her mother chastise her for her endless list of foibles had ensured Alex had a healthy sense of her own faults. That reminded her that tonight was the twins' weekly call with the family.

"Let's head over to Maggie's. Maybe we can brainstorm over there."

Drew opened the door to Alex's knock. He was looking spry and chipper for someone who'd been on the brink of death with pneumonia only a couple days ago.

"Hello. We thought we'd come hang out for a bit. We could use a fresh perspective on the case." Alex knew she should have texted or called first to make sure it was okay to come over, but she hoped the couple would forgive their social faux pas.

"Come on in. You can stay for lunch. Maggie is preparing sandwiches right now. Tom will be over in a little while as well." Drew held open the door.

"We don't want to impose." Alex was more than happy to take advantage of their offer and knew Hanna thought the same, but felt she should offer a little resistance. Maggie's food was always delicious, and Alex's stomach was starting to remind her it hadn't been fed in a while.

"Nonsense. Come in." Drew headed back to the sofa and raised his voice so Maggie could hear. "Alex and Hanna are here and will be staying for lunch." Drew pointed at the poster board. "What's that?"

"I'll show you when Maggie comes in." Alex leaned it against a wall.

Maggie came out of the kitchen, wiping her hands on her apron. "I'm so glad you're here. I have a few things to tell you both. The gossip was flowing faster than the water into the sacrament cups this morning. I'm almost done. Sit down and talk to Drew for a minute while I finish up."

Alex's offer to help Maggie was kindly, but firmly, declined.

"How are you feeling today?" Alex couldn't see any evidence of the cornucopia of medicines that had littered the table yesterday.

"Almost good as new. I didn't want to go to church, just in case I have a relapse from doing too much too soon."

"I have every confidence that won't happen." Alex smiled.

Uncertainty flashed across Drew's face. "Where were you two?"

"We were at the school this morning for the winding-up ceremony. They had a bit of a memorial for Kyle."

"What's going on at the school? Maggie saw some sheriff's cars there when she left church."

Maggie walked in with a tray packed high with sandwiches, cookies, and a bowl of chips. "Don't you tell him anything until I come back. I just have to go grab the plates and cups."

There was a soft knock on the door as Tom entered.

"Sorry, I'm late. There were more parishioners than I expected, wanting my words of wisdom." Tom took off his tie and shoved it in his pocket.

"Ha! If they only knew." Maggie came in, carrying a second tray.

Hanna quickly helped her distribute the paper plates and plastic cups.

"Everyone help yourselves." Maggie waved the new arrival in.

With everyone finally seated and food piled on their plates, Hanna put her plate on a side table and crossed the room to sit beside Maggie. Alex and Hanna had discussed it on the way over, and they suspected Maggie would have a hard time hearing the news.

"Someone else has been killed." Hanna said gently, and looked to Alex to finish telling the news.

Tom was about to take a bite of his tuna sandwich but lowered it to his plate. "Please tell me it was an accident."

"I'm sure there hasn't been an official ruling yet, but I have a feeling it's not going to be classed as an accident. I found Brooke in the parking lot by her car. She was dead." Alex said.

Maggie's face crumpled. "Oh no. I knew it was possible she had something to do with Kyle's death, but she's too young to die."

Hanna rubbed Maggie's back. "I know. But this puts another spin on Kyle's death."

"I'm okay. You go eat your lunch. I can hear your stomach rumbling. I've hardly seen Brooke in the past twenty years, but I just feel awful for her parents."

"Do you know how she died?" Drew gently patted Maggie's shoulder when Hanna returned to her seat.

"The ME thinks it was strychnine poisoning. He started to tell Duncan it had something to do with the body being arched. Duncan made me leave before the ME could say anymore. We've also been given a warning not to discuss this with anyone. Duncan doesn't want the details getting out." Alex took a bit bite of her sandwich.

Drew took a sip from his glass of water. "Strychnine poisoning can cause violent convulsions, and rigor mortis to set in quickly. Sometimes the body is locked into the position it was in during the final convulsion. Did you notice if she had a red face?"

"She did. I wondered about that." Alex had known strychnine could cause violent convulsions. A chart listing poisons and their symptoms was hanging in the shop.

"Where did I hear about strychnine recently?" Maggie face was scrunched up as she thought.

"Eudora mentioned Eddie found some rat poison in her shed." Hanna cocked her head and raised her eyebrows. "It seems rather coincidental that Eudora mentions she has rat poison in her shed and now Brooke is dead, and quite possibly from strychnine. Who knew about the poison?"

Drew rubbed his hands together. "That's an excellent question. I'm also wondering if that was what was used to kill Brooke, but how would she have ingested it?"

Alex thought back to Friday. "Nate, Lucy, Kyle, Brooke, Maggie, Hanna, and I were all there when Eudora mentioned the rat poison. Eddie knew about it. And those people may have told others. The whole village could have known. But I have no idea how Brooke would have been poisoned. I've heard it has a strong, bitter taste."

Drew was stroking his chin and looking at Alex. "The taste of strychnine would be hard to disguise. From a poisoner's perspective, it would be best if it was consumed in one go, or maybe in something like a cup of strong coffee or a shot of bourbon. Something like that would help disguise the taste. It could also be inhaled or absorbed."

"Brooke told me she doesn't drink," Alex remembered, "so it wasn't done that way."

Tom spoke up. "I wish this was a question I didn't need to ask. Who is on your suspect list?"

Alex brought out her murder board. "It's a work in progress. There may be people I don't know who had a grudge against Kyle. Lucy certainly disliked him. She didn't make a secret of that. But she claims she was by the bar all night, and I think everybody saw her there. And I have to ask, is a strong dislike for someone enough to turn you into a murderer?"

"I should hope not, because I've never liked a certain woman here in town, and I've known her all my life." Maggie sighed.

"Actually, Miss Vicky pointed out that there was a point where Lucy wasn't at the bar," Tom said.

"Which Lucy explained, though it should be kept in mind," Alex agreed.

"Since Brooke is now dead, can we assume she didn't murder Kyle after all?" Hanna asked. "And if she didn't kill Kyle, then how did she know about Fenton's text?"

Alex had been wondering that herself. It was possible Brooke was with Kyle when he got that text, but didn't kill him. "It's all circumstantial. Brooke may have been there around the time of Kyle's death. She and Kyle were arguing during the dance. She claimed it was over politics, but did Kyle seem to be the type of person who would spend his time at a dance talking about politics?"

"I want to say no, but I wouldn't have put him down as having a master's in business either." Hanna sipped her water.

"We know the police have questioned Fenton, but he hasn't been arrested. He sent a text requesting a meeting, but that doesn't prove he was actually in the basement. Plus, Fenton seems genuinely upset about Kyle's death, though that could just be a cover." Alex tapped her finger against her plate.

"What about Nate? He had that fight with Kyle. And you thought Kyle was threatening Nate in some way. Didn't you say Lucy saw him at the dance?" Hanna asked.

"Yes. She said he was in the entryway for a minute and then left. What if he'd already been in the basement at that point? Or maybe he went down there after she saw him." Alex's head was spinning. "Plus, a customer told me he saw Nate outside at the side of the community center around the time of Kyle's death."

"That certainly sounds more promising as far as motives go," Maggie said as she topped up Drew's water.

Drew spoke up. "You said Everett was also out of sight during the window of time Kyle was killed. He could easily have snuck down to the basement and claimed to be in the bathroom. No one saw him."

Hanna objected. "I don't think Everett would ever kill anyone. Besides, poison is more of a woman's weapon."

"When I worked at the jail I saw a lot of incarcerated people whose friends would have sworn they would never hurt anyone. I think just about everyone may have circumstances where they might be pushed into doing something they never thought they'd do." Tom looked around the room.

Alex interjected. "As it happens, I think we can take Everett off the list. I found out he was sneaking away to watch some basketball games on his phone. But don't let Isabelle find out."

"Zara has pretty strong feelings for Kyle as well. She said he was cruel and a liar and a cheat. I'm not sure if she has an alibi for the window when Kyle was killed. And Eddie said she and Kyle had words at the dance. Apparently, her brother had an accident that left him unable to play football, and Kyle was involved."

"That was a pretty big thing at the time. Kyle was driving, and there was talk that Kyle had caused the accident intentionally. I know there was a deep rift in the community between those who believed Jack and those who believed Kyle," Maggie said.

"Maybe Zara finally decided to even the score. Though, why wait all this time?" Hanna looked at the murder board. "Why do you have Eddie on there?"

"Because Eddie wasn't very happy about Kyle working at the dealership. Kyle was causing problems with the customers," Alex said. "Though, Eddie also said he was basically getting paid by

Kyle's dad to keep Kyle out of trouble. Thus Eddie actually had a reason to want Kyle alive." Alex looked at Tom. A scowl crossed his face at the mention of Eddie's name.

"What about Duncan? Did he know Kyle? They were on the football team at the same time. Maybe Duncan knows something," Hanna said.

"Trust me, I've been asking Duncan about it whenever he's home, which hasn't been often. But he says that since he was a year older, he didn't have much to do with him off the field." Drew looked disappointed.

"Now, it's time for me to tell you what I discovered this morning," Maggie said. "Miss Vicky and Penelope were helping me organize leftovers from the alumni dinner for families that are struggling this Christmas."

"Hey, wait a sec. I saw Miss Vicky at the school, talking to Penelope."

"They were there, but they came to church for Sunday school. They saw me in the kitchen, organizing the leftovers, and came in to help. Miss Vicky mentioned that Rose and Lucy are struggling financially at the moment and could probably use a little help.

"Of course, I was shocked. I had no idea the pharmacy wasn't doing well. Miss Vicky said the pharmacy has barely been holding on, and that Rose made a bad investment that tipped the scales. Well, you know Rose's mind isn't quite as sharp as it used to be, and she wouldn't tell Lucy anything more about it."

"Could that be the same scam I was helping Duncan investigate last week?" Drew seemed excited at the prospect.

"It could be. By the time Lucy found out, it was too late. The cash was gone. Lucy told her mom not to tell anybody. But Rose confided in Miss Vicky because they're close friends. That money was supposed to be for a quarterly loan payment coming up. Lucy had to lay off their employee and is working all the hours to try and make up the money they lost."

"That's terrible," Hanna said.

"There's more to the story. Lucy's mom hates being a burden to her daughter and wishes she could marry Fenton."

"Fenton Carver?" Alex wasn't sure she heard right.

"Fenton has been in love with Rose for over forty years. They dated in college, but she ended up marrying Lucy's dad. Miss Vicky made it sound as if there may have been some hanky-panky some years ago before Lucy's dad died."

Chapter
Twenty-One

*D*id Lucy's mom and Fenton have an affair? Yuck. Everyone in the room had been silent for a moment with Maggie's revelation. Alex was confused. "So if Rose and Fenton are in love, why can't they marry? She's a widow."

"Rose knows her condition is going to get worse, and she doesn't think it's fair to Fenton. He'd have to take care of her and eventually put her in a home."

"That explains part of the conversation I heard. Or more correctly, parts of a conversation." Alex shared the gist of what she'd overheard outside the stage locker room. "What did she do for Fenton, and why can't anyone ever find out? Would he be willing to kill to protect the secret they have?" Alex asked.

"People do all kinds of crazy things for love. I drove to Seattle and back one weekend when Maggie and I were dating, to bring her a jar of water from the ocean." Drew kissed his wife's hand.

Maggie smiled at Drew. "I'd told him I'd always wanted to dip my toes in the ocean, but I'd never left Montana. A few days later he brought me the ocean water."

"That's so sweet," Alex said.

"Why would you want to go spoiling her like that, Drew? It's better to set the expectations low at the beginning." Tom ducked as Maggie threw a cushion at him.

"I'm glad Drew wasn't listening to you for advice." Maggie gave her brother a dark look.

"One good thing is that Hanna was at the sheriff's station when Brooke died." Tom gave Hanna a thumbs-up and ignored his sister.

"Not so fast, Romeo. If Brooke was poisoned with strychnine, it wouldn't have taken effect immediately. There's a short window before the effects begin, about thirty minutes, and we don't know how long Brooke was lying in the parking lot before Alex found her," Drew said.

The pit of Alex's stomach sank. "That's true. Hanna was at the school earlier, but what motive would she have to kill Brooke?"

"I didn't even know Brooke—I'd only just met her. And how would I have gotten the strychnine and administered it to her." Hanna sounded frustrated. "Well, I'd better head home. I need to work on the recipe for the new chocolate I want to submit for the contest next weekend. Strychnine Strawberry chocolates definitely wouldn't be a good choice now." Hanna got up and Alex followed suit.

"Wait. Alex, let me get a yearbook from Kyle's senior year. I borrowed it from Mrs. Matthews. You might find something useful in it." Maggie went into an adjoining room.

"Did Mrs. Matthews have a child in school at that time? I would have thought her kids were older."

Maggie returned with the book in hand. "Oh, her kids are older, but her husband was the caretaker at the school. He used to get one each year. He died a long time ago, but Mrs. Matthews has kept all his things."

Tom reached for Alex's hand before she could move away. "How about we watch a movie tonight at my place? Seven?"

"I'd like that." Alex squeezed Tom's hand. She and Hanna thanked Maggie for lunch and headed home. Alex had the yearbook tucked under her arm.

"What are you going to do about the chocolate contest? It's getting pretty close to game time to be playing with recipes."

"I've got the one I've been working on for a while. It just isn't quite right. I need to sit and think about the right pairings for the ingredients. Tomorrow morning I'll head to the shop extra early to experiment with a batch and try and figure out what's missing."

"Well, you know I'm always there to help taste test a new creation. I'm going to make something special for dinner. Maybe I'll invite Tom over to eat, and then we can go to his place to watch the movie."

"Sounds like a plan. I've had a hankering for Mom's pork chops. That is, if you're looking for input from the peanut gallery."

"I'll take it under consideration." Alex looked at her watch. She texted Tom with the invitation and got a reply so fast she wondered that he'd even read the message. She could prep everything for buttery mashed potatoes, mushroom gravy, the breaded pork chops, and glazed carrots. That would be delicious and relatively easy. If she timed it right, she could take Watson for a quick walk while the pork chops were in the oven.

*   *   *

A couple of hours later, Alex had the potatoes cut up and sitting in a pot of cold water, and the mushrooms and carrots sliced and ready to be cooked. She'd even managed to whip up a quick dessert. Her frying pan was heating on the stove, and a large pan lined with aluminum foil and parchment was ready for the oven preheating to three hundred and fifty degrees Fahrenheit. She pulled out three large plates and put a few tablespoons of flour on one and seasoned breadcrumbs on another, then broke an egg onto the third and scrambled it with a fork. Next she took her three fresh pork chops and dried them with a paper towel. She dipped both sides of her first pork chop in the flour, then coated each side with egg, and finally gave each side a good coating of well-spiced breadcrumbs. She poured oil into the frying pan and laid the pork shop in the pan. After she repeated the process twice, she turned her pork chops once so each side was nicely browned.

Then she transferred the chops to the aluminum foil–lined pan that had a generous dollop of avocado oil in it and put them in the oven. She set the timer for thirty minutes and called Watson.

"Do you want to go for a walk, girl?" Alex went to the front hall and grabbed her coat and the leash out of the closet. Alex called out to Hanna to let her know she was leaving. Watson was sitting obediently by the front door, with her tail wagging. "Yes. You've missed our beach walk haven't you?" The dog nodded her head.

Alex set out at a fast pace. Hanna would look after things if she was a few minutes late, but she hoped to have time to fix her hair and makeup before Tom came over. After last night's conversation with Tom, she hoped things would move forward. Even though Alex tried to deny it, she was starting to wonder if her best years would soon be behind her. *No. I will not think like that.* There were women her age having children and going back to school. Forty-six was the new thirty. *Yeah, and chocolate doesn't have calories.*

The evening air was frosty. There was still snow on the ground among the trees, but the road was bare. Watson had stopped to sniff at some bushes and to listen to a woodland creature somewhere in the dark. They reached the parking lot of the public beach, and Alex let Watson off leash for a quick run around the lot. There were enough lights surrounding the parking lot that she could keep an eye on the dog. A year ago Watson had been so timid she wouldn't have left Alex's side, but the pooch had come a long way.

Alex could see lights approaching from the entrance on the opposite side of the parking lot. The spot was popular for teens to hang out after dark. Alex called Watson. Time to go. With Watson back on the leash, Alex headed home. She needed to make the return journey a little quicker if she wanted to be there in time to get the pork chops out of the oven.

The road from the parking lot curved south and then headed through a densely wooded area as it turned east. Further along there was a footpath that connected the road straight across the block, but cars had to go all the way around to continue on the other side. Alex and Watson walked in the middle of the road as it wound away from the parking lot. Alex could hear a vehicle approaching, likely the one whose lights she'd seen. She pulled on Watson's leash so the two of them were walking close to the side of the road, to allow the approaching vehicle plenty of room to pass.

Alex glanced back and saw the vehicle approaching slowly. It was about twenty feet away when the engine roared, and the tires spit gravel as the vehicle sped up. The sound reverberated among the silent trees and had Alex's heart up to full throttle as she glanced back again. The vehicle seemed to veer toward the edge of the road and barreled toward Alex and Watson. Without thinking, Alex yanked on the leash and jumped into the ditch, out of the vehicle's way. It flashed past in an instant. The slope was slippery, and Alex went tumbling down the side of the ditch. She lost her grip on the leash, and Watson remained halfway up the slope, looking at Alex, unsure if this was a new game her master was playing.

Alex's heart felt like it had jumped out of her chest. What an idiot. Hadn't they seen her? She hauled herself out of the snow. She was wet and could feel leaves and twigs stuck in her hair and on her jeans. She walked partway up the slope, then bent down and grabbed Watson's leash and finished the climb back to the road. The truck—Alex was sure it had been a truck—was long gone.

Alex replayed the scene in her head. Had it been an accident or careless driving? Could the driver have intentionally meant to run her and Watson down?

Chapter Twenty-Two

When Alex got home, she took off her wet shoes and dried off Watson's paws with a towel they kept near the door. She'd calmed down and was wondering if it might only have been a distracted driver or an idiot. Her jacket would have to be washed, as would the rest of her clothes. The buzzer sounded for the pork chops. Alex hurried into the kitchen to silence the noise and turn off the oven.

Hanna got there first. "The potatoes should be ready in a couple minutes for mashing." After she turned off the buzzer, she turned around. "I figured I'd help—" Hanna's jaw dropped when she saw Alex. "What happened to you? I've seen mice in better shape hanging from a cat's mouth."

Alex ran to the mirror in the hall. She looked like she'd gone sledding headfirst without a sled. "Can you handle the potatoes? I'm going to run upstairs and try and fix myself up."

Hanna had come to stand beside her. She looked like she was going to insist on an explanation.

Alex paused at the bottom of the stairs. "I went ditch diving. I'll explain when I come down. Give me five minutes."

"You're going to need more than five minutes to come back from that look. Come on Watson—let's get you some supper."

Hanna was right. Alex's hair was not going to be revived by a quick brushing. She removed the biggest bits of the forest with her fingers and then ran a large-toothed comb through her hair. A few brushstrokes later, and it didn't look too terrible. Depending on what she was being compared to. Alex finally decided to throw her hair in a ponytail. That would have to do. She wiped the dirt from her face and quickly touched up her makeup. Wearing clean jeans and a festive sweater, she headed downstairs.

Hanna had finished mashing the potatoes and was draining the water from the carrots. "Can you grab the butter, please?" Hanna completed what she was doing and turned around. She gave her sister an appraising look from head to toe. "Not quite red-carpet ready, but you'll do. Can you add the sautéed mushrooms to the white sauce and see if it needs any more seasoning? Now, tell me what really happened to you."

While Alex stirred the mushroom sauce and tossed the carrots, Hanna quickly chopped some fresh parsley and got the Parmesan cheese out of the fridge. "I'll tell you when Tom gets here, or I'm just going to have to repeat everything." The doorbell rang. "See? He's here already." Alex hurried to let Tom in.

He gave her an appreciative look when she took his coat, and he kissed her on the cheek. Wow, that was the closest she'd come to a real kiss yet. "Watch it—we're being watched." Watson was sitting a few feet away, tail wagging and waiting for her share of the affection.

Tom bent down to pet the dog. "You've got a couple of burrs stuck to your coat. Where have you been hanging out, Miss Watson?"

"That's an interesting story. I'll tell you and Hanna about it while we eat."

In the kitchen, Hanna plated the pork chops and sprinkled parsley over the top. She grated some Parmesan and added more parsley to the mashed potatoes, then put the bowl on the table. Once food was on their plates, Tom and Hanna looked at Alex expectantly.

"There's not really that much to tell." Now in the safety of her kitchen, Alex was beginning to wonder if she had overblown what happened. "Watson and I walked to the beach and then were headed back home. A little ways past the turn leaving the parking lot, a truck came up behind us. It had slowed down and we'd moved to the side of the road. I thought they were just being cautious, but all of a sudden the truck accelerated, and it seemed to be coming right for us. If Watson and I hadn't jumped into the ditch, we could have been hit. With the snow being so wet, I lost my footing and slid to the bottom of the ditch. Watson fared a bit better. That's it."

The look on Hanna and Tom's faces went from concern to outrage. "Whose truck was it?" Tom had put down his fork and had his fist clenched on the table.

"It happened so fast, all I can tell you is it was a dark-colored truck." In her mind, Alex could still see the bright lights as she'd jumped out of the way. "I'm not even positive it was intentional. You know what kids are like. It could have been someone who was on their phone or changing stations on the radio. They might not even have seen us. I was wearing a dark jacket and pants."

"We're going to call Duncan and tell him about it. Even if it wasn't intentional, they could have killed you." Hanna had her phone in hand.

"Wait until after dinner. I'm fine and the truck is long gone. There's no point in disturbing our dinner." Alex took a bite of her pork chop. "This is so good. Let's not waste all this effort."

Tom and Hanna reluctantly agreed to wait until they'd eaten, before contacting Duncan. The trio soon managed to restore some of their good humor, and Tom shared interesting experiences from his time working at the jail.

Once their plates had been cleared from the table and the leftovers covered and put in the fridge, Alex pulled out three Black Forest mini trifles. "I hope you like them."

"They look delicious." Tom's eyes had grown big and round at the sight of the desserts.

"Nice job, sis. What's in them?" Hanna asked.

"Just pantry staples and some of Maggie's leftover triple-chocolate brownies. I cut up the brownies into small chunks and put them in the bottom of the cups. Then I layered in some canned custard and cherry pie filling, another layer of brownies, and more custard and pie filling. I topped it with whipped cream and some shaved chocolate to garnish."

"I wondered where the rest of those brownies went."

"There are a couple more desserts in the fridge, so you and Duncan can have them later." Alex winked at her sister.

Minutes after Hanna texted Duncan with the news of Alex's incident with the truck, the deputy was at the front door. "You caught me at the perfect time. I just finished a quick bite of supper and was going to head back to the office. It's going to be another late night."

Hanna led the handsome man into the kitchen. "Sit down and you can eat some dessert Alex made while she tells you what happened."

Duncan's eyes widened when Hanna put the Black Forest trifle down. He started spooning it into his mouth with gusto. "Tell me what happened," he managed to say in between bites.

Alex repeated what she'd told Hanna and Tom. "Unfortunately, I didn't get a look at the driver, and the only detail I'm certain of is that the truck was a dark color. Maybe an older model." Alex's hand had a little scrape, and she rubbed it as she retold her story.

"Why don't you close your eyes and go through it in your mind again. Picture yourself there. What do you see?"

Alex obediently closed her eyes and was mentally looking back at the truck. "The lights were too bright to see anything. They weren't the bright LED lights. They were the regular yellow ones, so it was probably an older vehicle. I think there might have been a grill guard on the front of the truck. That's it I'm afraid. Not very helpful."

"I'll write it up. My mom showed me the post the *Harriston Confidante* put out. Now everyone in the village thinks you're investigating Kyle's murder. Even though you're not, right?"

Alex put on her most innocent wide-eyed look and shook her head. If she didn't actually say the words, then it wasn't really lying, was it?

"Mm-hmm." Duncan's expression suggested he didn't believe Alex's response. "Hopefully, it's just some kids joyriding."

"I need to show you something else." Alex grabbed her backpack and handed Duncan the note from her windshield. "This was left on my windshield sometime after I got home from work and before I headed to the alumni dinner. It has my fingerprints all over it. Sorry—I forgot about it."

Duncan gave Alex the stink eye. "I'll take that with me. I'm not sure if we can get anything from it at this point. It looks like someone thinks you're involving yourself in this murder investigation, and doesn't like it. I'd better head out. The sheriff is still waiting to hear if Brooke's death is a homicide."

"I thought she died of strychnine poisoning? It's not like she would have accidentally taken that herself." Hanna took the empty dessert cup and put it in the sink.

"I wonder how you got that information." Duncan gave Alex a hard look. "We haven't released the official cause of death yet, so until then it's simply suspicious. But the sheriff wants the killer found quickly. After last Christmas's timely resolution to the murders, she wants to keep her record looking good."

Alex raised one eyebrow. "Her record?"

Duncan shrugged. "You know she took the credit officially, even though people around here know the truth. I think she's trying to prove the sheriff's department is capable of solving the murders in her jurisdiction without the help of an amateur sleuth." Duncan got up and headed to the door. "So don't get in her way, Alex. She won't take kindly to any interference."

"Did you check the parking lot camera feed where Brooke died?" Alex wasn't sure if Duncan would share any more information, but it was worth a try.

"Actually, we did. Unfortunately, the security company hasn't finished installing the system yet, so it isn't live."

That was disappointing. Even if it hadn't identified the killer, the camera could have established Brooke's time of death. Alex and Hanna walked out onto the porch with Duncan.

"Is Hanna still a suspect in Kyle's murder?" Alex wouldn't rest as long as Hanna was on the sheriff's radar.

"She is, but so are some other people. You don't need to worry. I'm on the case, and I'm going to make sure the right person ends up behind bars. Alex, please be careful. If someone did try to run you down tonight, it may be because of your interest in Kyle's murder. " With a quick nod to Alex and a lingering gaze at Hanna, Duncan left.

After helping Alex and Hanna clean up the kitchen, Tom had gone to his house to cue the movie while the twins had their weekly call with their family.

Chapter
Twenty-Three

Hanna was invited to come watch the movie, but she insisted she was in need of an early night, as the following day would begin another whirlwind week of activity.

Alex walked to Tom's, wondering if anyone was watching her. Usually, the dark gave her a sense of privacy, but not lately. Tom whisked her in the door when she got there. He sent her to the living room while he headed to the kitchen.

"What would you like to drink?" Tom called from the kitchen.

"Just water, please." Alex was already on the sofa ready to press play on the movie.

When Tom was settled beside Alex, their drinks within easy reach, he put his arm around her and pulled her close. And then the doorbell rang.

Rats! Alex had become certain the universe was trying to send her a message: *"You will be a spinster forever."*

Tom came back to the living room with Eudora trailing behind him. "I'm so sorry to barge in on your evening." Eudora looked at Alex apologetically.

"No worries. We were just going to watch a movie, but we can do that anytime. What brings you out tonight? I'm guessing it's not a social call." Alex wasn't about to show her disappointment that she and Tom had had their evening interrupted.

Eudora was one of the sweetest and most helpful people she knew. For an eighty-year-old woman, she managed a schedule that most thirty-year-olds would find grinding.

Eudora sat on the fireplace hearth across from Alex and Tom and wrung her hands. "The sheriff's department came to my house a short while ago with a search warrant."

"What? They don't suspect you in one of these killings. They can't possibly." Alex was outraged on Eudora's behalf. First her sister, and now a woman in her eighties! What was the sheriff thinking?

"No, no. At least I don't think I'm a suspect. They came to get the rat poison from my shed. As you'll recall, I mentioned it to you and several others at your shop on Friday. They want to test it against the poison that was used to kill Brooke."

"Ah. That makes sense. It would be too much of a coincidence that there are other sources of strychnine randomly floating around town." Alex relaxed when she realized her friend wasn't about to be hauled off to the sheriff's station for questioning.

Tom leaned forward and looked pensive. "Actually, we live in a rural community. There could be any number of farmers in the area who use strychnine for pest control."

"That's true, but I have to agree with the sheriff's department. It seems too coincidental that strychnine is used in a murder right after I mentioned I had some in a shed that anyone could access." Eudora brushed a stray hair from her forehead. "The thing is, they didn't find it. The rat poison was gone. They searched every inch of the shed, and they're searching my yard right now. But it should have been in the shed. It was definitely there Thursday night."

"Is there any chance Eddie took it and disposed of it?" Alex thought perhaps he'd decided not to leave it there and hadn't mentioned it to Eudora.

"They talked to Eddie. He said he hasn't been back to my house since Thursday, and I watched him leave it in the shed at that time. He's had a busy weekend with all the reunion activities." Eudora looked so forlorn it broke Alex's heart.

"I'm sure the sheriff's department will figure out who did this. Just out of curiosity, how did they find out about the rat poison?" Every tidbit of news was treated like a commodity in Harriston. Alex would love to spend a day at the bakeshop, to hear all the gossip.

Eudora shrugged. "Everyone seems to know about it. One of the deputies heard about it from her cousin's husband. I feel absolutely terrible that my rat poison may have been used to kill Brooke. And what if the killer has their sights set on someone else? No one is safe until it's found."

Alex wondered if the two deaths were connected, and if so, how. She'd also wondered if Kyle had been taking steroids in high school. Maybe Eudora knew something. "Did you ever hear any rumors of Kyle taking steroids in his senior year?"

"You know I don't like to repeat gossip." Eudora looked at Tom.

"I'm sure it wouldn't be considered gossip in this instance," Tom said.

"Then under the circumstances, I'm willing to make an exception if you feel the information could be useful."

Alex nodded. "I feel like these murders may connect to something from the past. But I've only lived here four years, and I'm not privy to all the gossip. I'm still considered an outsider by lots of folks."

"People here are multigenerational and view anyone who has moved here in the past twenty-five years as new to town."

Alex agreed. You couldn't swing a nutcracker at a potluck dinner without hitting at least a couple dozen families related to one another.

"It certainly wasn't common knowledge, but I did hear something at that time. Back in those days we didn't have cell phones, social media, or Google. People just didn't know about those things like they do now. The GP in the village—he's in a senior's home now—mentioned something to me in passing when we were sitting together at a football game one Friday night. We were talking about a doping scandal at the Tour de France the year before, and he mentioned his concern with the use of steroids in athletes. He said he hoped Fenton knew what he was doing. He didn't specifically indicate what he was referring to. I took it to mean either Fenton was giving some boys the steroids, or he knew they were taking them and wasn't interfering."

"Would Fenton care if it came out he was supplying his players with steroids or letting them use them with his knowledge?" It had been a long time ago, Alex thought.

"Fenton has always cared what people think. But I certainly don't believe he'd kill over it." Eudora stood and looked at Alex. "You be careful. Whoever killed Kyle and Brooke isn't going to appreciate you looking into this."

"That's exactly what I've said." Tom led the woman to the door.

Alex and Tom had ended up forgoing the movie and watching an episode of a true crime show. Knowing someone out there might still have Alex, or anyone else, on their naughty list had dampened their spirits. At nine Alex headed home, feeling restless. If she tried to go to bed, her mind would just go round and round. She needed something constructive to do while her thoughts wandered.

Earlier, she'd pulled out a recipe for Christmas stollen and left it on the counter. The German yeast bread, baked with dried fruits, candied citrus peel, nuts, and spices, had been a staple in her home every Christmas growing up. Talking with her family earlier had brought to mind all their childhood traditions. Celebrating the Christmas season without a homemade stollen would be unthinkable.

It appeared she and Hanna were on the same page once again. Hanna had left Alex a note beside the recipe. She had started the dough and hoped Alex would finish it when she got home. The raisins, homemade candied citrus peel, and almonds were in a bowl, covered in rum. The dough ball was sitting in the ever so slightly warm oven in another bowl, covered in plastic wrap. It had been over an hour, and the dough was now more than double in size. Alex washed her hands and put on an apron.

As she prepared everything, she thought about the missing rat poison. She and Tom had done a little research on strychnine while they watched the television show. Handling the poison required some precautions. Even breathing in or touching the toxic substance could cause a fatal reaction. Through her research in conjunction with naming their chocolates for the shop, Alex had learned a bit about several poisons. She knew some substances could be absorbed through the skin, but she hadn't really ever thought about the danger of inhaling something like strychnine.

Would the person who took it have known exactly how to handle the substance? Nate was a vet—he certainly would have known, as would Fenton, who was not only a farmer but had also been a science teacher. Eddie worked with farmers; he might know about strychnine, and he certainly knew where to find some.

Alex punched down the dough and then added the soaked fruit and nut mixture to the dough after pouring out the excess rum. She could put it back into the stand mixer and let it do all the work, but kneading the dough by hand would be far more therapeutic.

Normally, she didn't make bread of any kind. Her skill set didn't seem to lend itself to bread making. Her mother had despaired over her. No matter how often she tried, Alex's bread resembled a weapon more than a food staple. Her outcomes with stollen were, happily, more successful.

Alex added flour to the slightly sticky dough until it pulled away from the counter easily. She proceeded to cut the dough in two equal halves and then pressed each piece into an oval shape about one inch thick. First she folded the left side of the dough into the middle, and then folded the right side over on top of the left side so it was slightly off center. She used the bottom of her hand to press down along the length of the stollen, to the right of the fold, to give the Christmas bread it's characteristic look.

Alex thought about her other suspects. Lucy or Zara could have searched the information about handling strychnine as easily as she and Tom had. Plus, Zara ran a hardware store that sold those types of products to local farmers. There were probably even directions on the can itself. But why would any of them kill Brooke? Did it have something to do with high school? Except Eddie and Kyle weren't in the same graduating class. As far as Alex knew, no one benefitted financially from either death, and Eddie actually benefitted more if Kyle was alive. Could Brooke have witnessed something the night of Kyle's murder if she was with him shortly before he died?

Alex placed the stollen on a baking sheet lined with parchment paper and covered it loosely with plastic wrap. She put the baking sheet back into the still slightly warm oven to rise for another forty to sixty minutes. While she cleaned up, she thought about Harriston's Class of '99. They'd lost two graduates this weekend. It was a class plagued with scandals. Almost every bad thing that had happened led back to Kyle. Were there others in that class who had been tormented in some way by Kyle? With all the events over, was it possible someone they hadn't even put on the list of suspects was driving or flying home thinking they'd gotten away with murder? Alex retrieved the yearbook Maggie had given her and sat on the sofa.

Instead of skipping around, Alex went through the book, page by page. Kyle dominated many of the pictures, but that was largely because of the number of pictures devoted to football games. There was a picture of the football team gathered on the field behind the school with Fenton. Nate seemed to be looking at Kyle with a dark, brooding gaze. In the background Zara and some other cheerleaders were practicing a complicated move. Zara must have been quite strong to pull off some of those routines. Several pages later there was a picture of Zara leaning against Nate on the grass among a group of other kids. Had they dated in high school?

Alex flipped a few more pages and found a picture of a pretty young girl with an RIP beside her name. It was the girl, Olive, that Miss Vicky mentioned at the alumni dinner. What caught Alex's attention was the girl's last name. It was Dunn. That was also Lucy's last name. In Harriston there wasn't much chance they weren't related.

Alex flipped through the school pictures fairly quickly until she came to the graduating class. She looked at each picture carefully to see if anything struck her as odd, but there was nothing obvious. Alex hadn't realized that Miss Vicky had been the school secretary. Her picture appeared with the other school administrators. Alex kept flipping pages and found the picture she'd seen at the school, with Fenton yelling at one of his players. It really wasn't a very flattering picture; you could count the man's teeth, his mouth was open so wide. Alex looked at the background more closely. She went into the kitchen to preheat the oven and put the stollen on the cooktop. She got a magnifying glass out of a junk drawer. Upon closer inspection, Alex could confirm it was definitely folders all the kids had. But even under magnification, Alex couldn't identify the one person turned away from the camera.

Alex went back to the pictures of all the various clubs. She couldn't find a club that had more than two of the people from that particular picture as members. Maybe they were all working on a project together. Alex wasn't sure if it meant anything, but she made a mental note to ask Maggie about it tomorrow. But for now, her stollen was ready to go into the oven.

Chapter
Twenty-Four

Monday mornings were always tough, but the next morning Alex felt like she'd been hit with a sandbag. The lack of sleep over the weekend had caught up with her. She went downstairs for some tea. Hanna had already left, and Watson was asleep on her doggy bed. When Alex peeked into the living room, Watson opened one eye before letting it slip closed again. The dog looked as tired as Alex felt. She let her gaze slide over the decorations that adorned every corner of the room. The tree was done in white, gold, and silver. The white twinkle lights on the tree were the only lights on in the room, and it gave everything a soft glow.

In the kitchen Alex saw a note on the counter. Hanna had taken Alex's car because it was blocking Hanna's. Hanna had left her keys on the table in the hall. While Alex waited for the kettle to boil, she sat at the island and scrolled through her phone. She had a notification that another one of Miss T's posts was available.

The post was titled "Local Sleuth Almost Killed."

What! Alex read down the article as quickly as she could.

Our local sleuth was almost run down yesterday. Does it have anything to do with her insatiable curiosity? She has been investigating the recent murders. Perhaps she's getting close to revealing the killer.

Hanna Eastham is still a suspect, but the sheriff's office is also considering other persons of interest in the case. If Brooke Gibson hadn't died in the school's parking lot, she would be on that list. It appears she had information that only someone who had been with Kyle shortly before his death could have known. Hopefully, Fenton Carver is one of the people deputies are questioning, because Brooke Gibson certainly thought he should be.

The article carried on by repeating several things that had been mentioned in earlier posts. How on earth had Miss T gotten that information? Alex hadn't told anyone aside from Hanna, Tom, and Duncan about her incident with the truck. Could Duncan have a leak in the sheriff's department? And how did Miss T know about Brooke's suggestion that Fenton should be a suspect?

Watson padded into the kitchen and rubbed her head against Alex's leg. "Are you ready for your breakfast, miss?"

Watson wagged her tail enthusiastically while Alex set about filling her bowl with food. "There you go. Don't say I don't do anything for you."

Alex prepared her tea and took her cup upstairs to sip while she got ready. She decided to wear her jeans and a white crew-neck top with three embroidered black snowflakes across the chest. She grabbed the red sweater that she'd worn to the dance the other night.

Emerging from the house with Watson beside her, Alex got into Hanna's car. She decided a quick stop at Cookies 'n Crumbs was in order. There weren't any empty parking spots in front of the popular bakeshop, so Alex headed to Murder and Mayhem. She parked the car and took Miss Watson in the front door. Once the pup was set up in her favorite spot, Alex went to the kitchen to let Hanna know she was heading to the bakery. Instead of finding her sister elbow deep in chocolate, she found her sitting at the island with a bag of ice on her knee and a cut on her forehead. "What happened to you?"

"I was attacked."

"What! Are you okay?" Alex rushed over to her sister, tilted her head to the light, and looked at the cut on her forehead.

"I'm fine." Hanna batted Alex's hands away. "I parked your car in the driveway and was coming in through the back door. The motion sensor light didn't come on, and I was trying to find my phone as I walked up the steps, so I could shine the flashlight to see what the problem was, and out of nowhere someone grabbed me from behind. They covered my mouth with one hand and had their other arm around me so I couldn't move. They whispered in my ear, 'I warned you to mind your own business.' Then they shoved me and took off. I hit my head against the door, but my right knee took the brunt of it. It's pretty sore." Hanna gingerly prodded her knee. "I think they thought I was you."

"I can't believe this. Do you need to go to the hospital? Could it be broken?" Alex bent down to look at her sister's knee. "It's impossible to see anything unless we pull up your pant leg."

"I think it's just bruised. I went into the washroom and looked at it, but there was nothing there."

Alex checked the back doorstep. She looked at the motion sensor and realized why the light hadn't gone on. It had been smashed. Pinned to the wall beside the exterior door was a note. It said, *NEXT TIME WILL BE WORSE.*

Alex went back inside to tell her sister what she'd found. "This was planned."

"I can't believe it. Why would anyone want to do this?"

"I think you were right. This may have been someone trying to warn me off from asking questions about the murders. Anyone who reads Miss T's posts knows what's going on, so it could have been anyone. Did you read today's post?"

Hanna shook her head. "I haven't had a chance."

"Wait till you do. It's lucky you weren't more seriously hurt. I don't want to touch the note in case there are fingerprints. We need to call Duncan."

While Hanna called Duncan to tell him what had happened, Maggie arrived. Alex quickly explained what had happened to Hanna. "Will you stay with her while I run to the bakery for some muffins?" There wasn't anything else Alex could do for now, and baked goods were Hanna's favorite comfort food.

"Of course. Is there anything else I can do?"

"Just don't let anyone touch the note until Duncan gets here."

Alex jogged to the bakeshop and was dismayed to find a line that extended down the steps of the shop. Great! Alex got in line and hoped it wouldn't be too long of a wait. Two women, standing ahead of her, were obviously talking about Miss T's article. One of them turned around to see who was behind them. She smiled, and then Alex watched the woman subtly nudge her friend and nod her head in Alex's direction. The other woman casually turned around.

Alex felt a tap on her shoulder and jumped. She swung around to see Eddie grinning at her. "Sorry. I didn't mean to startle you. Fancy meeting you here."

Alex wondered if Eddie was going to ask her out again. *Please no*. She'd never seen him before at the bakeshop in the morning. Was he following her?

"I'm just getting something for breakfast. You?"

"With everything that happened over the weekend, I thought I'd better get a box of goodies. I know everybody in the office will have a hard time today. Though the hardest part will probably be trying not to look too happy around Kyle's dad."

"It's hard to believe it's only been three days. It feels like so much has happened. My heart goes out to Kyle's and Brooke's parents."

The line was moving forward, and Alex advanced onto the first step. Kyle was close beside her. Alex was trying not to fidget.

"Did you know Miss Vicky worked at the school as a secretary? I suppose you did, since you went to school here."

"I think she spent her whole career there. When I went to school, she was kind, but no nonsense. Kids didn't have much luck pretending to be sick with her around. She could spot a fake at ten yards."

"I guess she knew most of the students."

"She knew every student by name, and usually their families too. There probably wasn't much that happened at the school she didn't know about." Eddie's face started to turn pink. "I know you're busy next weekend, but I'm wondering if you'd like to come with me to a show after that?

The moment she'd been dreading. Alex wasn't sure what to say. "Um, I'm not sure if you knew, but I've sort of been dating Tom Kennedy. We haven't really established that we're exclusive, but I'd feel odd going out with someone else until I figure out exactly what the status is with him. I'm really sorry."

"No, don't worry about it. I understand. But I'll keep checking in with you. He looked a little possessive on Saturday at dinner. I was wondering about that. If things don't work out with you and Tom, I'll be around."

Thankfully, the line was moving, and Alex and Eddie had made it inside the bakery. Alex wasn't surprised to see how busy it was. There wasn't a single chair available. Tragedy in Harriston had the residents flocking to the bakeshop for a cup of coffee with a side of gossip, and today was no exception. A few people stared at Alex. If Alex had to make a guess, she'd say some of these folks had seen the *Harriston Confidante*'s latest post. Who was Miss T? Alex would love to know how or where she was getting her scoops from. Alex got her order and escaped outside. She breathed in the clean, crisp air and headed back to the shop.

Murder and Mayhem's shop was housed in a 1926 mishmash of Victorian and Craftsman design. The two-story house had once been a residential home but had been converted to house a retail establishment many years ago. The twins had worked hard to restore the home's beauty, focusing on its Victorian elements. They'd painted the wood siding lemon cream and scraped and repainted all the exterior trim a clean white. White lights stretched across the porch roof and down the pillars holding it up. An enormous fresh evergreen wreath, decorated with pinecones and a giant red bow, hung on the heavy front door.

Inside, Alex could smell the delicious scent of sugar cookies. She knew Hanna must have lit one of their homemade candles. Alex stopped to give Watson a special dog treat the bakery had started making in the fall. Hanna insisted they make Watson earn her treat, so Alex had her shake a paw and then do a high five before handing over the tasty cookie.

Entering the kitchen, Alex wondered if she should make Hanna earn her morning muffin. "Ordinarily I'd make you shake a paw or give me a high five in exchange for this muffin, but under the circumstances, I'll give you a pass. It's the *leash* I can do. Just don't get used to having it this easy," Alex kidded her sister as she put the box of muffins on the kitchen island. Hanna scoffed and switched the hand she was holding the ice with, to grab a muffin. Maggie quickly took it from her, broke it in half, and buttered it for Hanna.

"Is Duncan coming?" Alex got plates for the three of them and grabbed a muffin.

"He'll be here as soon as he can, but he said it might be a while. He couldn't talk, he just said *paws* off the evidence until he gets here, and to tell you not to question anyone," Hanna joined in on the punning.

Too late. "Well, Duncan is *barking* up the wrong tree, so I've got some questions for Maggie." Alex retrieved the yearbook she'd packed in her bag. "Questions about things I found in here." She held up the book.

Maggie groaned. "Those are *a-paw-ling* puns." Maggie put down her muffin. "I'll help if I can."

Alex opened to the page with the girl who had died that year. "How is Olive Dunn related to Lucy?"

Maggie squinted at the picture. "She's Lucy's sister."

Alex's eyes went wide. "I had no idea it was Lucy's sister who had died."

"She drowned. They found her the day after she went missing in the water, near one of the summer cottages. It was closed up for the winter. It was really lucky they found her as quickly as they did." Maggie fingered her muffin. "There was talk that she'd killed herself because there was no other reason for her to be there. Officially, they put it down as an accident. But people always wondered."

"Lucy's never mentioned having had a sister." Hanna leaned over to get a look at the picture.

Maggie turned the book so Hanna could see. "It was so sad. Lucy and her mother never talk about it. I think it just about killed Rose. Olive was only a year younger than Lucy, but they weren't particularly close. I sometimes got the sense that Lucy was jealous of her sister."

"They certainly looked very different. Lucy is very—" Alex wasn't sure what to say that was kind. "Plain. Whereas her sister was the cheerleader type."

"They were both smart, but Lucy and her sister had very different interests. I sometimes wonder if Lucy's parents favored Olive. When we'd get together, it was always Olive this or Olive that. At any rate, Lucy's been a wonderful caregiver to her mother."

"That's interesting. The things you don't know about people."

"Sorry. Sometimes I forget you haven't lived here all your life, and just assume you know."

"No worries. Now, what really interested me was this picture." Alex flipped to the picture with the kids holding folders. "Do you know if these kids belonged to a common group or club?"

Maggie studied the picture for a minute. "Those are all kids from Kyle's class. Except for this one." Maggie pointed to the person Alex hadn't been able to identify. "I'm not sure who that is. But I don't think the others were in any kind of special group. Kyle definitely wasn't. He lived and breathed sports, and nothing but sports. This one"—Maggie indicated the boy in hippie clothes—"he was always part of the drama and music performances. I know Brooke was on the debate team and the school paper. I don't know if Nate participated in anything outside of sports. I think Zara was always a cheerleader. I'm not sure if she did anything else."

Alex rubbed her forehead. She needed to find answers.

Hanna asked them to turn the book so she could look at the picture. "What are they all holding? It looks like folders."

"Exactly. Why would a bunch of kids all be getting the same folders if they didn't have any particular interest in common?" Alex cupped her chin.

"Is this a pop quiz?" Hanna went back to her muffin. "I have no idea. But you need to stop touching your face. You're going to make your wrinkles worse."

"Seriously. My wrinkles. These are barely character lines. I don't have wrinkles."

Christina Romeril

"You will if you don't stop rubbing at your face."

Maggie was shaking her head. "Alex, I'm guessing you have an idea what the folders are all about. You're looking very pleased with yourself."

Alex tried to not to look too excited. "What I noticed is these kids cleaned up on the academic awards. Brooke's parents were both teachers at the school. She appears to be handing out folders to those kids. What if there were test answers in those folders? Could they have been cheating? I remember one of the teachers saying the same kids were getting the top marks on almost every test or exam in science, English, and math. But mind you, these kids did well in all their subjects."

"I've heard teachers mention they thought there was some cheating going on in Kyle's class." Hanna came and looked at the picture again. "But this is hardly conclusive proof."

"I agree. It's suggestive, but it could have been anything in those folders. Plus, why would some of them have resorted to cheating? They were already doing very well," Maggie said.

"That kept bothering me as well. Why cheat if you're already getting good marks. I did a little online research on each of them. Brooke became a lawyer and had her eyes on landing a judgeship. She had high ambitions. She wanted to get into a top school. Even back then she was a type A personality. Nate wanted to become a vet, and that's a very competitive program to get into. Kyle needed to keep his marks up for his scholarship. Go figure: the hippie kid ended up graduating from MIT. Zara is the only one who didn't really go on to a prestigious school."

Maggie squinted her eyes shut for a second. "As I recall, she started dating her husband right after her high school graduation. He was a few years older and had just come back from college. They got married in September. I think she had a baby rather short of the normal nine months. Her husband's parent's owned the hardware store in Swanson. Zara and her husband own it now."

"Well, that explains why she didn't go to school in the fall."

Maggie looked at the wall clock. "You may be right, Alex, but I'd better go get things ready. We're opening soon."

After Maggie left, Alex flipped to a page in the yearbook, listing the kids who had received academic awards. "You know there were two other kids in that graduating class who did really well."

Hanna put the bag of ice on the counter and started to stand up. "Who were they?"

"What do you think you're doing?" Alex walked around and gently pushed Hanna back onto the stool.

"I've got chocolates to make, and my knee feels much better."

"You wait until after Duncan comes. Then we'll see how you're doing. The two others who did exceptionally well were Lucy and Isabelle."

"You don't think they would have been involved?"

"Why not? Lucy was originally going into nursing and then switched to pharmacology. Both require good marks. Isabelle became a nurse. And the person with their back turned to the camera is wearing those tear-away pants. It could be Isabelle with her cheer-leading outfit underneath. And guess what award Isabelle received?"

Hanna shrugged her shoulders.

"Most improved. She had never been on the honor roll before that year."

"How do you know that?"

Alex flipped to Isabelle's graduation picture. "Read what she wrote for favorite sayings."

Hanna read it aloud: *"I'll get on that honor roll yet!"*

Alex looked at her sister significantly. "I think I'm going to go visit Miss Vicky. Eddie told me she knew every kid in the school, and what was going on. Even if she couldn't prove it, she may have had some idea who was cheating."

"You ran into Eddie? I think he's sweet on you."

"I know. He asked me out again this morning."

"Again? Girl, you are not keeping me in the loop. But now isn't the time. I've got to get this recipe perfected, and sitting here doing nothing is not helping. Tonight, we talk."

Alex and Hanna gave each other a fist bump. "Fine. But for now, you sit and ice the knee." Alex got her sister some fresh ice and went to help Maggie open up.

Chapter
Twenty-Five

D uncan hustled into the store and came directly to the kitchen, with Alex and Maggie following.

"Are you okay?" He looked at Hanna's face and saw the cut, then glanced down at the plastic bag filled with ice she was holding on her knee. His mouth was set in a grim line.

"I'm fine. Just a little banged up. Alex wouldn't let me get to work until after I talked to you."

"Tell me exactly what happened." Duncan gently tilted Hanna's head to the light as Alex had done. His touch may have been a little more gentle.

Hanna retold the series of events that had resulted in her injuries. "Alex can show you what she found on the stoop."

Alex led Duncan through the back hall and held the door open for him. "I thought it best to just leave everything the way it was." She waited a moment while Duncan took in the scene. "What do you think? Is this the same person who left the note on my windshield?"

"At first glance the paper and writing look similar on both notes. I'll take pictures of the scene and then bag the evidence. The sheriff isn't going to allow me to call in forensics. She'll just dismiss it as vandalism or a prank since no one was seriously hurt."

"Luckily, no one was seriously hurt. The injuries could have been far worse. Did you see Miss T's blog this morning?"

Duncan shook his head. "I've been interviewing Kyle's parents. They finally made it home from Palm Springs. They're devastated. Kyle was their only child."

Alex showed Duncan the article on her phone. "Anyone who reads this trash would think I'm investigating the murders. Whatever happened to integrity in journalism?" Alex shrugged.

"I think the attacker thought I was Alex," Hanna said, explaining their suspicion.

"And that's why you need to leave the investigating to us. I don't want anything to happen to you." Duncan was looking at Hanna. "To either of you." Duncan's gaze included Alex, though she got a frown Hanna hadn't had to endure.

After Duncan left, Hanna convinced Alex to let her carry on testing her new recipe. She pointed out that if their roles were reversed, Alex wouldn't be putting her feet up and resting. Hanna was right. In the end, Alex made her sister promise if she felt dizzy or nauseous, or the pain in her knee increased, she'd go see a doctor.

Alex wanted to find out more about what had gone on during Kyle's senior year. She felt as if understanding Kyle better would help her find his killer. After trying to think of a natural way to bump into Miss Vicky and Zara, now that there weren't any other reunion activities, Alex finally decided to go with a method she'd used before, but with a twist. She grabbed two boxes of chocolates and headed to Miss Vicky's house.

Alex drove past Everett and Isabelle's large home, decorated with pine garlands and colorful lights. They had a sled and reindeer on their front lawn that lit up at night. The remaining lots on that side of the street were as yet undeveloped and were dotted with ponderosa pines and western larches. Further down the street, on the opposite side, was Miss Vicky's house. She'd festooned the front stoop with multicolored lights. There was a hand-carved, knee-high bear to one side, holding a sign that said "Welcome." A Santa hat had been put on its head. Alex walked up to the door with a confidence she wasn't feeling, hoping Miss Vicky wouldn't see right through her flimsy excuse. She knocked on the door.

The pudgy older woman answered, wearing a bright pink sweat suit and a workout headband around her forehead. She looked like a female Richard Simmons. In her hand was a five-pound weight. She looked surprised to see Alex standing there.

"Hello?"

"I'm sorry. Am I interrupting your workout?"

"Yes. But that's okay. I've had enough of being physical—I'm ready for a break. What can I do for you?"

"Actually, I came to bring you this." Alex handed her the box of chocolates. "We had a special draw in honor of the reunion weekend, and your name was picked."

"That's strange. I don't recall entering a draw. But I'll never say no to free food."

Alex shrugged her shoulders. "Maybe someone else entered your name." Alex leaned around Miss Vicky and saw there was a wall of bookshelves in the living room. "You must be quite the reader. That's an extensive collection of books."

"Come in. Let's not let any more of the heat escape." The woman led Alex into a standard living room that opened from a small entryway common to many of the houses built in the same era.

Alex stopped short when she saw Rose sleeping in a reclining chair in the corner. "Is this a bad time?"

"When Rose is having a particularly bad morning, Lucy drops her off here. She usually sleeps a lot on those mornings. By noon,

Rose is usually doing better and I'll bring her to the pharmacy. A dump truck driving through the living room won't wake her until she's ready."

Alex slipped her shoes off and went to a comfortable-looking sofa that afforded her the best view of the entire room. The television was paused on a Jane Fonda workout. Miss Vicky sat down adjacent to Alex on a chintz-covered armchair. Alex let her decorator's eye rove over the room. It was done in dusty rose and blue and screamed Laura Ashley from the 1990s. Alex saw a certificate on one of the bookshelves that said Miss Vicky had retired after being the secretary at Harriston School for forty-one years. Alex pointed to the certificate. "I didn't know you were a secretary at the school." *A little lie—at this point I'm not keeping track.*

"Yes, indeed. I never had children of my own, thank goodness, but I had a part in rearing thousands of them. Imagine how many kids need therapy now because of me. Ha ha ha." Miss Vicky laughed at her own joke.

Alex couldn't help but laugh. She opened the yearbook she had brought. "That's why I thought I'd bring this over." Alex held up the yearbook. "I thought if anyone could figure this out, it would be you. Do you recognize who this is?" Alex pointed to the person partially turned away from the camera with the tear-away pants.

"Let me see." Miss Vicky took the yearbook and held it up to catch the light from the window. "Oh, that's Lucy. I can tell by the sweatshirt she's wearing and those horrible pants. Her mother despaired that Lucy dressed more like a boy than a girl. She was forever telling her to dress like her sister. Olive was a lovely girl. She used to come over on Sundays, and we'd have tea together."

It looked like Alex's guess might be right about another potential cheater. "I guess you knew Kyle and Brooke?"

The woman's face hardened. "I don't know what this world is coming to. Now, I don't mean to be cruel, but I don't believe in all that stuff about not speaking ill of the dead. Kyle was a spoiled brat as a child, and he turned into a right nasty adolescent. And it seems that, as an adult, nothing much had changed. Even so, he didn't deserve to be murdered."

"It does seem he had a bit of a reputation. In fact, I understand the year he graduated there were some suspicions about cheating in his class." Alex was keeping an eye on Rose, who seemed to be sleeping soundly.

"Can I get you a glass of water? I try and stay hydrated." Miss Vicky grabbed a bottle off the coffee table and took a sip.

Alex shook her head. "Do you think the rumor about the cheating was true?"

"I had my suspicions. So did a few teachers, but they could never prove anything. The same group of students kept getting exceptionally high marks on all the tests and exams. Teachers started to watch them like hawks, but they definitely weren't bringing in materials to copy from." Miss Vicky scooched forward. "Personally, I think they had copies of the tests."

"What makes you say that?"

"It was Olive who mentioned it. I'd told her about the suspicions a few teachers had. I asked if she'd heard anything. She pointed out that essay answers can't be copied from someone else, and that was a sure sign the kids must have copies of the tests. I did mention Lucy was one of the kids under suspicion. Olive said she'd keep her eyes open, but of course she died days later. Just between us, I think Fenton was giving the science tests to Kyle to study from. And Kyle wasn't the first one. There were other boys on Fenton's team in years before and after who did far better in science than they should have."

"But how would the other kids have gotten those tests?"

"I'd lay odds that boy sold those tests to other students. And I think Brooke was doing the same thing." The woman shook her head. "I liked that girl, but she was so focused on getting top marks, I'd say she might have cheated."

"How would she have gotten hold of the tests?"

"You have to remember, computers were still in their infancy. Teachers had hard copies of tests, and her parents were both teachers at the school. She and Kyle weren't friends, but it seemed almost like they were business partners. Mind you, I don't think she liked him; she just put up with him. Remember, this is all speculation. It was just talk among a few teachers, and I heard some of it. Since Brooke's parents were both teachers, and Fenton taught at the school, these things weren't discussed openly."

"I got the impression this past weekend that Kyle wasn't all that close to his former classmates."

"I don't think Kyle ever had any real friends. In fact, I think he was a narcissist as well as a bully. Textbook. I've been taking an online psychology class." The older woman paused to shut off her television. "Kyle was always running some kind of scheme and trying to make money off his friends. In elementary school, he started a poker ring. Unbelievable, right? Ten-year-olds playing poker."

"Can you think of anyone who'd want to kill Brooke? I imagine sales for Pink Bis will go down dramatically now that she's gone."

"I sold some Pink Bis on Saturday. I love the color. Did you know it was Olive's favorite color?"

Alex startled when Rose suddenly sat up and spoke to them. How long had the woman been awake?

"Now, now. You go back to sleep. There you go. Close your eyes." Miss Vicky rolled her eyes at Alex. She lowered her tone. "She does that sometimes, just wakes up for a minute and says random things. Olive hated pink. Her favorite color was blue, as I recall. Where were we?"

"I wondered who might want Brooke dead."

"That's a mystery. She was generally liked. Perhaps a bit bossy, but I can't think of anyone who might have harmed her. Kyle is another story."

"I heard he was using steroids in his senior year. Did you ever hear anything about that?"

"Fiddlesticks. Now, I'd best be getting changed. I've got errands to run later this afternoon after I drop off Rose. Thanks for these wonderful chocolates."

Alex got up and headed to the door. On the bookshelf was a familiar picture. "Isn't this the young man who had the car accident and ended up losing his football scholarship?"

"Yes. He's my cousin's son. That accident was another one of Kyle's legacies."

"Does that mean you're also related to Zara?"

"I am. We're second cousins or cousins once removed. I can never remember how that works. She's a fiery one, the complete opposite of her brother. Zara was sent to the office a few times for getting into fights. She was impetuous. Acted first and thought later." Miss Vicky opened the door for Alex. "Now you be careful. I read Miss T's article about you this morning. It sounds like someone isn't very happy to have you snooping around. There are lots of people that would prefer to leave old secrets dead and buried."

Chapter
Twenty-Six

Alex headed straight for Swanson after the visit with Miss Vicky. Her cover had been blown thanks to Miss T, so she hoped Zara would buy her story about a draw for chocolates. The road from Harriston to the highway wound leisurely through a beautiful valley dotted with stands of trees. Traffic was moderate, and Alex was entering the outskirts of Swanson less than fifteen minutes after leaving Miss Vicky's.

She felt like it was a good sign when she found a parking spot practically in front of the hardware store Zara and her husband owned. Now, if she could just keep the luck running.

Inside, the hardware store was packed tightly with rows of everything from paint to grass seed. The seasonal aisle was filled with Christmas decorations, and Alex had to give herself a stern reminder as to her purpose at the store to avoid going in that direction. Alex saw Zara almost immediately. She was changing the paper roll at the cash register while a young man watched. How to best approach finding out what she wanted to know. Should Alex lead with the cheating or the other questions she had? Ultimately, she decided the cheating wasn't likely to be pertinent to the murder.

Zara looked up as Alex approached. "Oh, hi. Alex, right? Give me a sec, and I'll be right with you."

Alex reasoned that since she was waiting, a quick trip down the Christmas aisle was warranted. It didn't matter that Alex had well over forty containers of Christmas decorations in her basement; she was always on the hunt for something new.

Unfortunately, Zara was true to her word and Alex had barely started looking at tree ornaments when Zara approached and asked what she needed.

Alex went through her spiel about the fake draw. "I wanted to deliver these. I know it was a difficult weekend, and I believe chocolate helps with everything."

Zara's eyes welled up. "It's been a terrible weekend. Kyle ruined everything."

Alex must have looked confused.

The teary-eyed woman quickly amended her statement. "I don't mean his death." More tears gathered and spilled over her lashes. "Let's go in my office—there's no one else there at the moment."

Alex followed Zara through to the back of the store. The office was a small cubby of a room, and every surface was covered with binders, piles of papers, and boxes of gadgetry that would make an electrician swoon.

"Sit down. Do you want some coffee?" Zara brushed away her tears, picked up a mug sitting on a credenza, and grabbed the half full coffeepot.

"No thanks. I'm more of a tea drinker, and I've already had my quota for the morning."

"It seems like I've done nothing but cry this weekend. What a reunion." Zara turned on a funny fan that looked like an ashtray and was sitting on her desk, and reached in a box that said "RECEIPTS." She pulled out a pack of cigarettes. She held it out to Alex. "Do you smoke?"

"No, thank you."

Zara took out a cigarette and put the pack back in the box. "I'm not supposed to smoke inside. In fact, I'm not supposed to smoke at all. But with everything that's happened this weekend, I need one." She took a long pull on the cigarette and blew the smoke directly at the contraption on her desk. It was pulling most of the smoke into the machine.

"I noticed you were pretty upset Saturday night at the dinner. I saw you talking to someone in the parking lot."

Zara looked away. Her hand holding the cigarette twitched so badly, Alex was afraid Zara would drop the cigarette and set the room ablaze.

"Oh, that was nothing. I was just overly emotional with everything that had happened."

"I was looking through a yearbook, and it looked like you and Nate were an item in your senior year." Alex was trying not to breathe in the smoke from the cigarette, and leaned as far back in her chair as she could to get away from some errant tendrils advancing toward her.

Zara busied herself brushing away cigarette ash from her desk, oblivious to Alex's contortions. "We dated for a couple of years, but we broke up right after graduation. Nate was going away to school to become a vet, and I was planning to go to a college somewhere else. Long distance doesn't really work." The hand holding the cigarette reached up, and a finger started to twirl itself around a chunk of hair.

Alex had visions of Zara's long beachy waves going up in flames.

"Yesterday, I was on my way to the school, and I saw you and Nate. I saw you slip him a note. It was all cloak-and-dagger. Are you two secret agents or something?" Alex tried to lighten her tone, but in the end it came out like she was interrogating a suspect.

Zara's eyes went wide, and she fiddled with her cigarette. At least it wasn't near her hair anymore. "That was just some information he asked for about a new brand of animal feed. Gosh. You really are quite the detective."

"I just happened to be in the right place at the right time. I noticed a picture on the wall outside the office of your family. How old are your kids?" Alex tried to sound interested in the woman's family.

The innocent-eyed mask disappeared, and a calculating look crossed Zara's face. "I'm guessing you already have a good idea how old my kids are. I met my husband the week after graduation, and we got married a couple months later. He'd already graduated from college and was working here at the store. You know how these things go."

"Yes. Plans so often don't happen quite how we envisioned them. I guess your brother found that out. It was so sad what happened."

Zara leaned forward and her eyes narrowed. "Kyle got what he deserved in the end. Karma. I'm only sorry it took so long. He wreaked nothing but havoc all around him. My brother wasn't the only person Kyle hurt. It's a long list, and it looks like someone finally evened the score."

"Did you want him dead?"

"No. I didn't want him to die. But since someone took it into their own hands, I can't say that I'm sorry."

"Kyle certainly stirred up strong feelings. Who else wouldn't have been sad to see Kyle meet his end?"

"Everyone. Honestly, he hurt so many people back in high school, and I'm sure he never changed. Everything he did was for his own benefit. Plus, he was just mean. I think he genuinely enjoyed seeing other people suffer."

"Do you have someone specific in mind?"

"My brother for one. My brother was a great football player. Scouts from colleges had been looking at him since his sophomore year. I think Kyle was jealous when Jack was offered a scholarship. Like, if Jack got a scholarship, it would somehow detract from Kyle."

"Do you think Kyle intentionally flipped the car?"

"Kyle had just got his driver's license. As they left the meeting, he grabbed my brother's keys and said he'd drive. My brother said Kyle had been drinking, and so he told Kyle no way. But what Kyle wanted, Kyle got. He didn't wait for my brother to buckle up, and sped down the driveway like a demon. If the car hadn't flipped, they were bound to hit a tree or something."

"Why would he do that? He could have been hurt himself."

"Kyle was always wild and reckless, and together with alcohol it wasn't a good combination." She shrugged. "Plus, he had his seat belt on. If my brother had been buckled in, he probably would have been okay as well. My brother was sure Kyle meant for him to be hurt."

"Why didn't Kyle get into any trouble?"

"It was my brother's word against Kyle's. Kyle said he hadn't been drinking. It was a couple days later before they checked that, and of course by then there was no alcohol in his system. Plus, they couldn't find proof that Kyle had purchased or stolen any alcohol. His parents didn't keep it in the house. Kyle acted all apologetic afterward. His parents paid for everything. Except the scholarship was gone, and my brother's dream of a football career was over."

"I can see where you'd feel angry at Kyle. Why did you get involved with him and the others cheating in your senior year if you hated him so much?"

"How did you find out about that?"

"I heard a few things, saw some things, and put everything together. I think Kyle and Brooke were selling tests to certain students in their class. I'm pretty sure I know who was involved."

"I guess now that Brooke is gone, it doesn't really matter anymore. She asked me not to say anything about it. You know, with her becoming a judge, it wouldn't have looked so good. I told her it was high school, and no one really cares what happened that long ago. But she was convinced it would hurt her chances."

"Why did you all cheat? From everything I've heard, all of you were doing okay in school."

Zara snorted. "Okay wasn't good enough. It wasn't back then, and it definitely isn't now. I wanted to be a nurse. If you want to get into the top schools or programs, you need to be the best. It's crazy when ninety-five percent isn't good enough; for some programs you need ninety-eight or ninety-nine percent to be truly competitive. There's so much pressure put on kids. I've seen it with my own two. My son is in his second year of college and wants to become a vet, and my daughter wants to be a chemical engineer. They have to work so hard, there's hardly time for fun anymore."

"Wasn't Brooke afraid one of the others might have said something?"

"She always seemed to know how to get people on board with her way of thinking. In some ways she and Kyle weren't that different."

"You, Kyle, Brooke, Nate, the hippie kid, Lucy, and Isabelle. Was that everyone involved?"

"Isabelle wasn't involved. Otherwise, you got us all. But like I said, that was high school, and everyone did stupid things. No one cares anymore."

"Do you know if Kyle was taking steroids in his senior year?"

Zara looked genuinely surprised. "I hadn't heard anything about that. If he thought it would give him an edge, I'm sure he would have done it, though." The phone in the office rang. Zara looked at the number on the display screen. "I've got to take this. Thanks for the chocolates. Can you let yourself out?"

Alex walked back to her car, thinking about everything Zara had said, or hadn't said. She certainly hadn't confessed to anything other than cheating on some tests. She still sounded bitter about her brother. Bitter enough to kill Kyle? Alex didn't think Kyle deserved to be murdered, but the more she found out about him, the more she understood why someone else might think he did.

Though she'd solved the mystery behind the cheating, she didn't see that it had gotten her any further in figuring out who killed Kyle. Alex thought the only person who might have considered that to be a motive for murder was Brooke, and she was dead. Could there be two killers? Maybe completely unrelated? Could Brooke have killed Kyle, and then she was murdered for a completely different reason? Could there be more people from the Class of '99 on the killer's list? Or had Brooke found out who killed Kyle, and had to be silenced? And what about the five thousand dollars in his pocket?

Alex headed back to Harriston as she continued to consider her suspects. Fenton could be the killer? But what was the motive? Kyle was giving Fenton a hard time about a loan, but that hardly seemed a strong enough reason to kill his former student. Who could tell her more about Kyle and his relationship to Fenton? Certainly Fenton wasn't going to tell her anything. He was a cranky old fart on the best of days. She didn't think she could get him to frame himself.

Alex had harbored the distinct impression that Miss Vicky knew more than she was saying. But how could she get her to talk?

Alex was driving into town and could see Valley Vets, Nate's vet clinic. Parked off to the side of the lot was a truck. Alex slammed on her brakes and pulled into the parking lot, then drove up beside the blue truck with a grill guard over the front. She recognized the logo on the passenger side door. It was a circle with a horse and a dog in the middle, and around the edge it said "Valley Vets Clinic." A memory flashed through her mind. This was the same logo that had been on the door of the truck in the church parking lot on Saturday night. Alex walked into the clinic and approached the receptionist at the front desk.

The perky little brunette, who didn't look old enough to have a driver's license, asked, "Do you have an appointment?"

"No. I'm actually just wondering whose truck is parked out front. It has the clinic's logo on the door."

"That depends. Is the truck white or dark blue?"

"Blue."

"Then that's Dr. Baxter's truck. Is there anything else I can help you with?"

"Nope. Actually, while I'm here, I might as well make an appointment for Miss Watson's annual shots and checkup." Their dog got more regular medical care than either Alex or Hanna.

After Alex made the arrangements, she got back in her car and drove away. It appeared Nate had been the cause of Zara's emotional reaction the other evening.

Well, well, well. What could that mean?

Not only that, but Nate drove a dark-colored truck. She'd seen it at the community center the day Nate punched Kyle, and that's probably why it had seemed familiar. But it was a newer model, and Alex still thought it was an older model that had tried to run her down. It had all happened so fast, she could be mistaken.

*   *   *

Back at the shop, Alex told Hanna what she'd discovered. "I think Zara and Nate are having an affair. I think that's what Kyle was taunting Nate about when I saw Nate punch him. He must have known about the affair. When Nate came to the dance, he could have been looking for either Kyle or Zara. Nate told me someone keyed his wife's car Friday night. What if he broke off the affair with Zara? She might be angry enough to key his wife's car."

Miss Vicky had said Zara had a temper and was impulsive in school. Maybe she hadn't changed that much.

"Or could Nate have been angry enough with Kyle to kill him? If Nate's wife and Zara's husband found out about the affair, it could jeopardize both marriages." Hanna was just putting her trial batch of chocolates in the special fridge they had that kept their chocolates at the optimal temperature. "When these are set, you and Maggie can try one and tell me what you think." She pulled out one mold from the fridge and slammed it upside down on the counter. Hanna wiped her hands on her apron and sat on the stool she'd left by the island.

"Could this be what Miss T was talking about on her blog yesterday? It was something about the key to a good breakup."

"That could be."

"Maybe Zara and Nate didn't care if anyone found out about their affair. What if they were going to leave their spouses? They used to date in high school." Alex thought about what she'd seen in the church parking lot. There was trouble in paradise, judging from Zara's reaction. Alex was looking at the chocolates. She pulled the mold away to uncover forty shiny bonbons. "Those look perfect." She reached out and popped one in her mouth. "So good. How are you feeling? You look a little pale." Alex was worried her sister wasn't resting like she should be doing after this morning's incident.

"I'm fine. Maggie's been checking on me regularly," Hanna said impatiently. "Those are the last batch I made, but I've made a slight variation in the group I just put in the fridge. I think you're right about Nate and Zara having an affair, but we don't know if it has anything to do with either murder." Hanna stood up. "I'm going to make some of the chocolates we're getting low on. Alone. Maggie's actually been pretty busy. Maybe you should go help her. That's my not so subtle way of telling you to get out of my kitchen."

"I'm going. I know when I'm not wanted. But if you decide you need my help making chocolates, you come get me, or if any more dead bodies show up. Definitely get me then."

"You're so weird."

"But you love me."

Alex went into the hall, and four women who looked to be in their forties entered the shop. Alex welcomed them. "If you need help finding anything, let me know."

The tallest of the bunch approached Alex as the others dispersed throughout the shop. The woman had "wild child" written all over her. She had her hair buzzed short and colored pink. Her ears had a row of piercings any punk rocker could be proud of. There was a butterfly tattoo creeping up her neck above a tie-dyed long sleeve T-shirt, and she wore wide-legged jeans. "Do you have any mysteries with birds as a theme?"

Once again, Alex was reminded not to judge a book by its cover. "We do. Let me show you." Alex led the woman to the Meg Langslow Mysteries, where each title had a bird theme. "Do you live in town?"

"I used to. I was supposed to come for the reunion last weekend, but my psychic told me there was a bad aura happening, and my chakras were out of balance. She said I should wait until after Sunday to come. Maybe I would have been murdered too, if I'd been here."

"Did you belong to the Class of '99?"

"No. I graduated in '95. No one's been murdered from that class, have they?"

"Just the two from '99. Where are you and your friends from?"

"We drove up from Missoula. One of the other ladies came to adopt a dog from a rescue shelter in the area. I happen to know the lady that runs it."

"That's wonderful. I heard the shelter is full, so they really need the adoptions."

"I find it amazing how people that have difficult upbringings often end up being so nurturing."

"How so?"

"The lady that owns the shelter practically raised herself and her younger siblings. No mother, and the father—well." Wild child tilted her hand by her mouth, indicating the father must have been a drinker. "She had a rough time. But I really wanted to come to Harriston to see what's changed. Does Zara Hobbs still live here?"

"Her married name is Nichols. She and her husband own a hardware store in Swanson. You know her?"

"I used to babysit Zara. She was a bit crazy, so her parents had me come over until she was thirteen. She had a real temper. Her parents had her see a psychologist for a while. They couldn't leave her alone at home. She actually took apart her friend's bike and threw the pieces in the lake when she was eleven, all because her friend got the lead part in a class play. She's probably nothing like that anymore."

"Wow. I did hear she was a bit impulsive. Who was the friend whose bike she took apart?"

"I think it was the woman who was killed. Brooke Gibson." The woman looked over her shoulder. Her friends were heading to the cash register, where Maggie was waiting to ring up their purchases. "I better hurry and choose my books. We'll be going to the Festive Foods event on the weekend. We were going to support Choco Choco, but after what happened, I guess we'll be there to support your shop."

Other customers had come into the store, and Alex went to help them. Wow. Zara had some issues as a child. Could her resentments toward Kyle and Brooke have been unleashed at the reunion?

Later Alex stood at the counter and checked off books on an invoice as she unpacked them from a box. She looked up when the bell over the front door jingled. She was surprised to see the sheriff and two deputies enter.

Sheriff Summers approached Alex and handed her a piece of paper. "This is a search warrant. It allows us to search your premises, including any outbuildings. You'll need to close the store until we're done, though you're welcome to stay here during the search."

Chapter
Twenty-Seven

A lex looked at the search warrant. It said they were looking for strychnine. "What reason do you have to base this on? This is crazy."

"You'll need to let us do the search. You're welcome to call your lawyer." Sheriff Summers pointed to the sleeping pooch under the table behind the counter. "You'll need to secure your dog."

Alex put a leash on Watson and looped it around the table leg. Watson opened one eye briefly before going back to sleep. Apparently, being a professional sleeper was Watson's chosen career. Alex waved Maggie over and explained what was going on. While Maggie dealt with the customers in the store, Alex turned their sign to "Closed" and let Hanna know what was happening, and then she called Everett.

The lawyer was there in minutes, since he'd been working from home. Alex let him in and showed him the warrant. He took it and went to talk to the sheriff. Maggie had texted Duncan to find out if he knew anything about the search, but hadn't heard back.

A few minutes later Everett came back to Alex, Maggie, and Hanna, who were huddled together by the counter.

"An anonymous tip was called in early this morning. The individual claimed they saw Hanna's car near Eudora's shed early Saturday morning, around four. They were able to give a description of the vehicle, the license plate number, and a description of Hanna. The sheriff got confirmation today that Brooke died of strychnine poisoning. They think it was the rat poison in Eudora's shed. They need to find it to confirm that, though."

"That's impossible. I was with Hanna all night and early that morning." As Alex talked, deputies were systematically searching the house. "Plus, Duncan was with us at four that morning. He can verify her whereabouts even if they don't believe me."

"I just got a text back from Duncan. He had no idea the sheriff was coming here with a search warrant. He's been at Kyle's work, searching through things there. Kyle's dad gave the sheriff's office permission earlier today." Maggie glanced at her phone again. "Duncan's on his way here."

"If he can verify you were with him, then I'll talk to the sheriff and see if she'll discontinue the search."

While they waited, Alex told Everett what had happened to Hanna that morning.

"Alex, maybe you should leave the investigating to the sheriff's office. The whole village knows what you're doing. I think it's too much to hope that the killer isn't aware as well."

"Maybe, but this just makes me more determined to find the truth." Alex realized that all her life she'd been more determined to do something if someone told her she shouldn't or couldn't.

Twenty minutes later Duncan arrived. He and Everett talked first, then went to the sheriff. A few minutes later the deputies left, and the sheriff approached Alex and Hanna. "It looks like whoever called in the anonymous tip was lying, if my deputy is to be believed. Miss Eastham, you are still a person of interest in Mr. Allerton's murder. Please come to the sheriff's station no later than four PM tomorrow to sign your revised statement. Your statement has more drafts than most novels."

Hanna turned to Duncan after the sheriff left. "Are you going to be in trouble over this?'"

"She's not very happy about it. I did put it in my report, but I may have buried it a little, and I didn't point it out to her. There's not a lot she can do, but I'd better tread carefully for the next little while." He lowered his voice. "In case you're interested, we got the report back on the bottle of Pink Bis found by Brooke's bag in the parking lot. It contained a large amount of strychnine, and only her fingerprints were on the bottle. And Brooke's fingerprints were among those on the five thousand cash we found on Kyle."

Duncan headed to the door with Hanna.

Everett turned to Alex. "I know you won't listen, but my advice is to leave the investigation with Duncan and the sheriff."

"You are one hundred percent right." *I won't be leaving the investigating to the sheriff,* Alex thought. Then she asked, "Before you go, I have a question about Kyle. Back when you were playing football against him, did you see any evidence that he was taking steroids?"

"This doesn't constitute as evidence, but he did bulk up quite a bit between his junior and senior year. Of course that could just be from hitting a growth spurt and working out. I really don't remember anything else, other than his temper. Could have been roid rage, as they call it now. Of course, he always had a temper, but I guess it was worse senior year. I heard a kid on another team they were playing against made a joke about his acne, and Kyle tried to attack him. Several members of the team and his coach had to hold him back."

"Where would he have gotten them from if he was using?"

"Back then he might have gotten them from his doctor, if he could convince him he needed them. Or his coach, his parents, a pharmacist, or even on the street. I know of at least one kid on my team that used steroids, and he got them from his parents. His dad got them prescribed for himself and then gave them to his kid."

"How could a parent do that? Don't they have potential side effects?"

"Have you ever been to a high school football game? There are parents that would mortgage their homes or sell an organ if they thought it would give their son a chance at the big leagues. I've got to go, but call if you have any more trouble with the sheriff."

Alex turned back to her sister and Maggie. "Let's just clean up and go home. There's no point in opening this close to the end of the day."

"Okay, but first I want you guys to taste my new chocolates." Hanna untied Watson from the table and led them to the kitchen.

Alex was dismayed at what she saw there. The deputies had pulled so many things out of cupboards and just left it all on the island. It was going to take them a while to clean up.

When they were finally done half an hour later, Hanna had several chocolates on a plate. "I'm calling them True North Nicotine Chocolates. It's a milk chocolate shell with a creamy maple-flavored caramel center. I have a hint of something special in there. See if you can guess what it is."

Maggie and Alex each took one. Maggie closed her eyes. "These are delicious." Maggie reached for another one. "Heavenly."

Alex could taste something. It was very subtle. "Nutmeg. It's barely there, but I can taste it, and it wasn't in the one I ate earlier."

"I'm impressed. Your tasting skills are improving." Hanna fist-bumped with her twin.

Alex was about to reach for another chocolate, when there was a knock at the door. "I'll get it."

Walking down the hall Alex wondered what she'd say to whoever was at the door if they asked why the shop had closed early.

She opened the door, prepared to say they were doing a chocolate tasting, but to her surprise it was Tom. "Hi." She looked at him quizzically.

"Why is the store closed? I thought you were open until five thirty."

"Come in and let me tell you all about it." Alex led the way to the kitchen.

Tom explained his unexpected visit as they walked to the kitchen. "Mrs. Matthews called on me this afternoon with a loaf of bread and hoping for a chance to tell me about her visit with the podiatrist. Don't ask."

In the kitchen, Alex waved Tom to a chair. "So, we're all dying to know. Did Mrs. Matthews show you her feet?"

"No. She did not show me her feet, but I got the impression there was something else on her mind. She finally brought out a note and showed it to me. She said she'd been very foolish. I took a picture of it." Tom pulled out his phone, tapped a few screens, and handed it to Alex. "She was being blackmailed but told her son it was an investment, so she wouldn't have to say any more about it."

Alex quickly read the note on Tom's phone.

Do you want all of Harriston to find out about your husband? How he used to buy liquor for minors while he was the school's janitor?

At least one car accident happened because of his actions. Maybe that family will sue you if they find out. Make the right decision and save some money.

Put $5,000 cash in the garbage can on the west side of the public beach parking lot by 6 p.m. on December 6.

Alex handed the phone to Maggie. Hanna had come around the counter, and they read it at the same time.

"Mrs. Matthews was very embarrassed. Mr. Matthews used to be the caretaker at the school, as Maggie mentioned yesterday. Two years before Kyle graduated, he asked Mr. Matthews to buy him alcohol and offered him twenty dollars for every time he got it. She said they didn't have a lot of money and that extra twenty bucks every two weeks, sometimes more often, really helped out. Mr. Matthews figured Kyle would get the alcohol one way or another, so it might as well be him getting paid for it." Tom took the phone from Maggie and put it in his pocket.

"Oh dear," Maggie said.

"The last time Mr. Matthews bought the alcohol was the weekend Jack was injured in the accident with Kyle driving. Mr. Matthews told his wife all about what he'd been doing. They never went to the police because they were afraid he would lose his job, maybe his pension. He was retiring the next year. She said he was never quite the same afterward. He died several years later. Mrs. Matthews was afraid that Zara's family might sue." Tom shook his head.

"That note had to be from Kyle. He was truly lower than scum." Alex couldn't believe it.

"Mrs. Matthews wanted to make sure that 'nice woman at the end of the block who solves murders' saw this. She asked if I would share it with you." Tom looked at Alex. "Mrs. Matthews assumed the note was from Kyle and wondered if Kyle preyed on any others in a similar way."

"Miss Vicky said things were tight at the pharmacy and that Rose had made a bad investment. Could she be another victim?" Alex thought there was something familiar about the note.

Maggie spoke up. "What about Fenton? He's been short on money as well. Drew said Fenton was usually very generous in his donation to the Toy Drive, but this year he only gave a token amount. He said things were tight on the farm, but this past year was a great year for farmers and ranchers. Fenton should have had some extra money."

"When I asked Miss Vicky if Kyle could have been using steroids, she said, 'Fiddlesticks' so fast, she couldn't even have considered it. Yet everyone else I've asked said it was definitely possible. Could Kyle have blackmailed her as well?" Alex wondered out loud.

"Why doesn't Mrs. Matthews just tell the sheriff's department?" Maggie asked.

"She doesn't want people to find out. Her husband is gone now, and she wants to protect his good name. She said she'll deny it if the sheriff asks, but she wanted Alex to know. She said she knew Alex was investigating Kyle's death because she read it on Miss T's website. I didn't even know Mrs. Matthews knew what a website was," Tom said. "It turns out she's active on social media. She goes by the handle 'BakingBad.' She takes pictures of all the treats she bakes and posts them."

Tom had church business to attend to, and left the shop after forwarding the picture to Alex's phone.

As they tidied up before going home, Alex mentioned her conversation with the pink-haired woman. "Maggie, did you ever hear anything about Zara?"

"It's so long ago. There are bound to be things I've forgotten. I do remember that she could be a bit wild. But I don't really remember anything specific. Though I do recall Brooke getting a new bike. She never mentioned what happened to her old bike, but it was in sixth grade, and she got a ten-speed. That was the last year I babysat her."

"Even if Zara was a little cray-cray when she was a kid, it doesn't mean she's still like that." Hanna was checking her appearance in the mirror hanging on the back of the kitchen door.

"Might I remind you of the gouge in Nate's car that we saw on Sunday? Does keying a car sound like the actions of a stable adult?"

A Nutcracker Nightmare

Alex raised her eyebrows as she looked at her sister's perfectly made-up face.

"She has a point, Hanna. If Zara could do that to her lover's car, what might she have done to someone she hates?" Maggie wiggled into her jacket.

"You guys go home. I'll lock up. Then I'm going to pay Miss Vicky another call. I don't think she was being completely truthful earlier today," Alex said.

"Are you sure you're safe? Someone is out to hurt you. We should all leave together," Hanna insisted.

"I'll be two minutes behind you. If it makes you feel better, you can wait in your car and watch me lock up."

Chapter
Twenty-Eight

Once Alex was in her car, Hanna and Maggie drove off. Alex headed in the same direction but turned south when Hanna and Maggie continued the short distance to their respective houses. Miss Vicky only lived a few blocks away. Alex parked on the street in front of the house.

Lights were on, so Miss Vicky must be home. Colorful lights around the front window blinked cheerfully as Alex walked up the pathway wondering how she would approach the topic. Accusing Miss Vicky of lying might be tantamount to attacking her very moral fiber. The woman seemed to see things as either black or white. Plus, there was always the remote chance Miss Vicky was the killer. Alex played it out in her head. *Hi, Miss Vicky. Did Kyle by any chance try to blackmail you because you sold him steroids in high school?* Maybe a more indirect approach would be better. The woman answered the door before Alex had finished knocking.

"That was fast." Alex was still trying to figure out what to say.

"I saw you coming up the path." The pink tracksuit had been replaced by a white fleece lounge outfit. Miss Vicky looked like a giant marshmallow.

A Nutcracker Nightmare

Alex guessed there was a whole posse of seniors lurking by their windows, keeping an eye out in their neighborhoods. It was a wonder there were any secrets in the village. "I wondered if I could come in for a minute? I have a few questions, and I'm sure you know more about what's going on in the village than Miss T."

The senior preened. "That may be. Come in. I was just watching *Jeopardy*."

Miss Vicky turned the television to mute and looked at Alex expectantly. "What can I help you with?"

"Earlier today I found out that Kyle may have been blackmailing several people. Might he have been blackmailing you as well?"

Miss Vicky laughed. "That little punk wouldn't have dared approach me. He wouldn't have gotten one red cent, and I would have reported him. Assuming I even had something he could blackmail me with. Which he didn't."

Looking at the recliner in the corner, it had come to Alex in a flash. How protective Miss Vicky always was of Rose. Alex cut in, "You're right. I bet you're straight as an arrow. Probably never fudge on your taxes or even speed in your car. But I bet you know of someone else he blackmailed. And I bet you'd tell a little white lie to protect them."

Alex watched the woman's face freeze. She'd hit the mark. Alex decided to go all in. "Did Kyle blackmail Rose?"

"Why would he do that?" Miss Vicky's voice went up an octave.

Alex could tell the woman was bluffing. "I think Rose was somehow involved in selling steroids to Kyle. She and Fenton had some kind of romance. She was a pharmacist. I bet Fenton asked her to sell them to him, and then he gave them to Kyle, or something like that. Kyle must have known or found out. Had he threatened to expose what she'd done?"

Miss Vicky blinked rapidly and kept pulling at the neckline of her sweatshirt.

Bingo. Alex was sure the look on Miss Vicky's face confirmed Alex's theory. "When I asked if you thought Kyle was taking steroids, you said, 'Fiddlesticks,' but every other person I spoke to thought it was entirely possible. And yet you probably knew more of what was going on at the school than anyone else."

Miss Vicky's face crumpled and her shoulders slumped. "It's true. I just wanted to protect Rose. She and Fenton were having an affair for years. He asked her to sell him the steroids for some of his team, and she felt she couldn't say no. Then when Olive died, she broke off the affair with Fenton. Sometimes the death of a child splits a couple apart, but in this case it drew her and her husband together again.

"Rose came to me after she got the blackmail note. She showed it to me. It told her to leave a bag with five thousand dollars in cash in a garbage can by the public beach parking lot on a specific day. She didn't want Lucy to find out what she'd done. That's why she decided to pay it. She got me to take her to the bank and to drop off the cash. She said it was better if Lucy thought she was addle brained than to know the truth of what Rose had done. We assumed it was Kyle, but the note wasn't signed, and we never saw the blackmailer."

"Wasn't she taking a chance? After all, the blackmailer could have kept pressuring her for more money."

"That's what I told her. It made sense that it was Kyle. He had a gambling addiction—I'm sure of it. He was always going to need more money. She said by the time he came around again, she might be too far along to worry about it. Her Alzheimer's is progressing, and some days she really struggles to remember things."

Harriston was a hotbed of sex and secrets. Alex was shocked by the revelation but tried to keep a neutral expression. Rose looked the perfect grandmother. How had this woman gotten involved in this? "Could she have killed Kyle?"

"It's not possible. I'm not sure she could even find her way across town most days. She's not operating with a full load, if you catch my meaning. Lucy won't let her drive anymore."

"What about you? Did you kill Kyle?"

"If I was going to do anything, I would have reported Kyle's activities. But Rose begged me not to say anything. We've been friends all our lives. I couldn't betray her."

Alex couldn't picture Miss Vicky attacking Hanna or trying to run down Alex. But she'd learned that appearances could be deceiving. "You don't have that note, by any chance?"

Miss Vicky shook her head. "Rose made me promise I'd burn it, and I did."

"I appreciate your candor." Alex got up to leave. She reached into her pocket, hoping for a tissue, because she could feel a sneeze coming. Instead, she found the Weight Watcher's number and the wrapper she'd stuffed into her pocket at the dance just before she'd found Kyle's body. She'd completely forgotten about them. She glanced at the papers and was about to stuff them back into her pocket when she realized where she'd seen a similar wrapper recently.

Alex thanked Miss Vicky for her time and headed to the car. As she walked down the porch stairs, a vehicle passed the house and pulled into the driveway next door. Alex recognized the truck, or at least one very much like it. It was a dark color, older model, and then she remembered. The truck that had tried to run her over definitely had a grill guard on the front, the kind that protects the front end in case you hit a deer. Just like this one. Alex stepped back into the shadow of some dogwoods and watched as Fenton got out of the truck and walked up to Rose's house.

Alex pulled the candy wrapper out of her pocket. It was actually a wrapper for a cough candy, the same kind she'd seen Fenton popping in his mouth. She'd bet dollars to donuts Fenton was the killer, and here was the proof he'd been in the basement, in her pocket all along. She raced to her car and fumbled with the key fob to unlock the doors. As she paused to open her door, she looked up at Rose's house. Standing on the front step was Fenton. When she got into the car, the interior light came on. She looked up at Rose's front step and locked eyes with Fenton. In that second, she was sure he knew that she knew what he'd done. He rushed down the steps toward her, and she yanked her door shut, locked it, and started the car.

Fenton came running up alongside the car and pounded on her window.

Alex's heart rate went from zero to sixty in two seconds.

He yelled, "We need to talk."

Alex shook her head and put the car into drive.

Fenton grabbed the door handle and tried to open the door. "Come on. I just want to talk to you. Open up."

She wasn't about to open the door. She'd let Duncan do the talking. She slowly drove forward, hoping he would let go. The last thing she wanted to do was drag a senior citizen, even a murderous one, along the streets of Harriston. With the seniors at their windows and the fact that half the population over seventy had a cell phone now, she didn't need to see a video of her dragging Fenton with her car.

Thankfully, with one more pounding on the window, he let go and she drove away. She raced straight home, parked the car, and locked it as she sprinted inside. As soon as she opened the door, she yelled, "Hanna, lock all the doors!" Alex locked the front door and met Hanna coming down the hall. "Did you lock the doors?"

"They're already locked. What's going on?" Hanna's brows were knit together.

"I know who the killer is and who tried to run me down. He's probably the one who attacked you too. It's Fenton."

Chapter
Twenty-Nine

"Fenton? The killer. Are you sure?" Hanna's mouth hung open.

Alex quickly explained what had happened at Miss Vicky's house. "I was afraid he might try and follow me. Please, call Duncan right now."

While Hanna made the call, Alex went into the kitchen and tried to calm down. She was shaking so hard, she had to clench her teeth to keep them from chattering. As soon as Hanna put her phone down, Alex looked at her expectantly.

"Duncan is going to be here as fast as he can. He wants to talk to you first, and then he'll get Fenton picked up and taken in for more questioning."

Hanna had been in the middle of making lasagna when Alex rushed home. To keep busy, Alex took over browning the ground beef while Hanna grated the cheese.

"Do you really think Rose was involved in selling steroids to Fenton for his team? She seems like such a nice lady."

"Women do crazy things for men when they're in love. But when Olive died, the family kind of pulled together. I guess Fenton's been trying to rekindle the romance." Alex couldn't imagine being so in love that she'd be willing to do something so wrong.

They'd just popped the lasagna into the oven when the doorbell rang. Alex and Hanna looked at each other and by "twin-tuition" went to answer the door together. Alex checked the peephole and saw Duncan standing there. She opened the door to let him in.

They all sat around the kitchen table, and Alex began her explanation. She tried to shine the light away from why she'd been visiting with Miss Vicky. She focused on what she'd learned, though the frown on Duncan's face suggested she wasn't fooling him.

"It was when I was leaving and found the wrapper in my pocket that I put it all together. I'd picked up the wrapper at the bottom of the basement stairs just before I found Kyle's body. At the time I thought it was just garbage, and in all the excitement I forgot about it. Then when I saw Fenton's truck, I was sure I remembered seeing the grill guard as the truck whizzed by the other night. Tonight when I looked up and saw Fenton looking at me, I'm sure he realized that I'd recognized his truck."

"We're going to find him and bring him in for questioning. Someone back at the station is already working on a request for a search warrant for his truck and his house. We'll get something on him. Keep your doors locked until we pick him up. I'd like to think he's smart enough not to come here, but desperate people don't always do the smart thing." Duncan stood up and made his way to the door. "I'll call this information in. As soon as we have something, I'll let you know."

Alex called Tom to let him know what had happened. "We've got lasagna in the oven. Would you like to come over and keep us company? Though I guess I may be putting you in danger by inviting you over."

"In that case, how about if I call Maggie and invite her and Drew over as well—safety in numbers. Maybe we can have a potluck. I'll bring Mrs. Matthew's bread along, and I happen to know Maggie's got soup and a salad she could bring."

"That sounds wonderful. We'll feel much better having a full house here tonight."

Alex and Hanna set enough places at the table to accommodate their impromptu dinner party. When they were done Hanna grabbed a brush and lip gloss out of the kitchen junk drawer. She quickly ran the brush through Alex's hair and applied some gloss to Alex's lips.

"There. Now you're ready to receive male callers."

"What would I do without you?" Alex gave her sister a high five.

When the group was finally assembled around the table, Tom asked if he could say the blessing for the meal. Everyone heaped food onto their plates as soon as amen was said.

"I don't remember the last time I ate." Alex buttered half a piece of the bread Tom had brought. It reminded her that she needed to figure out what she could do with the information Mrs. Matthews had given her.

Drew piled lasagna on his plate.

Maggie gave him a dirty look. "Don't you think you should take it easy? You've been sick. Your stomach may not be ready for such a big meal."

"I'll be fine. I'm almost as good as new. Besides, pasta is easy to digest."

Maggie rolled her eyes and took a bite of the pasta dish. "You're *impastable*."

Everyone groaned.

"This has been such an interesting turn of events. After all, there were endless *pastabilities* because Kyle had made so many enemies." Hanna dabbed a napkin to her mouth.

Alex looked at Tom. "I'll give you a *penne* for your thoughts."

"You are all being far too *saucy* for a serious topic like this," Tom responded.

"Since I started this, I'll end it. I'm sure Fenton has been *ravi-lonely* all these years." Maggie stood up and bowed.

Everyone laughed.

"I feel a little sorry for Fenton. He finally tried to rekindle his romance with Rose, and then Kyle tries to blackmail her. Maybe Kyle's also been blackmailing Fenton. Do you think Fenton tried to get Kyle to stop, and things got out of hand?" Maggie glanced at everyone.

"Those are a lot of maybes." Hanna looked curious. "But why? What did Kyle need the money for?"

Alex paused her fork on its way to her mouth. "I think Miss Vicky might have figured it out. She thought he had a gambling problem. When I looked at his social media, I thought some of the pictures were taken at a casino. He was already gambling in elementary school. Maybe he struggled with it his whole life."

"When I worked at the jail, there was more than one person who was there because of a gambling addiction. People start losing money, and they think they can win it back if they play just one more time. Before you know it, they've lost their cars and their homes, and some go on to steal from their employers, or worse." Tom buttered another piece of bread.

Hanna's phone rang. Everyone was instantly quiet. She answered and listened for a few minutes. "Okay. Let us know when you find out more." She ended the call, and her gaze scanned the table. "They've picked up Fenton. They told him they were working on a search warrant for his truck, and he told them to go ahead and search, they didn't need a warrant. He said he had nothing to hide. When they checked, they found the can of rat poison in his truck. They're pretty sure it's the one from Eudora's shed. It was hidden in a tool chest under a tarp in the back of his truck. He claims it wasn't his, but they've taken him in for questioning."

"I know Fenton's always been kind of cranky, but I never would have believed he was a killer." Drew looked shocked.

Maggie nodded. "I agree. But I never would have suspected he gave steroids to the boys on his football team. How could he abuse his position in that way?"

"I know winning meant everything to him. It seems like he took it too far." Tom helped himself to another piece of lasagna.

When everyone was done eating and the dishwasher was loaded, they all found a comfortable spot in the living room.

Alex grabbed some cookies from the freezer. She set the box on the table. "Help yourselves."

Talk slowly moved away from Fenton.

Maggie asked, "Are you donating any cookies to the bake sale this Saturday?"

The bake sale was held every year to raise funds for the historical society. If they took in more than they needed, they donated the difference to purchase toys for families in need of help over the holidays. Fenton always donated generously to the Toy Drive and helped deliver the toys each year. Alex wondered who would be taking over his responsibilities now.

"We baked these German Lebkuchen cookies in November, and there are more in the freezer. We knew we wouldn't have time this week, with the competition and everything. We hadn't planned on a murder. What do you think?" Alex asked.

"These are good. What are they?" Drew was already on his second cookie.

"They're a traditional Christmas gingerbread cookie. It's not quite like what you're familiar with. They're softer and made with honey, almonds, and marmalade. We'll still add chocolate or icing to them before we donate them. They're one of my personal favorites." Alex took one cookie from the tin.

"I'm going to be doing nothing but making chocolate for the rest of the week." Hanna got up and went to the kitchen. She returned almost immediately with a small box of chocolates. "I brought a few samples of the chocolates I'm working on. I still have time to tweak the recipe, so try them and tell me what you think."

Tom and Drew both reached for a chocolate immediately. There was a fair deal of grunting as they let the flavors melt in their mouths. "Delicious," both pronounced simultaneously.

"I was going to include the Strychnine Strawberry originally. After what happened to Brooke, I decided not to include that one for the Festive Foods contest. I'll still have it available for tasting, though."

Hanna still hadn't heard from Duncan by nine thirty, so everyone decided to head home. It had been a nice night to get together, without too much talk about murder. The five of them stood outside on the doorstep and appreciated the crisp air.

Drew and Maggie went down the stairs. "Make sure you girls lock up tonight. Even though Fenton is with Duncan, until we know if he's being arrested for the murders it's best to play it safe."

Alex looked down from the porch at her friends. "We will. I'm not taking any chances. He looked furious when he was pounding on my car window earlier tonight."

Hanna waved to their friends and said good night to Tom and went inside. Tom and Alex were alone. He looked down at her. "Danger seems to follow you. Or do you chase after danger? You seem to love all this sleuthing, even when it puts a target on your back."

Alex hadn't really thought about it, but Tom was right. Even before Maggie had asked her to get involved, Alex had put her nose

right into the middle of everything. If that was going to be a problem for Tom, then Alex wasn't sure how their relationship would
survive. "Does that bother you? Because this is who I am, a little
bit nosy . . ."

Tom shot her a look.

"Okay, a *lot* nosy. Impetuous. Bossy. Unfiltered."

"And kind, thoughtful, generous, courageous, helpful. It's the
sum of these qualities that impresses me. I don't want to change a
hair on your head. I'll probably keep telling you to be careful, but
I accept you for who you are. I'm even beginning to think I can
handle all these Christmas decorations. Now, I'd like to kiss you,
but we have an audience."

"Who? If it's Watson, I promise she'll get over it."

"Mm, not Watson—your neighbor across the street. I can see
her at her curtains, with binoculars. She should really learn to turn
off all the lights if she's going to do that." Tom took a step back.
"So for the benefit of our audience, I'll just say good night." Tom
stepped back and made a sweeping bow, then turned and went
down the stairs. As he walked away, a car slowly drove past the
house. It looked like Lucy and Rose.

Alex shut the door and leaned on the back of it. Penelope had
cost her a kiss. Alex was going to have to do something about that
ghastly woman. Alex smiled. Maybe things were going to be okay.

Chapter Thirty

Alex and Hanna had agreed the night before to go to work together the next day. Until Fenton was behind bars, they weren't going to take chances.

They were both up by six on Tuesday morning. There were only ten more days until Christmas Eve, and still so much to do. Alex had come downstairs first and put the kettle on for their tea. She decided they had time to stop at Cookies 'n Crumbs for some goodies on their way to work.

Hanna came down looking fresh, wearing jeans and a long sleeved T-shirt that said "A Balanced Diet Is Chocolate In Both Hands."

"I just got off the phone with Duncan. He's going to stop at the store at seven. Poor guy has only had three hours of sleep. He's been up questioning Fenton most of the night. He wants to tell us what's happened in person."

"What? You couldn't get him to tell you?"

"I tried. He said if he told me over the phone, he wouldn't have an excuse to see me in person."

"Ah. That's so sweet. It sounds like the two of you have worked out your issues."

"Well, hopefully if I'm not a suspect anymore, we can have a real heart-to-heart talk." Hanna filled her travel mug with tea.

"But I want to know what's going on with you and Tom, and you and Eddie. Tom was all googly-eyed over you last night. Spill."

"We had a moment last night. In fact, Tom was going to kiss me, but Penelope was watching us with binoculars. There's got to be something we can do about her."

"Nice! Penelope is just jealous because she's had her eyes on Tom. She'll ease off once she sees there's no hope. What about Eddie?"

Alex sighed. "He's so good-looking. I think he's great, but he's younger than I am. And Tom and I have a relationship of sorts. I'm not entirely sure yet what that relationship is, but I want to explore it." Alex took a sip of her tea. "Eddie basically said he's waiting in the wings if things don't work out with Tom."

"Perfect. You've got a backup. Things will all work out."

"Fingers crossed. I've fed Watson. She's just outside doing her business." Alex went to the sliding door that led to their deck and called the pooch, who came running back.

Hanna stopped in front of Alex and fixed the scarf Alex had tied around her neck. She could never get it quite right, the way Hanna did.

"What are you going to do if we don't live together anymore?" Hanna asked.

"What do you mean? If you get married and move out, I'm just going to stay in your guest bedroom." Alex grabbed her tea.

"What if you get married first?"

"I'd say there's not much chance of that. Tom and I are barely dating. Besides, I can just let myself go, then." Alex laughed and grabbed her car keys from the entryway table. As she did, her phone chimed.

"Hmm. I set an alert to tell me if Miss T posts another article." Alex swiped at her phone a few times and started to read. "What the—!"

Hanna moved closer so she could read the screen on Alex's phone at the same time.

Miss T has discovered that one of the school's former coaches is currently being questioned by the sheriff. This reporter has it on good authority that he tried to harm our local bookshop owners and may also be responsible for the recent murders in our cozy village.

I'll be keeping my ear to the ground for the latest scoop in this double homicide.

"How did she find out? This only happened late last night. Does she have a source inside the sheriff's department?" Alex was dumbfounded.

Hanna shrugged. "She must, but we need to get going so we can stop at the bakeshop before we head to the store."

Despite the early hour, the bakeshop was standing room only. Hanna and Alex were stuck in line near the door. Hanna was looking at all the advertisements on the bulletin board while Alex wondered what they should order.

"Oh, look—here's an ad for a handyman. We're going to need someone to fix or replace the motion sensor light." Hanna looked at the ad. "Though, I guess we can ask Eddie."

Alex glanced at the homemade flier with phone numbers at the bottom that could be torn off. Beside it hung the poster advertising the rescue shelter. The rescue shelter flier was professionally done. *I wonder where they get their posters made.* "I hope it won't be awkward with Eddie."

The sisters were called up to order. Hanna looked at the pastry case. "Can we get a half dozen of the cranberry and white chocolate scones?" She looked at Alex for confirmation.

Alex nodded. While they were waiting for their order to be bagged Alex listened to a woman at a table nearby.

"Did you hear? Nate's car was keyed sometime this weekend and he took it to a body shop in Kalispell yesterday for a new paint job. But guess who's paying for it? My sister's husband's cousin's wife is the receptionist there, and she said Zara's husband came in and made the arrangements for them to bill him."

Alex raised her brows and leaned a tiny bit closer.

"So who do you think keyed the car?" The other woman at the table was leaning closer to her companion.

"Probably Zara's daughter. The apple doesn't fall far from the tree. Nate and his wife have a son around the same age. You know kids these days."

Hanna nudged Alex. She had the scones and had already paid for them.

Alex and Hanna drove the short distance to the shop while Alex told her twin what she'd overheard. "I think we know it wasn't Zara's daughter that keyed Nate's car."

"I'd say this makes it certain. But does that mean Zara's husband knows she had an affair?" Hanna grabbed the treats and got out of the car.

"It sure seems that way." Alex balanced her backpack and her travel mug as she let Watson out of the back seat. "Let's go in the front door."

Hanna unlocked the door and when the three were in, Alex closed and locked it. She breathed in the mingled scents of evergreens, chocolate, paper, and vanilla. It never got old. Alex put her tea on the counter beside the cash register and Watson went to her bed behind the counter under the table.

"You never can tell. I always thought Nate and his wife were so happy together." Hanna stopped in the doorway on her way to the kitchen.

"When I talked to Zara, I got the impression she and Nate were pretty serious in high school. She tried to make it seem like it was no big deal when Nate went away to school, but maybe the flame never died." Alex looked at her sister.

"Even if Zara keyed the car, it has nothing to do with the murders. The killer is in jail." Hanna headed to the kitchen. She returned a minute later with their treats on a large plate. Hanna continued with their conversation. "If Zara's husband paid for Nate's car to be repainted he must know what's really been going on?"

"Maybe. If he found out about Zara's affair, that would give him a motive to kill Nate, but not Kyle. But if Kyle was threatening Nate about exposing the affair in the parking lot last Friday then Nate had a great motive for killing Kyle. Was that only three days ago?"

"Did you hear what I said? The killer is in jail." Hanna took a sip of her tea.

"About that. I'm not sure Fenton is the killer. He's got to be the one who tried to run me down. And I can believe he attacked you, but I just don't see him as a killer. I don't know how to explain it. It just doesn't feel right."

"But you're the one who put the sheriff's department onto him."

Alex cringed. "I know. But I may have been too hasty. I was so upset by what happened at Miss Vicky's house, I just assumed if he was our attacker, then he must be the killer. But I've been thinking about it and I don't necessarily think that's true."

"So are you saying Nate or Zara killed Kyle?"

"I don't know. If Kyle threatened to expose the affair, then either Nate or Zara would have a strong reason to silence him."

"You have a point, but what about Brooke? Why kill her?"

"I know. That's what doesn't fit. Unless Zara is still upset Brooke got the role in their class play. Or maybe she was jealous of Brooke's success. It's the same for Fenton. Why kill Brooke? Did Brooke see the killer? She had to have been with Kyle in the basement shortly before he was killed. There's no other way she could have known about Fenton's text. And we know Fenton had to be in the basement at some point too."

Hanna looked at Alex with raised eyebrows. "That's a lot of activity in the basement."

"Here me out. What if Brooke was with Kyle just before he was killed? She goes back upstairs to the bathroom, and the killer confronts Kyle. Kyle is murdered, and the killer puts his body in the utility closet and either leaves up the main stairs or the back exit. Then Fenton comes along a couple of minutes later and looks down the hall. Drops the candy wrapper. Since he doesn't see Kyle, he goes up to the bar. Maybe Brooke saw the killer somehow? The killer would have walked right past the women's washroom where Brooke was, if he went up the main stairs. And you can see the front door of the hall from the washroom as well."

"I guess that's possible. But Everett was in the bathroom. Eddie was in the storage room. Lucy was standing at the bar, watching people come and go. How could no one else have seen the killer?" Hanna looked perplexed.

"Unless it was one of those three, or maybe the killer came back inside through the door at the smoking area."

There was a knock at the front door. Hanna ran to open the door. "It's probably Duncan," she called out.

Alex envied her sister. She seemed to know what she wanted. For over three years she had patiently waited, knowing Duncan was the right guy for her. It looked like things were going well between them. Alex really liked Tom, but as soon as Eddie with his come-hither smile and charming ways came along, her head had been turned. Hanna had known all her life she wanted to be a chocolatier. Alex was still trying to find her niche. She loved the bookshop, and she enjoyed helping Hanna with the chocolates, but it was when she was puzzling out a mystery that she really felt like she was doing what she loved.

It's not like amateur sleuth was a profession. She couldn't hope for bodies to keep coming her way. *That would be sick and morbid. Right? It would be wrong, so wrong.*

Maybe she could talk to the theater in Swanson about organizing several murder mystery nights in conjunction with one of the restaurants over the summer months. Was that something she could take on to feed her love of mysteries? Alex would definitely need to think about it.

"Hello ladies." Duncan came in. "I can't stay long." He saw the Christmas scones on the counter. "Well, maybe long enough to have one of those." He helped himself to a scone drizzled with a creamy white glaze.

"You must have a leak at the sheriff's department. Miss T already knew about Fenton being questioned early this morning." Alex handed Duncan a napkin.

Duncan shook his head. "No way," he said with his mouth half full. When he was finished chewing, he continued. "He didn't get picked up until late last night. There's no way anyone let that out overnight. I suppose someone might have seen us taking him in."

"Has he admitted to killing Kyle and Brooke?" Hanna asked.

Duncan looked at Alex. "He's admitted to trying to run you down and to attacking Hanna. He said he thought it was you he went after here at the shop. He wanted to get you to stop asking questions." Duncan frowned at Alex again.

She was going to get a complex with all the frowns she had been getting from Duncan.

"But he's adamant he didn't kill Kyle. He says he went to the basement, but no one was down there. Then he turned right around and went upstairs to the bar. Lucy was there, and he said she could vouch for him. He claims he was only in the basement for a minute at most."

"I remember Lucy did mention that she saw Fenton come in around ten," Alex agreed.

"He claims he was just trying to scare you with his truck, not hit you. He was afraid you'd find out that he and Rose were distributing the steroids to some of the players on his team. He said someone— he assumed Kyle—was using that information to blackmail him and Rose." Duncan took a big bite of his scone. "That's why he wanted to talk to Kyle. He'd looked into it and found out the statute of limitations had run out, and Rose couldn't be prosecuted anymore for selling him the steroids. The note she got said she'd go to jail, and Lucy would lose the pharmacy. That's why she gave him the money."

"What's going to happen now?" Alex asked.

"We're holding him on the charges involving you and Hanna. Hopefully, he'll confess to the murders. Though we're not sure what the motive would have been for killing Brooke. It's possible she may have witnessed Kyle's murder."

"Yes, but why wouldn't she have said something right away if she'd seen something?" Hanna asked.

"We don't know." Duncan looked tired.

Alex carried on. "How did he know about the rat poison, though?"

"He must have heard about it somewhere. I swear half the village knew Eudora had some in the shed. He claims he'd never seen that tin before. Unfortunately, the only viable prints are Eddie's. We know Eddie handled the can, so we expected to find his prints on it. I'm guessing the killer wore gloves." Duncan popped the last bite of his scone into his mouth. "Gotta go. I'll be questioning Fenton again today."

Hanna walked Duncan to the door. When she came back, she started preparing the store for opening. "That seems to wrap up this case. It sounds like Duncan is on the same track you are, except it was probably Fenton who killed Kyle and Brooke. I'll be making chocolates for the rest of the day. You know where you can find me."

Alex decided to do some dusting while she thought about Duncan's information. Despite Hanna's opinion that the case was solved, Alex wasn't as certain. There were several things bothering her. Before she could go through them in her head, Maggie arrived. She had a large container in her hand.

Maggie flourished the container. "Homemade soup for lunch. I thought we could grab some sandwiches from the deli, to go with it. I'll just pop this in the fridge and be right back."

When Maggie returned, Watson came out from under the counter for some attention. Once Maggie had given Watson enough affection, the dog barked and started to head to the hall. When no one followed, she came back and barked again.

"What is it, Watson?"

Watson looked at Alex like, *"Hey you dummies. Follow me."*

Alex followed the dog into the conference room. Watson jumped onto the bench in front of the television and looked at Alex with a soulful gaze.

"Okay. I'll let you watch television for a bit, but not all day. Is that understood?"

Watson had a grin on her face as if to say, *"Get a grip. You know I've got you at my beck and bark."*

Alex wandered back onto the sales floor, where Maggie was eating one of the scones. "Maggie, did Duncan update you on Fenton?"

Maggie had just taken a big bite and nodded her answer.

"There are a few things bothering me. Maybe if I talk about them out loud, I can figure out why I've got that funny niggling feeling in the back of my brain."

Maggie gave Alex a thumbs-up.

"Okay, bear with me. First, how did Fenton come upon the nutcracker? The candy wrapper was at the bottom of the basement stairs, but the nutcracker was by the back door. You couldn't see that box from the utility closet. I suppose he could have come in through the back door, killed Kyle, then walked up the main stairs, hoping no one would see him."

Maggie looked thoughtful. "That's a good point. If he didn't want to be seen and came in through the back door, then why leave the other way, where there was a much higher risk of being seen? Especially since no one knew he was there."

"Second, Brooke was likely with Kyle when he got the text from Fenton. Did she stick around to wait for Fenton's arrival? Did she really see something? Or is there a motive for her murder we've totally missed?"

"It seems unlikely that Fenton would have killed Kyle in full view of Brooke. So you have a point there."

"Third, did Fenton know about Brooke's Pink Bis issues? How would he have gained access to her purse or the bottle?"

"It sounded like Brook's love of her little pink bottle was no secret. Maybe he went to see her? Would it be that hard to get at her bag?" Maggie licked some icing from her finger.

"Realistically, the poison would have had to be administered within half an hour of her symptoms beginning. That means some time Sunday morning. Brooke was at the B&B. So would he have had an opportunity to put the poison in her bottle?"

"Those are all good insights. We should all get together again and talk it out. But we'd better open the store—it's nine."

Alex greeted her first customers with a big smile. For the next hour she made book recommendations, rang in purchases, and helped gift-wrap three books, a candle, and a jar of jam. As she wrapped the jam, she managed to get a paper cut. A second later Maggie reached over Alex to grab the scissors Alex had been using. In her haste, she dropped the scissors and they landed within a hair of Alex's hand.

"Oh, I'm so sorry. Are you okay?"

"I'm fine."

"No, you're not. You're bleeding. I'm so sorry. I should have been more careful. Let me get you a tissue."

Alex looked at her hand and realized it was the paper cut that was bleeding. "Don't worry Maggie—it's just a paper cut. The scissors didn't touch me." Alex finished wrapping the gift after she dabbed away the blood on her finger.

When the customer had left, Maggie insisted on looking at Alex's hand. "I was so sure I'd cut you when I dropped those scissors." Maggie fished a bandage out of the first aid kit in a drawer.

Alex was looking at her finger as Maggie put on the bandage, and she had an epiphany.

"I think I know why Brooke wouldn't have reported seeing the killer."

Chapter Thirty-One

"Why wouldn't Brooke have reported seeing the killer?" Maggie looked at Alex curiously.

Alex held up her bleeding finger to Maggie. "A minute ago you thought the scissors you dropped were the reason I had blood on my fingers."

Maggie nodded. "Yes. I didn't realize they didn't actually hit your hand. It was so close."

"Exactly. I'd just given myself a paper cut seconds before. Remember Kyle also had a cut on the back of his head? What if Brooke shoved him and that caused the cut. He hit his head where I saw the blood on the wall, and maybe he passed out." Alex started pacing behind the counter. "Brooke thought she'd killed him and took off. Then the killer comes along and hit Kyle on the head with the nutcracker, and that's the blow that actually killed him. The sheriff's department still hasn't released that Kyle had two injuries to his skull. Brooke would still have thought she'd killed him. If she saw the killer coming up the stairs, she might even have thought they knew that Brooke was the killer."

Understanding flashed across Maggie's face. "And the killer may have thought Brooke would eventually realize she hadn't killed Kyle and realize who had. That makes perfect sense."

When the shop was empty, Alex and Maggie checked on Watson. Despite the dog's pleading looks, Alex shut the television off. As they left the room, Maggie slipped Watson a treat. "I saw that," Alex said.

Alex and Maggie went to tell Hanna their theory.

"It makes perfect sense. Right?" Alex looked at her sister for confirmation.

"That's a good theory. But what if the murders aren't related? Maybe there are two killers. Or maybe there's a connection between Kyle and Brooke no one has figured out yet. They were both from the same graduating class. Alex already figured they were involved in the cheating ring. Maybe there's another connection."

Alex looked at Maggie. The woman's shoulders had sagged, and she looked as deflated as Alex felt. Alex had been so sure they'd come up with the perfect solution. "I guess those are all valid points. It just seemed like such a good theory."

"Keep it in mind, sis. But just remember there are other possibilities."

Alex and Maggie went back to the sales floor, somewhat less excited. "Maggie, if you don't mind, I'm going to go check the mail and see if I can pump Eudora for some information."

"You go ahead. I've got to get the books ready for next month's book club read."

Alex couldn't be bothered getting her jacket. The weather was still relatively mild, and she was only going across the street. Their post office box was crammed full with Christmas cards and magazines. She went into the post office proper, which was empty. Alex tapped the bell on the counter, and Eudora bustled out from the back room.

"Oh, I'm glad it's you. I've been wanting to talk to you since I read Miss T's article."

"Is there anyone in town who hasn't read it?" Alex asked.

"Unlikely, dear. That woman has an uncanny knack for discovering things."

"Any ideas on her identity?"

"Surprisingly, no. I just don't know who could be getting this information so quickly. At any rate, I wanted to make sure you and Hanna were okay. This is a nasty business. I can't believe Fenton was behind it all. And yet when I think back twenty years, it's a little easier to understand."

"Is he so different now from then? I just assumed he was always a cranky old guy."

Eudora smiled. "He wasn't really cranky back then. He was very competitive, though. I think he felt like he had to prove himself, and the way to do it was to have one of his students or football players go on to become famous. When that didn't happen, he became bitter, or cranky as you say."

"There's something niggling at me, and it feels like I missed something important." Alex filled Eudora in on what she'd found out and what she suspected. "Did you know about either Nate and Zara's or Fenton and Rose's affairs?"

"I didn't know about Nate and Zara until recently. But I suspected the affair between Fenton and Rose. I'd heard a few things and thought perhaps she was planning to leave her husband when the girls were finished school. But then Olive died. I think Fenton was devastated when Rose stayed with her husband. He never married."

"Do you think Fenton could have killed Kyle and Brooke if he thought he was helping Rose? What about Miss Vicky? She's very protective of Rose as well. Do you think she could have killed Kyle for her friend?" Alex asked.

"I'd have a hard time believing that about Miss Vicky," Eudora replied. "Plus, she went home early that night. There's no way she would have come out on the roads again in that weather. She's always been a nervous driver."

"Miss Vicky didn't leave until ten. It's possible she could have killed Kyle before she left. But I do wonder if she could have moved his body. Kyle was a big guy. What about Nate or Zara? Does it seem like everyone around here is having an affair? I'm struggling to get kissed by a man I've dated for a year. I digress. If they were having an affair, and Kyle threatened to expose it, that could be the motive for murder."

"Well, perhaps for Zara, but I have it on good authority that Nate confessed his affair to his wife and broke it off with Zara. There's a brand new vehicle sitting in Nate's driveway. I've heard it's an apology gift. It sure beats a bouquet of flowers."

"I guess if Nate decided to confess, there wouldn't be much point in killing Kyle. But that doesn't clear Zara," Alex said.

"You know what they say. Hell hath no fury." Eudora raised her eyebrows. "There is something else. I was helping to prepare all the grad photos for the display at the school. I also happened to see a recent picture of Zara with her kids in an ad for their hardware store. You should take a look at the picture of Zara's son, and then compare it to Nate's graduation picture. You might want to check the date of when Zara's son was born. I'd say the boy is the spitting image of Nate."

"Oh my goodness. What if Kyle knew that? That would certainly be a motive for murder."

"From what I knew about that man, I would think he'd use anything he knew to blackmail someone. Though what Fenton did to you and Hanna is inexcusable, and he needs to pay for that. I'd hate to see the wrong person put in jail for murder. I feel a certain responsibility in all this because it was the poison from my shed that killed poor Brooke."

"You don't have anything to feel guilty about. It's the killer who should feel guilty. It would be so much easier if Fenton would just confess. Thank you for the information, but I gotta run."

Back at the shop Alex checked on Maggie and then went to help Hanna. "Put me to work. Whatever I can help with."

"Why don't you take over coating these molds with this white chocolate. I need to make the salted caramel filling. We're almost out of the Cyanide Salted Caramels. They've been selling really well."

Tom came into the kitchen. Alex's stomach did a flip-flop again. "What do we owe this unexpected visit to?"

"I just came to see you because I like you a *choco-lot*. Isn't that reason enough?"

Alex groaned. "Did you come see us just so you could say that? I think you're really here to see if we have anything good to eat. And you're in luck."

Hanna nodded to the counter by the fridge. "Those chocolates on the tray are waiting for you. Help yourself."

"I think I will. But that really isn't why I came." Tom looked over the selection on the tray and popped a truffle into his mouth. "These are so good. As I was saying, I thought you'd want to know Mrs. Matthews got another blackmail note. She's going to turn it over to Duncan and tell him everything. It can't be from Kyle because he's dead, and she has no idea who it could be. She's supposed to put a thousand dollars in the garbage on the north side of the beach parking lot today. She brought over a pan of cinnamon buns and told me her big toe had a fungus infection. She was sorry she couldn't show it to me, but she had to hurry since she was heading to visit Rose with some of those buns as well."

"You are so lucky. Those cinnamon buns are delicious. I'm sorry to hear about her fungus infection. Maybe you'll get a peek next time." Alex laughed. "Why would she be going to see Rose?"

"Mrs. Matthews is a good woman with no sense of what's appropriate." Tom shuddered. "She used to clean for people in town. Rose is one of her former clients. It seems Rose is taking Fenton's actions very hard."

"That's so sad. Murder has so many far-reaching consequences."

Chapter Thirty-Two

After Tom left and Alex finished helping Hanna with the chocolates, Maggie suggested Alex write the bookshop's newsletter. "You probably want to let everyone know about our upcoming pre-Christmas sale. Have you thought about having fliers made and distributing them throughout the Valley?"

"Actually, I had thought of that, but it slipped my mind with all the action of the past few days. I took a picture of the flier for the pet rescue that was pinned to the bar at the reunion dance. I wanted to find out where they had it done. I love the graphics and fonts that were used. It's just so perfect. I'm hoping we can get something similar done for us."

Alex got on her computer and made a list of all the information she'd need for the flier. Then she found the picture of the pet rescue flier on her phone. She studied it and then texted the number on the flier. She identified herself and asked where they'd had the fliers made. She got a response immediately.

My brother does all our advertising and created those. He created our website as well. The guy's a saint—we wouldn't be open if it wasn't for him. His name is Eddie Mills. Here's his email.

Alex was surprised. Eddie hadn't mentioned it was his sister running the pet rescue. Though, it wasn't a surprise that he was helping her. He was just one of those genuinely nice guys. Alex offered to make a donation and got instructions on how to do that.

She stared at the picture of the flier on her phone. Did she want to contact Eddie? Would it make it seem like she was chasing him? She was definitely attracted to him, but she didn't want to lead him on.

Maggie brought her out of her reverie. "Did you get the information you were looking for?"

Alex looked at Maggie for a moment in silence. "I did. It just wasn't what I was expecting."

"Great. Hopefully, we can get them done this week, and then I can get Drew to put them up for us."

"Yeah. That would be terrific." Alex gave her head a shake. Focus. She created the newsletter and had Maggie check it over before sending it to their subscribers. Hanna came out of the kitchen with a small plate of chocolates. "These are for customers, except for those two on the edge. Try them. I tweaked them slightly."

Maggie and Alex each tried one of the designated chocolates. Alex's eyes widened. "These are perfect. They're the new maple ones for the competition. Right?"

Hanna nodded. "I've been tasting so much chocolate, I need a second and third opinion. Maggie, what do you think?"

From the rapturous expression on Maggie's face, it seemed obvious what her thoughts were. "I think I could give up just about everything, Drew included, but not chocolate. These are perfection. You've hit everything about them exactly right. I think they're your best yet."

Alex agreed. "You've hit all the right notes. They're a winner."

"Alright. That's three yeses. That's good enough for me. I'm going to make another five hundred exactly like this." Hanna went back to the kitchen looking pleased.

The rest of the afternoon went quickly. There was a burst of traffic half an hour before closing. Alex was grateful when the last customer left and she turned their sign to "CLOSED." "Let's get things cleaned up and go home."

"You got it." Maggie started putting books and other items away.

Alex went to see if Hanna was almost done.

In the kitchen Hanna was just doing the final scraping on a batch of chocolates. "I'll be a little while yet. Why don't you go home and take Watson for a walk? By the time you get back, I should be done."

"Works for me. Maybe I'll see if Tom wants to join me for the walk."

"That's sounds like a good idea. If you're right and Fenton isn't the killer, you shouldn't be out by yourself. Plus, you two need more time alone." Hanna paused what she was doing. "I've noticed a different vibe between the two of you. Anything you want to talk about?"

Alex sighed. "Not right now—maybe later tonight. I've got a few things on my mind. I'll leave the car for you. Keys will be on the counter by the register."

"Come on, Watson—it's time to go home." Alex pulled the leash off a hook by the door. She debated whether to text Eddie and ask him to create a flier for the shop. They also needed the motion sensor light fixed. Hanna would probably tell her to contact him, and she was probably right. However things turned out with Tom, there was no reason she and Eddie couldn't be friends. Alex and Watson meandered home. When they got to the house,

Alex went inside and turned on the lights, leaving her purse in the hall.

"Let's get our walk over with. Then we can relax afterward. Maybe watch some television?" Alex and Watson walked next door, and Alex rang the doorbell.

Tom came to the door with a jacket in his hand.

"Did you want to come with me to walk Watson?"

Tom looked apologetic. "I'm actually just headed to Hickory Smokehouse. I'm meeting someone there."

"Oh, no worries. Maybe I'll see you later." Alex hurried down the stairs with a reluctant Watson, who seemed more inclined to stay at Tom's than go for a walk.

It was just as well Tom couldn't go. Alex had so much on her mind, and her thoughts were a complete jumble. As the day had gone on, she'd been more and more certain that Fenton was many things, but not a killer. But she was no closer to figuring out who was. If Fenton wasn't the killer, whoever it was probably felt safe with Fenton in jail. Zara certainly had her reasons for disliking Kyle, but why Brooke? Did Nate even have a reason to kill Kyle? And she had no idea why he'd want to kill Brooke.

The sticking point was Brooke. Could Brooke's death be completely unrelated? Maybe Brooke had had an enemy to do with her work as a lawyer. Did someone follow her here? Was that too much coincidence? Alex could understand the many reasons someone might have wanted to kill Kyle, but why Brooke? Unless, Brooke saw something she shouldn't have. Alex was certain Brooke had been with Kyle shortly before his death. Could she have seen the murderer or something that pointed to the murderer? If Kyle was blackmailing her, what was it about? Could that be what had gotten her killed? Was there something in her past that had sparked the murder?

Alex thought back to her conversation with Brooke after Kyle's murder. What had she said? She'd talked about the distinction between being innocent versus being proven guilty. She'd also said something about bartenders and lawyers knowing lots of secrets. Was Brooke hinting that she knew something? Lucy had spent most of the night near Eddie, a bartender. Had she told him anything? She had claimed to be at the bar all night, but Miss Vicky had pointed out that wasn't actually the case. Everyone had assumed Lucy was at the bar all night, but she may have had an opportunity to run down to the basement to kill Kyle. Was there more to their history than she had let on?

Alex was surprised to find they were at the edge of the parking lot to the public beach. She'd been so wrapped up in her thoughts she hadn't been truly aware of her surroundings. Alex could see a lone car parked in the lot. Alex let Watson off her leash and headed to the water. It was a beautiful night. There was no wind, and the temperatures were still unseasonably warm. Someone was walking along the retaining wall. When she was a few yards away, she saw it was Lucy. Maybe she could shed some light on Alex's questions. "Hi, Lucy," Alex called out so she didn't scare the woman.

Lucy stopped and turned to look at Alex. "Oh, hi." She pulled earphones out of her ears. "I wasn't sure if I heard something or not. I was listening to music."

"Do you come here much? I haven't seen you before." Alex glanced around to see where Watson had gone. The dog was sniffing at a tree at the edge of the parking lot.

"Not really—too many sad memories. My mom is at Miss Vicky's place right now, so I thought I'd get out of the house for a bit."

"Your mom must be so unhappy about Fenton. I gathered they were seeing each other."

Lucy looked out toward the water. "My mom will be fine. Fenton wasn't what she thought. Better she found out now. Besides, with her Alzheimer's she'll forget him quickly enough."

"I'm not wholly convinced he killed Kyle and Brooke."

"Are you kidding? Didn't Fenton try to run you over with his truck? A guy who would do that wouldn't think twice about killing someone. Especially someone like Kyle. Fenton did the world a favor. Unfortunately, he got caught."

"I understand why he might have killed Kyle, and I know he had the opportunity, but why would he have killed Brooke?"

"Who knows? They found the rat poison in his truck, so there's the proof."

"I know. But there were others who wanted Kyle dead. Zara seems a bit hot tempered. You've known her longer than me. Could she have killed them?"

"I doubt it. She doesn't seem the sort. She gets her anger out pretty quick. You've probably heard about the car-keying incident. Most of the village has. The sheriff's department have Fenton in jail, and if they think they've got the right person, shouldn't you leave it to them?"

"You may be right. I'd better head back. It was nice to run into you." Alex had been watching Miss Watson and was about to call the pooch so they could head home, but then she remembered something and paused. She turned back to Lucy who was still in the same spot, watching the water. "The night Kyle was killed, you weren't at the bar the whole time."

"No, I stepped away briefly to clean up the drink Kyle spilled around ten, and I went to the washroom once, earlier in the evening. I wasn't gone long. Oh, and I guess while Duncan questioned me, I was elsewhere. Other than that, I was within a few feet of the bar all night."

"How did you find out about the rat poison in Fenton's truck? That information hasn't been released. Not even Miss T knows that." Alex watched Lucy in the dim light.

Lucy walked toward Alex. "I think Fenton must have called my mom when he was arrested. I'm sure she was the one who mentioned it to me. I should probably head home too. I want to be there when she gets back."

Was Lucy telling the truth? There were so many little inconsistencies. Alex turned back toward the parking lot and walked beside Lucy, then paused. "Lucy, did your sister find out you were getting copies of the tests in your senior year?"

"How did you find out about that? Oh, what does it matter! Yes. I was cheating. Kyle and Brooke were able to get copies of the tests, and they sold them to a few of us. My sister, the little snoop, searched my room and found copies. She told me she was going to confront Kyle and Brooke and tell them to end the cheating or she'd tell the school administration. But it's ancient history. She died before she ever said anything."

"It wasn't ancient history for Brooke. She was worried about that coming out since she was up for a judgeship."

"I know. She asked me to forget it ever happened. It's not like I would have said anything anyway. I just want to forget that whole time of my life."

"Is that because you had something to do with Olive's death? Maybe you and Kyle were in it together. You were both at the Chinese restaurant the night before he died. Was he blackmailing you, or was it the other way around?"

"Are you crazy? You're accusing me of my sister's death?" Lucy was standing in front of Alex. "I can't believe you. Whatever. I'm too tired to deal with this." Lucy turned away and then faced Alex again. "I keep forgetting, I've got something for you. It's in the trunk of my car."

Lucy's car was only a few feet away. Alex wondered if accusing someone of being a killer in an empty parking lot, after dark, was a great idea. She debated making a run for it.

Lucy walked to the car and popped her trunk open. She reached in for something. When she turned around she was pointing a stun gun directly at Alex. "I mentioned I had one of these, but with Mom's condition, I've been afraid to keep it in the house. I've had it in the trunk of my car for a few days, waiting to run into you."

Alex couldn't believe she kept getting herself into these situations. "Lucy, I don't know anything. I was just taking a shot in the dark about your sister." *Bad choice of words.* "Don't do something you'll regret."

"What are you talking about? Here, take it." Lucy held out the gun to Alex. "I figured with all the trouble you've been having you should have some kind of personal protection." Lucy pointed to the trigger. "Just point this sucker at your attacker, press this trigger, and make sure both prongs hit him. Then hold the trigger to give him the shock of his life." Lucy pressed it into Alex's hand. "It's fully charged. I couldn't find the manual, but you can find them online."

Alex held the gun and looked at Lucy. "You really didn't have anything to do with your sister's death?"

"No. My sister was a little pain in the behind, but I loved her." Lucy started to turn around but paused and turned to face Alex again. She had tears in her eyes. "I didn't push her into the water, but I was partly responsible for her death. The other night at the Chinese restaurant, my mom and I were sitting in the booth beside Kyle and Brooke. We were in one of those tall booths you can't see over, and they didn't know we were there. They were having a private conversation."

Alex remembered the comment Lucy had made to Kyle, in the shop, and how he'd looked uncomfortable. Lucy had been letting him know she'd overheard his conversation. Alex realized she still had the gun in her hand and shoved it in the pocket of her jacket.

"I overheard Kyle and Brooke talking about my sister. After she found those tests, she asked to see both of them. Kyle had her meet them at one of the summer cottages he'd broken into in the past. They were standing by the boat launch when she told them she was going to turn them in if they didn't stop cheating." Lucy swiped at a tear on her cheek. "Brooke and Kyle offered to pay her to keep quiet, but my sister, for all her faults, was the most honest person alive. She refused to give in to their bribes, so Kyle got angry and threatened her. When that didn't work, he ripped her necklace from her throat and threw it out on the ice."

Alex could imagine Kyle doing that. Everyone said Kyle's temper was worse in his senior year, probably because of his steroid use.

"Olive went out on the ice to retrieve the necklace. But there'd been a warm spell, like now, and she fell through the ice. She was too far out for them to reach her. Brooke wanted to go for help, but Kyle said it would be too late to save her and their lives would be ruined. So, they walked away."

"Kyle was blackmailing Brooke about that." Now it all made sense, Alex realized.

Lucy nodded. "Brooke was trying to convince Kyle that he had just as much to lose as she did. He said he was already ruined, but she had a lot to lose. She agreed to pay him the next day."

That was where the five thousand dollars had come from. Duncan had already told them Brooke's fingerprints had been found on the money. "Brooke must have met Kyle in the basement to pay him. Who knows what happened? Maybe she did kill him. But then who put the strychnine in Brooke's Pink Bis bottle?"

"Is that how she was killed? I'd heard she was poisoned with strychnine, but not how she'd ingested it. How ironic. She probably drank one or two of those bottles per week since high school." Watson sidled up to Lucy's leg, and she bent down to pet the dog. "We sell quite a bit of that stuff at the pharmacy. I know Zara buys it regularly. Just a few days ago I was watching my mom on the hidden camera at the pharmacy, and I saw Eddie buying some. I guess everyone has their problems."

"Why haven't you told the sheriff what Kyle and Brooke did to your sister?"

Lucy shook her head. "It won't bring back Olive. Kyle and Brooke are both dead. I'm feeling enough guilt. I don't need the whole world to know. Please don't say anything. My mom doesn't need any more upset in her life at this point."

"I can respect that. I'm really sorry." Alex felt terrible for having accused Lucy. Their family had seen more than its share of trauma.

Lucy wiped her eyes and headed back to her car. She had her hand on the door handle and looked back at Alex. "Be careful. I'm not crazy about Fenton, but I don't think he's a killer."

Chapter
Thirty-Three

A lex didn't know what to think. Had she just seen the best snow job ever? Were Kyle and Brooke really responsible for Olive's death? Alex called Watson over. The dog had wandered off to the shore again and came running back. Lucy turned on her car, and her headlights illuminated the parking lot. Alex was staring across the lot, and she was sure she caught a glimpse of something moving on the edge of the parking lot, by the trees. But maybe she was mistaken.

Lucy drove off and the other side of the lot was just a shadowy void once again. *It feels creepy.*

"Let's go home, Watson." Alex walked toward the exit and decided to leave Watson off her leash until they got to the road. She threw one last look over her shoulder at the spot where she thought she'd seen something. Her stomach knotted. There was definitely someone there. The person had moved to the edge of the pavement, and Alex could see the form, though whoever it was wore a hoodie that shadowed their face. There was something familiar about the stance.

She squinted to try and get a better look. "Eddie?" Her voice sounded loud in the silence. If it wasn't Eddie, she was going to feel very stupid. Maybe she should just go. The figure walked toward her. Alex stood rooted to the spot, unsure what to do.

Halfway across the lot, the figure reached up to the hood and pulled it back. "Hey, Alex. What are you doing out here at night?"

Alex could make out his easy smile and smooth voice. Alex put her hand over her heart. "You gave me a scare. I wasn't sure who you were." Alex smiled in return as the man got within a few feet. Watson was busy sniffing at the pavement and ignoring the humans.

"I'm heartbroken. You didn't recognize me, and here I've been trying to get you to go out with me for months." Eddie put his hands into the pockets of his hoodie. "So what's got you here tonight? Please, tell me you and Tom broke up, and you're here communing with nature to get over it."

Alex shuffled her feet and cringed inwardly. "I'm afraid not. Watson and I walk here most nights. I just ran into Lucy a few minutes ago. You must have seen her car."

"That's who it was. I just got here as a car was leaving. I've been working so much, I felt the need to get out of the house for a break. You know I haven't given up on you. I can be patient."

Alex desperately wanted to change the subject. "Your sister told me you've been helping her with the rescue shelter. She said you made the fliers and created her website. You really are a man of many talents. In fact, I was going to call you and see if I could get you to make a flier for the bookshop similar to the one you did for the rescue." Alex held up her phone and quickly scrolled through the pictures on her camera. "Here, I'll show you what I mean."

Eddie edged closer until he stood behind Alex's shoulder and could see her phone.

Alex tried not to move. She had so many conflicting emotions.

She scrolled to the picture of the flier. "I love this font you've used. It's unique. But it's the whole vibe, the colors, the graphics—I'd love something similar for Murder and Mayhem." Alex accidentally scrolled back to Mrs. Matthew's blackmail letter. She hadn't looked at it closely before, but now she saw that the last sentence with the instructions for where to put the cash were in the identical font as the one used in the pet rescue flier.

Alex quickly shut the app and flicked her finger across the screen as she tried to keep her voice even. "Well, you get the idea. I should go. Where has that dog gone?"

Eddie's arms shot out and encircled Alex.

"Hey! What are you doing?" Alex struggled, but Eddie's hold was firm.

"You know, don't you?"

"Know what? I've no idea what you're talking about. Let me go. Watson, go get Hanna!" Alex shouted at the dog. Watson, who'd been sniffing at the pavement, took off like a bat out of hell.

Eddie laughed. But not the sexy one she'd heard so many times. This time it was almost maniacal. "Even if your dog manages to get someone's attention, you won't be here anymore." Eddie started to push Alex forward. "We need a chance to talk, so I can explain everything. Then you'll see what a great guy I am. Really."

He was much stronger than Alex had ever thought. "I don't know what you think I know, but I assure you I don't know anything."

"I saw the way you closed your phone after you saw that letter to Mrs. Matthews. You realized I used the same font as I'd used on the shelter flier. Don't deny it—you're not a good liar." Eddie was trying to drag Alex toward the other side of the parking lot, but she'd dug in her heels. "Using that font was a mistake. I'm not going to hurt you. I just need you to understand."

Alex was in a steel vise. She couldn't move her arms to reach into her pocket. Alex knew she couldn't bluff her way out of this. Eddie was right. She had realized he was involved in the blackmail scheme when she'd recognized the same font on both items.

"I don't understand. You don't strike me as a blackmailer. How did you know all those personal details about Kyle?"

Eddie had stopped trying to drag her across the pavement. She knew she needed to keep him talking until help arrived. At least, she hoped help would arrive.

"I didn't want to be part of Kyle's blackmail scheme. He forced me into helping him. He had me create the letters, deliver them, and pick up the cash and bring it back to him."

"How could he force you into doing that?"

"Just before Kyle moved home, I'd used part of the down payment for my house to help my sister with some unexpected expenses at the shelter. If she didn't get certain things done, she wouldn't have been able to open. She's my big sister, and she's sacrificed a lot for our family. I admire all she's trying to do, and I've been trying to help her where I can.

"But then I needed that money for the house. So I borrowed from the dealership. I figured I'd have it paid back before the end of the year, and no one would ever know. That's why I was working so many odd jobs."

"Let me guess. Kyle found out when he became the CFO."

"Yes. And he threatened to tell his father if I didn't cooperate. I paid back every cent. But Kyle had the proof of what I'd done, and he kept threatening to tell his dad. We had a huge fight about it the day before the dance. He said he was going to tell his father about it when he got back from Palm Springs, and then he could take over my job."

"Do you really think Mr. Allerton would have fired you?"

"Kyle's parents always ended up doing what he wanted. I didn't plan to kill him. I just wanted to talk to him alone. I overheard him and Brooke arguing at the dance, and I knew they were meeting in the basement. When Brooke headed downstairs, I just went out the front door and ran around the building and in the back door. I knew it was unlocked because I'd gone in that way earlier in the day."

Alex interrupted. "But Everett said he heard you talking in the storeroom."

Eddie sneered. "I put my phone on a box and played a recording of me listing all the renovations I need to do to my new house. I figured no one would come in if they thought I was talking on the phone. I was just inside the basement door and listened to them argue. Brooke didn't want to pay Kyle to keep quiet. He was blackmailing her too."

"I know. Lucy told me."

"I didn't realize anyone else knew that. Anyway, after Brooke gave him the money, he told her it was just a down payment. She got really angry and shoved him. Hard. His head slammed into the wall, and he was out. She took off like a bullet. I saw that nutcracker in the box, and I don't know what came over me. After I hit him, I dragged him into the storage room and used my bartending towel to clean up my fingerprints and the blood."

"Where did you put the towel?"

"I just turned the good side out and kept it on my apron. I sat and talked to Duncan and the sheriff with it in full view."

"Did you kill Brooke?"

"I had to. When I was going upstairs, I passed the bathroom just as she opened the door. We looked at each other. She thought that I knew what she'd done. I just went back to the storage room and pretended I'd never left. But I figured at some point, Brooke might realize that I was the one who actually killed Kyle. So you see, I had to kill her. After I left the dance, I went straight to the shed to get the rat poison."

"How did you get the poison into her Pink Bis?"

Eddie snorted. "That was easy. I bought a bottle at the pharmacy on Saturday while Rose was working. She told me weeks ago that she usually worked alone over the lunch hour while Lucy ran errands. Rose would never remember me, and even if she did, nobody would believe her. At the dinner I watched Brooke. I saw how much was left in her bottle, so I went home after and poured out what I needed to and added the poison." Eddie had loosened his grip a little.

Alex managed to bring her forearms up and close to her chest

"On Sunday morning I waited until everyone else at the B&B had left for church, then I pulled up with my truck. I went in wearing my coveralls, with my tool belt on. I told Brooke I was there to fix a plumbing issue. The bottle was sitting on the kitchen table. She really made it too easy. I had her go to one of the bathrooms upstairs to turn on the water. While she was out of the room, I just switched the bottles. She never even questioned the gloves I was wearing."

Alex thought back to her walk to the school that morning with Hanna. She'd seen a truck headed in the direction of the B&B. Could that have been Eddie? She had been letting Eddie move her a little ways across the parking lot, to keep him talking. She asked, "What about Mrs. Matthews? She got another blackmail letter after Kyle died."

"Actually, that one was supposed to be delivered Friday night after the dance. Kyle planned to start on round two of his blackmail scheme. After Kyle was dead, I thought I'd deliver that last one because my sister really needs the extra cash right now. That's why I was here tonight. Mrs. Matthews was supposed to drop the cash in the garbage can today."

"I hate to burst your bubble, but she had no intention of paying again. She turned that letter in to the sheriff's department. Plus, Lucy had a hidden camera at the pharmacy. You're on video buying the Pink Biz. I think you might want to consider making a run for it."

"You're lying." Eddie's voice was uncertain.

Alex realized Eddie's hold around her had slackened since she'd stopped struggling. Thank goodness for her self-defense classes. She knew what she needed to do. She took a deep breath and then flung her body forward and down.

Eddie wasn't expecting the sudden movement, and she was on the ground before he realized what had happened. Eddie had gone down with her, just like at the line dancing class. He'd rolled over her and was sprawled on the ground a few feet away.

Knowing what was coming, Alex had jumped back to her feet immediately and got the stun gun out of her pocket. She pointed it at Eddie. "Don't come near me, or I'll shoot you with this." She carefully backed away from Eddie, who was still on the ground.

"That's not a real gun. Why don't you give it to me before you hurt yourself?" Eddie got up, lithe as a cat, and moved toward Alex.

"I'm serious. I'll shoot."

Eddie smiled and turned on the charm. "Hey. I'm one of the good guys. Let's go for a walk and we can talk. You'll see." Eddie had been creeping forward ever so slowly.

"Don't move," she said. "You're an embezzler, a blackmailer, and a murderer. Trust me, you're not a good guy."

"You know, I really like you. We have something. There's a spark between us. Don't tell me you haven't felt it."

"The only spark you need to think about is the one that's going to light you up like a Christmas tree if you take one more step." Alex couldn't believe she'd thought this guy was hot. Looking at him now, she noticed his eyes were beady and a bit too far apart, giving him a crazy look. Why hadn't she noticed that before? Alex was watching Eddie's eyes and knew the moment he decided to jump at her. And it was in that second she pulled the trigger. And held it. The two prongs shot out of the gun, attached themselves to Eddie's chest, and delivered fifty thousand volts.

As the shot zapped through Eddie's nervous system, he collapsed and was flat on his back faster than eighty-year-old Mr. Olafson wielding his shovel. "I told you to freeze, you scum!"

Alex had to remind herself to let go of the trigger after several seconds. She wasn't sure what to do. Her hands were shaking as she continued to point the gun at Eddie. Her phone had fallen to the ground when he first grabbed her. She didn't want to leave Eddie to go search for it. Though from the looks of him, he wasn't going anywhere right now.

As Alex stood watching Eddie, she could hear the sounds of a car approaching. *Oh, please let that car be coming here!* A minute later she could make out a small bundle racing across the parking lot. The bundle threw itself at Alex's legs and nuzzled her before trotting over to Eddie and growling. While Watson watched Eddie, Alex watched the car as it approached. It stopped ten feet away, and a second later Hanna was shouting and running toward Alex.

Hanna threw herself at Alex and hugged her. "I was so worried we wouldn't get here in time."

Alex had quickly moved the stun gun to the side so it wasn't pointed at her sister's midriff. "I'm fine. Did Watson get you?"

Duncan had jumped out of the vehicle at the same time as Hanna, and he ran over to Eddie. He pointed his gun at the prone figure as he yelled, "Freeze!"

Alex was pretty sure Eddie wasn't capable of doing anything else at that point. Duncan rolled Eddie over and handcuffed his wrists behind his back. The former heartthrob wasn't offering any resistance. Then Duncan carefully pried the stun gun out of Alex's hands.

Duncan gave Alex's shoulder a squeeze. "Good work. He won't be going anywhere for a bit."

Alex gave her sister a hug and then knelt down to hug Watson, who was now huddled close to Alex's legs. "You are the best!"

Hanna bent down and encompassed her sister and dog in a hug. "Watson came out of nowhere just as I got home from work. She was barking like crazy, and I knew something was wrong. You weren't anywhere in sight. She kept jumping forward and then racing back toward the road. I ran to Maggie's house because Duncan's car was in the driveway.

"I pounded on their door until Duncan answered, and I told him something had to be wrong. Watson refused to get in the car, so we followed her and she led us straight here. I was so afraid we wouldn't make it."

Duncan draped a blanket over Alex. "You go sit in my car. The sheriff will be here any minute. You'll need to give a statement. Are you okay?" He looked Alex over from head to foot.

Alex stood. "I'm fine. Just tired of dealing with killers. It's putting a real damper on my holiday plans."

"What about me?" A feeble voice called out from the ground. "Help me! That crazy woman attacked me for no reason! Just because I told her I wasn't interested in dating her." Eddie's voice was shaky but audible.

"I'd use your right to shut up if I were you, Eddie." Alex marched over to the area where Eddie had first grabbed her. After only a moment of searching, she found her phone and picked it up. She pressed a button and walked back to Duncan. She made a few swipes. The sound of Alex's voice filled the air. "Well, you get the idea . . ." The entire conversation had been recorded. It was still recording when Alex picked up the phone.

Chapter Thirty-Four

Hanna tried to insist they go to the hospital to have Alex examined, but Alex refused and reminded Hanna she was the one who had delivered the fifty thousand volts, not the one who'd received them. Instead, Alex elected to go to the sheriff's department to give her statement immediately.

While Alex talked to the sheriff, Hanna called Maggie and filled her in on everything.

Tom was with Maggie and Drew, and they were all anxious to hear what had happened. Some of the deputies had given Miss Watson some water while she was at the station, and made her a little certificate that read "Hero of the day."

When Alex was done, she just wanted to go home, shower, and crawl into bed. On the drive home, Hanna praised Watson. "It's a good thing she learned that trick. That is one smart dog. We owe her a wonderful Christmas present."

Alex had never been so well looked after. After they got home, Hanna fussed over her. She plumped Alex's pillows and pulled her blinds shut. "I thought you were going to go with Tom on your walk?"

"He was busy. If this is the treatment I get every time I shoot someone with a stun gun, I might do it again soon."

"I'm still sensing some tension between you and Tom. What's been going on?" Hanna sat on the edge of the bed while Alex was propped against her headboard.

"Nothing. Tom said he was a little concerned what people would think about the age difference between us. And that's part of it, but I'm sensing there's more to it. And I'm wondering what I really feel. I was flattered and a little excited by Eddie's attention. Your sister almost dated a murderer. Don't tell Mom."

"Now that Eddie's out of the picture, it might be easier to focus on Tom." Hanna helped Watson on the bed. The dog had come to see what was going on.

"I know, but I like my nice quiet life. I don't need all this relationship angst."

"Quiet? Someone just tried to kill you?" Hanna crossed her arms and looked at Alex.

"That's different. It doesn't cause me inner turmoil."

"Right. It's just another ordinary day when someone tries to scramble your innards."

"We don't even know if Eddie wanted to kill me. He said he just wanted to talk. This thing with Tom is way more serious. Getting involved with someone in a relationship is scary. There are so many pitfalls, especially at our age. You may not have noticed, but I can be a little set in my ways."

"Trust me. I've noticed. But I also see what a kind, caring person you are. And you deserve to be happy. Do you want me to have a chat with Tom?"

Alex laughed. "No, thank you. I'm pretty sure that would do more harm than good. Now that the real killer is locked up, maybe Tom and I can have a conversation that doesn't include words like *murder* and *suspects*."

"You're right, as usual. But for now I'm in charge, and it's time for you to get some sleep. I want your light out in ten minutes."

"Yes, ma'am." Alex gave Hanna a mock salute. She managed to turn her light off two minutes early, but she wished she could turn her thoughts off as easily. Her mind chewed over everything that had happened. There were still some things gnawing at her, but the more she tried to think about everything, the more she wanted oblivion. She finally resorted to counting sheep and fell into a fitful sleep.

* * *

The next morning, Alex awoke to the smell of bacon and cinnamon. She put on her robe and headed down the stairs. Hanna was at the stove, pulling out a pan of fresh-baked cinnamon buns. "Just like Mom's." She sniffed them and put them on the counter. "Bacon is ready, so all that's left is to pour some orange juice. Sit down at the island."

"How can you be so chipper? You must have gotten less sleep than I did." Alex sat on a swivel stool and hooked her feet on the bar at its base.

"Because I am focusing on my blessings. And that includes having my sister alive and well, and having Kyle's and Brooke's killer behind bars."

"Have you heard from Duncan?" Alex was hoping she'd get more answers.

"Eddie made a full confession. Duncan called me a little while ago." Hanna smiled.

"There are a few points I'm not clear on. I hope Duncan will answer all my questions."

"Tom stopped by about half an hour ago. I told him you were still sleeping. He said he'd talk to you later today, if you're up for visitors."

"I'm tired, not sick. I plan to go into work like usual. We have a competition this weekend." Alex's appetite hadn't been impaired by all the excitement yesterday. She gobbled up the breakfast Hanna had made and washed it down with a glass of juice and a cup of tea. After she changed into jeans and sweatshirt that said "Sleighin' It," she and Hanna drove to the bookshop.

Alex got out of her car and stood still for a moment. She drank in the peace and tranquility of order restored. In the shop she prepared everything for opening while Hanna went to the kitchen. Alex decided she would visit the hardware store later in the morning to purchase a new motion sensor light. It turned out when Fenton smashed theirs, he'd damaged it in such a way it couldn't be fixed. Until then, Alex decided to create a flier advertising their pre-Christmas sale. When she finished, she had it checked over by Hanna and Maggie. A quick glance at the time told her she could head into Swanson.

Alex was perusing the lights in an aisle at the back of the hardware store when Zara rounded the corner. She seemed surprised to see the bookseller. "Can I help you with anything?"

"I'm looking for a new motion sensor light." Alex looked at the woman. She looked like she'd lost weight, and there were dark circles under her eyes. "Are you doing okay?"

Zara gave a wan smile. "I'm fine. You've probably heard about our family troubles in the *Harriston Confidante*."

"Yes. I'm sorry everything was made so public. In fact, I'm completely puzzled by it. When you were in the bathroom talking to Brooke at the alumni dinner, she said something about stopping something if you knew what was good for you. What was that about?"

"She heard about Nate's car being keyed and guessed it was me. She was warning me I'd end up in legal trouble if I didn't stop doing stupid things like that. But I have no idea how it ended up in that evil woman's blog."

Alex waffled about bringing up something that had been on her mind. It really wasn't any of her business. After a brief internal argument, she finally spoke up. "Do your husband and Nate know who the father of your son is?"

Zara looked surprised and she blinked rapidly. After a moment's hesitation, her shoulders caved, and she nodded. "Nate's always known. He's pretty good at math, and it doesn't take much effort to count nine months. I think my husband suspected, but he knows now. I'm not sure what's going to happen. My son doesn't know. Please don't tell anyone."

"It's really not any of my business. But I am curious, what was really in the note you handed Nate?"

The corners of Zara's lips rose in a wry smile. "I asked Nate not to press charges. My husband agreed to pay for the damage to the car."

Alex felt sorry for Zara and her family. There would be a few things to work out there. Alex had emailed the flier she'd created to a print shop. She stopped there to pick up the copies she'd had made. After she had the fliers, she drove back to Harriston and went to the pharmacy.

Rose was behind the counter when Alex entered. She looked at Alex uncertainly. "I know you, don't I?"

"Hi, Rose. I'm Alex. I'm one of your customers. We were at the same table at the alumni dinner."

"Oh, of course. Sometimes my mind just can't quite remember things, and it's difficult to put the name and the face together. Are you here for a prescription?"

"No. I just wanted to see how you're doing and to thank Lucy for something she gave me."

"Lucy's such a good girl. She's my little Nightingale. Let me get her."

A moment later Lucy came to the counter with her mother. "Hi. What can I do for you?"

"I wanted to thank you for the little item you gave me last night. It may have saved my life." Alex told Lucy the bare bones of what had happened after the woman left the parking lot. Alex gave Rose and Lucy each a box of chocolates. "A little something to make your day merry." Alex was going to say goodbye, but thought of something. "You said you hadn't heard from Kyle since you graduated high school. But someone called Nightingale_91 kept pretty close tabs on his social media. I think they were a bit of a thorn in his side."

Lucy smiled. "Funny, that. I guess they'll have to find someone new to torment now, or maybe retire from social media."

Next, Alex stopped at Cookies 'n Crumbs for a treat. Usually, she was in a rush when she came in, and she rarely took the time to relax over a fresh-baked treat and a cup of cocoa. She ordered herself an eggnog sandwich cookie and a large cup of peppermint cocoa. The two flavors didn't pair particularly well, but that was what she was in the mood for.

Seated at a table in the back corner of the packed bakeshop, Alex looked at one of her fliers. She'd leave one on the bulletin board on her way out. It had turned out quite nicely, if she did say so herself. Alex glanced up from her cocoa and saw Penelope sit down at a table in the middle of the room. The woman had been waiting for that particular table to be free. How odd. Of course, Alex thought most of Penelope's behavior was odd.

As she watched, the woman casually reached one hand under the table and peeled something from it. Was she picking gum off the table? Certainly things weren't that bad in the antiques business. Alex continued to watch as the woman slowly pulled a tiny device out from under the table and slipped it into her purse. No one else was paying any attention to Penelope, who quickly ate the cookie she'd purchased and left.

Something turned over in her mind, like flipping a page in a book. How could Alex have been so blind? Alex finished her treats and pinned up her flier on the way out. She headed back to the bakeshop with a lighter step. She parked her car in the bookshop driveway and walked to the north corner of the block and into Penelope's antique shop.

"When what to my wondering eyes should appear, but a middle-aged peer who hasn't darkened my doors in a year." Penelope had a little device, like a memory stick, plugged into her computer on the counter. She had casually laid her hand over it as Alex approached.

"You're so quick witted, Penelope. I have an early Christmas present for you." Alex leaned her arms on the counter in front of the woman. Penelope had a fine bead of sweat on her forehead.

"Why would you give me a gift? We don't do that sort of thing." Penelope blustered.

"This is really from Hanna, because I'd like to see you fry. You are going to retire Miss T and the *Harriston Confidante* immediately. And if you don't, I'm going to tell everyone in this village how you've been secretly recording their conversations with your little mini recorder, currently plugged into your computer."

Penelope face had drained of color, and her hand over the recorder spasmed. She blinked rapidly, and her gaze flicked to the hand covering the device.

"You can drop your act. I know what you've been doing. I bet that little thing has traveled to all sorts of places recently, including the women's washroom at the church, my front porch, and under a table at the bakeshop. You've been a naughty girl. If you're not careful, you'll have a lump of coal in your stocking Christmas morning." Alex turned around and grinned as she walked away.

At the bookshop Alex assisted customers for an hour and then helped Hanna as she prepared dozens and dozens of chocolates. Alex hummed along to the Christmas tunes that were always playing softly in the shop. She'd been thrilled with the bonbons Hanna made using the new food colors she'd ordered. The new True North Nicotine Chocolates had a combination of white and red on their tops. Hanna had done pink on the Strychnine Strawberry. Alex was sure their chocolates would take home a prize at the Festive Foods competition.

"I have a few things I'm still curious about." Alex put her piping bag down and watched her sister at the stove. "Where did that bloody rag under Kyle's car come from? And why did the washroom smell like smoke when Brooke came out? And what was the ash in the sink?"

"Duncan thinks the rag came from Nate's truck. Nate was on a vet call just before he came to the community center. He thinks it blew out of Nate's truck. I have no idea about the smoke, though."

"Could Brooke have been burning a blackmail note from Kyle after she thought she'd killed him?"

Hanna stirred the mixture in the pot. "That's certainly a possibility. I guess we'll never know for sure."

*   *   *

As soon as Maggie locked the door at five, Alex called for a quick meeting. They gathered in the kitchen so Hanna could continue working.

"I wanted to let you both know, Miss T isn't likely going to be continuing her blog."

Maggie shot Alex a look of amazement. "Where did you get that piece of information?"

Alex couldn't help but grin. "I figured out who Miss T really is, and I told her if she published another blog post, I'd unmask her to the whole village." Alex told them what she'd seen at the bakeshop. "As soon as Penelope pulled that device from under the table, I knew. All the puzzle pieces clicked together."

"That woman. Has she no shame? What did I say? Cheaters never prosper." Maggie was triumphant.

"I don't think what Penelope did was cheating, but it did cross some moral and possibly legal boundaries. However, I have to admit cheating was the root cause of much of the troubles this past week."

"How do you figure that?" Hanna asked.

"It was the kids cheating on their tests that caused Olive to snoop and ultimately resulted in her death. That came back to haunt Brooke when Kyle tried to blackmail her. Nate and Zara cheated on their spouses, and we saw how that worked out. Eddie embezzled money from his employer, and I think that's a form of cheating, and it ended in murder, and now he's going to prison. Lucy lost her sister and ended up losing out on the opportunity to become a nurse. Fenton has lost the respect of the community," Alex said.

"Duncan said he thinks Fenton will end up getting time served and probation for what he did to you two. Plus, if Olive hadn't died, Rose might have married him back when they were having their affair." Maggie frowned. "That was another instance of cheating, Fenton and Rose having an affair. In the end it didn't turn out the way Fenton had hoped."

Alex nodded. "So, I guess you were right, Maggie. Cheaters never prosper. Except for Everett. He seems to have gotten away with it."

Hanna banged an upside down tray of molded chocolates on the counter. The chocolates all had a beautiful, glossy finish. "Actually, I spoke to Isabelle yesterday. She told Everett he had to go see the doctor because she was quite concerned about his constant need to use the washroom over the weekend. He ended up having to confess about his basketball games. She was not impressed."

Alex laughed and held her hands up in mock surrender. "I give up. Cheaters never prosper. Maggie, I bow down to your wisdom."

Chapter
Thirty-Five

The Festive Foods event had been a hit.

Alex and Hanna had practically sold out of all the chocolates they'd brought with them. And best of all, Hanna won first place for Best Tasting Chocolate with her True North Nicotine Chocolates. Sales at the store were booming as well, and Alex knew the last week before Christmas would be a crazy one.

She and Tom still hadn't had a heart-to-heart talk because she'd been working so much. They were supposed to take a walk that afternoon. As she and Hanna got ready for church Sunday morning, the day after the Festive Foods event, Alex wondered what she really wanted. She couldn't imagine life anywhere else. Harriston and the people there had come to mean so much to her.

She loved the friendship she had with Tom, and there was something deeper as well. She wanted to explore their relationship and maybe take it to the next level, but it was her fear of getting hurt that held her back. She sensed something was holding Tom back as well. He'd confessed his fear of what other people thought of their age difference, something Alex didn't worry about anymore, but she was sure there was more to it.

Alex and Hanna sat at the back of the chapel in a pew with Maggie and Drew. There had been traditional Christmas carols, a reading from Chapter Two in the Book of Luke, and Tom had reminded everyone as they celebrated the birth of Jesus Christ with its many traditions, to also celebrate what His birth symbolized, especially the love. He suggested when they saw shepherds, to let it remind them to be humble, and that the wise men would remind them to be generous. Finally, when they saw a little child, to remember to love unconditionally with forgiveness and compassion in their hearts. Alex was touched by the sermon, and it reminded her of the many blessings she'd been given. Including the love she had for her friends and family.

After church she hugged Maggie and Drew and thanked them for all their help the past week. Maggie invited Alex and Hanna over for dinner. Duncan promised he'd be home early in the afternoon, and Tom would be there as well. Alex promised to bring the twin's special rhubarb slush punch and a plate of cookies.

Eudora flagged down Alex and they hugged. Eudora looked Alex over carefully. "No visible damage, I'm happy to see. My faith in humanity has been shaken, but today's sermon helped to restore it. Thank you for finding the killer. Now I'll be able to sleep well again." But I'm very disappointed it was Eddie. He was one sexy young man."

Alex laughed. "I had no idea you thought that way."

"My dear, I'm old, not dead." Eudora winked. "It's odd that Miss T has been silent for several days now. I think our community has enough gossip spreading through it without its being posted online. I won't be disappointed if I don't see another blog post from that woman."

Alex held up her crossed fingers.

Hanna came from behind Alex and looped her arm through her sister's. "Let's go to Sunday school. Duncan is coming over this afternoon. I'm so happy."

A Nutcracker Nightmare

Alex was overjoyed that Hanna and Duncan seemed to have found each other again. There were bound to be challenges— there always were in life—but it was important to savor the happy moments as they happened.

Alex sat beside Miss Vicky in Sunday school. The woman leaned closer to Alex and whispered, "Rose and Fenton are seeing each other again. Lucy's not thrilled, but I pointed out that she might appreciate the extra help with her mother down the road. I'm sure they'll work it out."

"I heard Fenton will probably just get probation. One thing I'm still wondering about. I overheard Fenton and Nate arguing at the school. Nate said he wouldn't lie for Fenton. Do you know what he might have meant?" Alex asked.

"I imagine he was asking Nate to give him an alibi for the time Kyle was killed. He asked me to say I was with him during that time. Well, you can imagine what I told him. Honesty is the best policy. Our politicians need to embrace that principle."

Alex only half listened as Miss Vicky droned on about lying politicians until the teacher in the class glared at her and she was finally quiet. Alex said a quick goodbye and took off at the end of class before Miss Vicky could start round two on the dishonesty of politicians.

Alex waited at the doors for Hanna to catch up, and Tom came out of his office and stood beside Alex.

"We're still on for our walk?"

"Absolutely—it's a beautiful day. I'm going home to change. Just come get me when you're ready."

At home, Hanna made sandwiches while Alex tossed a salad. They made short work of the light lunch, and both went to change into casual clothes. When Alex came downstairs, Hanna had lit a scented candle, and vanilla and cinnamon were wafting through the house. Every set of twinkle lights had been turned on, and Hanna had cookies and chocolates set out on a platter, and their hot cocoa station was stocked and ready.

"Looks like you have a cozy, romantic afternoon planned." Alex had her hand slapped when she tried to take a cookie from the platter.

"I want everything to be perfect. Duncan's been working like crazy, and this is his first afternoon off in over a week."

The doorbell chimed and Alex grabbed her coat on the way to the door. She slipped her shoes on and opened the door. Tom wore jeans and a blue plaid flannel shirt under a black puffy jacket that hung open. He'd opted for hiking boots and wore a smile.

"I've been looking forward to this all morning." He held out his hand.

She liked the way her hand felt in his and the feel of his rough skin against her smoothness. "Shall we head to the beach?"

"Are you okay going there? No bad memories."

Alex shook her head. "No. I'm okay with everything. I'm sure Eddie's memory of the beach is more scarring than mine."

Tom laughed. Alex liked the sound of it. It was so honest and came from his belly, nothing held back. As they walked along the road in silence Alex drank in the view of the trees and the sun glinting in the cerulean-blue sky overhead. A hawk soared way above them, scanning the ground for its lunch. As the silence stretched on, Alex wondered which of them would say something first.

Tom finally cleared his throat. "You look gorgeous. I'm glad you were at church today. I missed seeing you last Sunday. In fact, I've missed seeing you this whole week. You've been so busy, there hasn't been much time to be together."

Alex felt a modicum of guilt. She'd intentionally stayed busy the past few days as she pondered their relationship and what she wanted from it. She also couldn't escape the feeling that there was still something going on that she wasn't aware of. "Yeah. It has been a crazy week. But I have to be honest with you. I've felt like you haven't been completely honest with me. Is there anything I should be aware of?" Alex looked up at Tom, who was keeping his gaze locked forward.

They'd reached the beach, and Tom led Alex to a bench that faced the water. Even though it looked frozen, Alex knew the ice was too thin to walk on. The weather forecast was calling for a significant drop in temperature tomorrow and snow in the evening. Hopefully, they'd have a fresh blanket of white for Christmas.

Tom still held Alex's hand, and he turned to face her. "There is something that I've been working through. I'm sorry I wasn't completely honest with you."

Tom seemed to be choosing his words carefully.

"When we started dating last Christmas, my kids made it clear they weren't happy with me for going out with you after their mother's death. They felt it was too soon. I was devastated, but then my brother got sick, and I realized I wasn't going to be around that much for a while. I thought it would work itself out. By the time I was back in Harriston full-time, I thought the kids would have gotten over their reluctance to see me dating again."

Alex sucked in her stomach as the implications hit her. That's what had been holding Tom back.

Tom continued. "Unfortunately, for them nothing had changed. They expressed their displeasure when I came home, and I told them of my intention to start seeing you again." Tom sighed. "I've been thinking about it ever since, and you may have felt a certain hesitance on my part. I'm sorry for that. I should have been honest with you from the beginning. I met with them at Hickory Smokehouse the night you zapped Eddie, to tell them the decision I'd made."

Alex felt angry that Tom's kids were putting their dad in this position. She felt disappointed that Tom hadn't felt he could talk to her about it. Alex's body was tense. She also realized she would be deeply disappointed if Tom decided to end their relationship. She wasn't sure if he was waiting for her to say something.

"That explains a lot. I've felt like there was something holding you back. I thought maybe you'd realized you made a mistake or had discovered you wanted to be with someone else."

Alex thought back to Penelope. Despite her quirks, she was closer in age to Tom. Maybe it was Alex's age that his kids objected to.

"I really am sorry if my silence hurt you in any way. As I said, I've been thinking about us. I finally decided it's my decision to date when I'm ready to do that."

Alex felt like she was holding her breath. Was he going to tell her it was over? They'd just be friends from now on?

Tom gently took Alex's other hand. "I want to see where this relationship leads us. I'm not going to stop seeing you. My kids will have to adjust. You are too important to me to let go." Tom leaned forward and gently kissed Alex on the lips. He pulled away and looked in her eyes. "I hope you agree."

Alex smiled. "Yes. I want to keep seeing you." And in that moment Alex realized that whatever challenges there would be, she very much wanted to continue their relationship. As she gazed back at Tom, she could hear bells jingling.

They both looked toward the parking lot, and there was Santa, guiding two horses pulling a hay wagon filled with children and their parents, laughing and waving. Santa held up the bells and gave them a jingle as he shouted, "Ho ho ho!"

Recipes

Hand-Molded Chocolate Recipes

Tools

digital kitchen scale (with metric)
digital thermometer
glass or plastic bowls
bench scraper
silicone spatulas
disposable plastic piping bag
polycarbonate plastic molds (mine are from Amazon)
gloves
wax paper

Gather all your tools. Your work surface should be clean and dry. Cover surface with wax paper. I like to weigh out all my ingredients and have them in small bowls beforehand. *Note:* If you choose to make the Gingerbread Gelsemine Truffles and choose *not* to dip them in tempered chocolate, you can skip right to the recipe; none of the information on chocolate tempering and sealing is applicable.

Prepare Your Molds and Temper Your Chocolate

Ensure your molds have been wiped clean with a paper towel or soft cloth and that they are free of any residue. *Do not* touch the inside of your molds with your ungloved hands. You will leave fingerprints that will mar your finished chocolates. Also ensure your molds are completely dry. Seriously, water is your mortal enemy in the chocolate-making process. Even a drop of water can ruin all your hard work.

Your house should be about 18 degrees Celsius [64 degrees Fahrenheit], if possible. If it is much warmer, your chocolate will not set properly. (I found this out the hard way the first time and had to move the chocolates all around the house and into the fridge briefly, on and off—such a headache.) Ideally, you do not want to put your chocolates in the fridge for long, as this can cause moisture issues. Remember, water is not your friend. So put on a warm sweater and lower your thermostat, or turn up the air-conditioning.

We will be using the microwave method of tempering chocolate. Pour about 300 grams of Bernard Callebaut chocolate callets (or, if using a slab, first chop what you will need into small pieces) into a glass or plastic bowl. You can use other good-quality chocolate, but this is not the place to skimp. Quality counts. Use milk chocolate with a three-drop fluidity for the mold.

Microwave for 30 seconds, then take out and stir. Microwave for 20 seconds and stir. Repeat until most of your chocolates are melted, but not all. Don't overheat. It is better to microwave in shorter bursts, and this doesn't take long. When most of the chocolate is melted, stir, stir, and stir some more (about 2 minutes.) Movement is essential in the tempering process, as is not melting all the chocolate in the bowl in the microwave. If you did accidentally do that, just add a few solid callets to the mixture and stir until they are melted. (If you're preparing chocolate for dipping truffles, just ensure the chocolate is the right temperature, and proceed to the dipping instructions now.)

For milk chocolate you need the tempered chocolate to be 29°–30°C [84°–86°F] before coating your molds. Use your thermometer to check the temperature. At the appropriate temperature, a metal spatula coated with chocolate and placed on the counter should be solid in about 1 minute.

Heat your molds briefly with a heat gun—I use an embossing heat gun from my card-making days (a blow dryer will work in a pinch.) The molds should be about 2–4 degrees cooler than your chocolate.

Pour tempered chocolate into the mold. Keep your mold tilted at an angle over your bowl. Use your bench scraper to scrape off the excess from the top and sides of the mold back into the bowl. Tap the sides of the mold with the handle of your bench scraper. Then tap the mold on the counter. You want to ensure you get any air bubbles out.

Turn your mold upside down over the bowl so the excess chocolate can drip out. Tap the sides of the mold. Scrape again while the mold is upside down. Place the mold upside down on the wax paper for about 5 minutes. Then pick up one end, but still holding the mold upside down, and scrape again onto the wax paper. You want a nice clean edge on the chocolates. Place the mold upright on the counter or a cool place, 18°C [64°F] for 5–10 minutes.

Make your filling/ganache. The recipes and instructions are after the sealing instructions.

Sealing The Chocolates

Once your chocolates have been filled and set, you are ready to seal them. Have your tempered chocolate ready. Follow the same tempering instructions as above, but you won't need quite as much chocolate. You can just add some new callets to the leftover chocolate from filling the molds. But ensure you follow all the steps properly.

Briefly heat the filled shells with the heat gun. This will allow the sealing chocolate to stick to the shells. Apply your chocolate over the shells—not too much, but ensure each shell is completely covered. Scrape the mold.

Tap the mold on the counter and check for air bubbles. Add more chocolate and repeat if necessary. Store at approximately 16ºC [61ºF] for at least 2 hours.

Ensure you have a completely clean work surface, and cover it with clean wax paper. You are going to flip your mold over quickly and give it a gentle crack onto the wax paper to unmold. If some shells stick, move your mold to a free spot on the wax paper and repeat, giving the mold a good crack on the counter—but not so hard that you break the mold. (And watch that stray fingers don't get caught between the counter and the mold. Yes—I did that.) Use gloves to turn over the chocolates, and put them in containers. I use cookie tins.

Store them at cool room temperature, away from humidity and light, for up to 2 weeks.

Check out the tutorials at BernardCallebaut.com to see how the experts make hand-molded chocolates.

Cleaning your Molds

Don't use soap and water. Ideally, you will only wash your molds once or twice a year with hot water. Wipe the inside of the shells dry, so there is no residue from the water. Normally, you can heat briefly in the microwave and wipe clean with a paper towel or a soft cloth. Remember, no ungloved fingers inside the mold. Ensure molds are clean and dry before using again.

True North Nicotine Caramel

Makes 20–30 bonbons (depending on size)

Ingredients

6.9 oz. [196 g.] granulated sugar
2 oz. [59 ml.] water
2 oz. [59 ml.] light corn syrup
5 oz. [148 ml.] heavy cream or whipping cream (it should have about 35% fat)
2 T. [28 g.] unsalted butter, room temperature, cut in pieces
2 T. real maple syrup
⅛ tsp. nutmeg (optional)
¼ tsp. salt
1 T. real rum or ½ tsp. rum flavoring

Directions

In a medium-sized saucepan with a heavy bottom, combine the sugar, water, and corn syrup. Stir. Wash down the sides with a pastry brush dipped in clean water. Then place over medium to high heat for 7–10 minutes. The mixture will begin to darken. Give the mixture a quick stir with a rubber spatula. Allow the caramel to turn a deep amber color (but not too dark—this can be tricky). Then stand back and slowly add cream. The mixture will sputter, rise, and spit. Turn off heat. Once it's safe, whisk the cream, until smooth. Then whisk in the butter until completely melted. Whisk in the remaining ingredients, and allow the mixture to cool.

Once the caramel is 27°C [80°F], pour it into a disposable piping bag. Cut a very small opening at the tip. Don't press hard: you want the caramel to come out slowly. Carefully fill each shell, and ensure you leave at least 1.5 mm [1/16 inch] space from the top of the mold. Ensure that space is across the entire chocolate. (I overfilled some of mine in the center and couldn't get as much chocolate over them as I would have liked for a really good seal.) Don't spill or smudge the filling onto the chocolate edges of the shells because this can cause problems with sealing them. Work quickly, and heat the caramel as necessary with a heat gun.

Cool at room temperature for at least half an hour, and then seal.

Gingerbread Gelsemine Truffle

Ingredients*

¾ c. [180 ml.] or 174 g. heavy whipping cream (35% fat)

14.39 oz. [408 g.] bittersweet couverture chocolate, very finely
    chopped (or just use callets)

2 T. [30 ml. gingerbread syrup (I use Torani)

½ tsp. molasses

pinch of cloves (approx. ⅛ tsp.)

pinch of ground ginger (approx. ⅛ tsp.)

*You will also need ingredients for rolling or dipping the truffles.
If you're using superfine sugar, you'll need about 2 T. Options for
rolling include superfine sugar, coconut sugar, cocoa, nuts, etc. For
dipping you will need milk chocolate callets (see tempering chocolate
section)*

Directions

Place the cream in a 2-quart saucepan over medium heat until it
barely comes to a simmer. Remove from heat and immediately
sprinkle the chocolate into the cream. Cover and let sit for 5 minutes. The chocolate should melt. Stir gently until smooth.

Stir in the syrup, molasses, and spices. Pour mixture into a shallow
bowl or pan. Cool to room temperature, cover loosely with plastic
wrap, and allow to sit overnight, or until firm enough to roll (or
refrigerate ganache until firm, about 4 hours.)

Coat your hands in cocoa powder, and roll ganache into ¾-inch balls. Place in a single layer on a jelly-roll pan, and refrigerate until firm. The mixture will still be on the softer side. I suspect it's due to the addition of the syrup, but I decided not to change the recipe because it's so good. Just work very quickly.

Now you will either roll them in your chosen coating or dip them in chocolate. If you choose to use non-tempered chocolate (or chocolate candy melts) for dipping, then the truffles will need to be stored in the refrigerator.

For rolling

Remove from fridge, and coat truffles in superfine sugar or whatever ingredient you've decided on. Place in truffle cups for presentation (optional).

If dipping*

Follow the tempering chocolate instructions. Start with 300 g. of milk chocolate callets—this is approximate. Prepare everything before you begin dipping. Set out your dipping tools or dinner fork (I'll just refer to a fork in the instructions, but it applies to a dipping tool as well.) Cover a baking sheet with a clean piece of parchment, waxed paper, or aluminum foil for placing the finished truffles on. Once you have your bowl of tempered chocolate, slide your fork gently under the truffle, drop into the chocolate, and ensure it is fully immersed. Lift it out with the fork, and tap the fork a few times against the side of the bowl. Slide the bottom of the fork over the edge of the bowl, to remove excess chocolate. Place the truffle on the prepared baking sheet. Tilt the fork so the edge of the truffle touches the sheet, and slide the fork out from under the truffle.

If you're adding decorations or garnishes, do it now, while chocolate is still wet. Repeat. You can leave your chocolate to set if your room temperature is around 16º–21ºC [60º–70ºF], but if your room is warm, you can put the chocolates in the fridge for about 10 minutes. If the chocolate is non-tempered or you've used candy melts, the chocolates should be kept in the fridge after dipping.

* I would recommend rolling because the truffles are really a bit soft for dipping.

Acknowledgments

Thanks once again to my family, who put up with my endless talk about murder. And especially, to my husband, who always lets me practice scenes from my book with him to make sure it's all real and possible.

Special thanks goes out to Rose Kerr for beta reading the manuscript on a tight deadline before I submitted it to my editor. Thanks as well to Gloria Larson for letting me ruin the ending (when she eventually reads it) so I could work out who the killer(s) was going to be just a couple weeks before Rose read the almost final manuscript. Thanks to Spencer MacLean and Dawn Criddle for reading the manuscript before I submitted the copy edits and providing feedback and encouragement.

All of this is only possible thanks to my incredible agent, Dawn Dowdle, of Blue Ridge Literary Agency, and Tara Gavin, my amazing editor at Crooked Lane Books, for giving me the chance to bring my books into the world. A special mention to the Crooked Lane team, including Dulce Botello, Madeline Rathle, and Rebecca Nelson, for all that you do behind the scenes to get a book into the hands of readers. A special shout-out to the copy and line editors who have the tiresome job of correcting all my mistakes.

Acknowledgments

Most of all, thanks to you, the readers, for letting me share the adventures of Alex and Hanna in the fictional setting of Harriston, Montana. Thanks to those who have written reviews and commented on social media letting me know you enjoyed the first book. It means so much to hear from you.